MURDER AT THE CLASS REUNION

Savanna stopped me as I entered the main corral. "Have you seen Miss Diaz?" she asked. "I haven't seen her in ages."

"Yes," I said. "I just saw her in the rest room."

Savanna smiled. "Maybe she's hiding out."

Sometimes I have a hunch. I've learned to pay attention. Turning on my heel, I headed back to the lobby, forcing myself not to run. I gestured to Zack to come with me. He didn't hesitate.

I called out Reina's name as soon as I entered the women's rest room.

There was no response.

"What's up?" Zack asked.

"Miss Diaz. Reina. I think something might be ..." I broke off as I got up on tiptoe and tried to look over the door. It was taller than I am, so I bent down and looked under it instead. The shoes were still there. I knocked on the door. "Reina, are you okay?"

I wanted her to be okay. I really did.

But she wasn't okay at all. . . .

Books by Margaret Chittenden

DYING TO SING

DEAD MEN DON'T DANCE

DEAD BEAT AND DEADLY

DON'T FORGET TO DIE

DYING TO SEE YOU

Published by Kensington Publishing Corporation

A Charlie Plato Mystery

DYING TO SEE YOU

Margaret Chittenden

Kensington Books
KENSINGTON PUBLISHING CORP.
http://www.kensingtonbooks.com

This book is dedicated to Kip Varela, of Nashville, Tennessee, my country-music consultant and very dear friend.

I owe a debt of gratitude to the following people, who kindly gave me advice, information, or help. Any errors of fact in this novel are mine, not theirs.

P. Casey Morgan, public-radio program producer

Detective III Paul Bishop, LAPD, Major Assault Crimes Investigations, author of the Fey Croaker mysteries

Dale Furutani, author of the Ken Tanaka Mystery Series and the Samurai Mystery Trilogy

John Giacobbe, Forensic Anthropologist (at large)

Michael McGregor, volunteer, Ocean Shores Fire Dept.

Jaki Girdner, author of the Kate Jasper Mystery Series

Cheryl Trahan, Academic Coordinator

Emily Cohen (for the use of her wonderful car)

CHAPTER 1

Everything has calmed down at CHAPS now. We've had excitement before, of course—that skeleton in the flower-bed, the corpse in Zack's car, the Internet bride, and that terrible experience with the storage locker—but this event really got wild. It even started off wild.

And seriously embarrassing.

I'd better give some background for those of you who haven't met me before. If you've previously hung out at CHAPS, just shoot on past the exposition.

Zack Hunter, TV star and all-American sex god, Savanna Bristow (formerly Seabrook), Angel Cervantes, and I, Charlie (originally Charlotte) Plato, own CHAPS, a country-western nightclub on the San Francisco Peninsula: We're all thirty-something, which is a trendy age group to belong to right now.

We had agreed recently that our outgoing expense was overtaking our income. There didn't seem to be much we could do to shrink the overhead, so we'd sought creative ways to make more money, instituting a cover charge, charging higher prices for drinks—including water—giving dance lessons every night we were open, and renting CHAPS out on Monday evenings and the occasional daytime.

On a very warm Monday night in August, I was sitting in the office at CHAPS with my feet up on the desk, reading the latest novel in a mystery series I really liked—written by a California author. I'd just picked it up from M is for Mystery, in San Mateo, that afternoon and was thoroughly engrossed, though a little surprised that this one had more violence than its predecessors. Benny, my Netherland dwarf rabbit, was keeping me company in his cage beside my desk.

The group that had rented CHAPS for the night kept breaking out in cheers, interfering with my concentration. They appeared to be having a high old time in the main corral, which is the largest dance-floor area in the club.

According to Zack, who made the arrangements, tonight's renter was some kind of environmental club that wanted to give line-dancing lessons to raise funds for a summer camp. The music was fabulous. I decided I should go find out the combo's name and bring them in to play for our patrons sometime. We usually had live music on Wednesdays and weekends.

I was still concentrating on that mission as I entered the main corral, so it was a while before I saw the reason for all the cheering. I stood there happily for several minutes inside the doorway, watching the dancers, making a mental note of the band's name, and listening to an out-of-sight instructor giving directions through a mike for "Walk The Line."

And then the dancers got confused. Some went one way and the rest the other, leaving a gap through which I could see the instructors, who were demonstrating the steps. Angel and I usually demonstrate for *our* customers. Savanna helps out sometimes. Zack mostly hangs around, looking decorative, which he does very well.

This group of dancers had *seven* instructors. I wasn't so much struck by the *number* of instructors, however. Or the fact that they were all excellent dancers. It was their *condition* that caused my mouth to drop open. Of the seven instructors, four were naked men, three were naked women.

I headed back to the office at top speed and punched Zack's number into the telephone. I was relieved to get his answering machine. When he was home, he preferred it to voice mail because he could screen calls as they came in and decide if he wanted to answer. God forbid he should miss a call from his agent, or a director, or a woman.

"Pick up, Zack," I ordered as soon as his seductively voiced outgoing message stopped. "This is Charlie and it's an emergency."

When Zack picked up the phone, he was saying something to someone in the room with him. In the bedroom, probably. "What's up, darlin'?" he asked me.

Somehow, I kept my voice even. "That group you rented CHAPS to. What did you say it was called?"

There was a pause. Someone at Zack's end said something in the background. A man.

"You hosting a group grope?" I asked.

I wouldn't have put it past him, in spite of the fact he was on probation. Not court directed. Charlie Plato directed. I'll explain later.

"Poker," he said laconically, which was the way he said most things. He paused. "The Natural Line-dancin' Club?" he said tentatively. "Scratch that—the *Naturist* Line-dancin' Club. They givin' you trouble, Charlie?"

"Depends how you define trouble, I guess. The instructors are wearing cowboy hats, boots, and spurs."

"So?"

"That's *all* the instructors are wearing, Zack. This is not an environmental group, this is a nude dancing group."

He laughed uneasily. "You razzin' me, Charlotte?"

I hate to be called by my real name, and Zack knows it. I also hate being called Red because of my long frizzy hair, which is actually closer to orange. I was never too fond of my nickname in high school, either. The kids called me "Stretch," because I topped out early at five feet ten inches. Unless you enjoy having your shins kicked, just call me Charlie.

"This is no joke," I said. "The summer camp they are raising funds for has to be real summery!"

"I'll be right there." He hung up on me.

By rights, as senior partner in CHAPS, Zack should have arrived with guns blazing, yelling for everyone to get out of Dodge before sundown. He looked the part in his usual all-black cowboy gear, and he seemed quite menacing as he shouldered through the crowd, with me in his wake. But then he stopped at the main corral bar. After ordering a Pellegrino water—we have an agreement that the partners don't drink alcohol at CHAPS while it's open—he leaned a hip on a bar stool, put an elbow on the bar, propped his chin on his hand,

and fixed his gaze on the instructors in all their naked swinging glory.

"You have to get them out of here." I spoke under my breath, so as not to inflame the bystanders, who already looked inflamed enough. "This can't be legal, even in California. What if Taylor Bristow were to drop in?"

"Not too likely," Zack said, without taking his gaze off the dance floor. I followed his line of sight to a Valkyrie blonde, who had a fat braid hanging over each of her ample breasts. Not only is it impossible to braid my hair, but being terminally skinny I don't have much in the way of a bosom, so there were two strikes against this woman already. The music had picked up a distinctly rock sound and the dancers were stomping right along with the beat. Including the blonde. A sight to behold.

"Taylor only shows up when Savanna's here," Zack added after drawing in a breath on a slow wheeze.

Detective Sergeant Taylor Bristow didn't always do even *that* nowadays, not since a couple of months ago when he'd gotten himself a needle-stick injury from a criminal he'd been patting down—a young punk who'd turned out to be HIV positive. The possibilities inherent in that situation had eroded the edges of what had been a fine and joyous marriage. Mostly because Bristow was acting far too cautiously around his wife— our own Savanna—and her little daughter, Jacqueline. I could sympathize with both sides of that problem. Four months to go until the results were in. I could only hope they'd make it.

"It's probably not against the law anyway," Zack

assured me. "There are plenty topless bars in California. What's the difference? It's not as if there's anyone lap-dancin' or actin' lewd. Everyone seems to be behavin'." He took his gaze off the buxom blonde long enough to frown at me. "Unless I missed somethin' interestin'?"

He swung around on the bar stool to evade the booted kick I'd aimed at his shin. Zack's reflexes are well honed.

"It's almost closing time anyhow, Charlie," he added as he lifted his water bottle for a swig.

About then, the nearest couple of gyrating dancers noticed him and came leaping over to get him to autograph their T-shirts. At least the customers had clothes on.

In case you are one of the few who haven't run into Zack before, I'll explain briefly that he's the Zack Hunter who played Sheriff Lazarro in the long-running, manically popular, most idiotic drama series in the history of television. Obviously, my view of *Prescott's Landing* was jaundiced—the show would not have run as long as it did if a majority had shared my opinion. The series had come to an end about three years ago, had enjoyed a brief resuscitation this last spring, but appeared to be dormant for now, though daily reruns on two cable channels were providing Zack with an appallingly huge income.

Because people see Zack on the television set in their living room, bedroom, or airport waiting area on a regular basis, they recognize him instantly when he appears in public. Depending on their personalities, they act in one of three ways: Some get right in his face, demand autographs, and want their photo taken with him. Others stand back, watching his every move with awed fascination. Some sneak furtive glances at him, pretending they are far too sophisticated to be interested.

Once noticed, Zack was soon surrounded by people wanting a little piece of him, and I was stuck on the edge of the crowd, nervously chewing my fingernails as the naked instructors strutted their stuff to a suddenly distracted audience.

Fortunately, Zack was right—closing time and deliverance were nigh.

After resisting Zack's usual offer to accompany me upstairs to the loft I lived in so he could tuck me in for the night, I gratefully locked CHAPS's heavy front doors against his impudent green-eyed glance and watched through the side windows as the entire line-dance group scattered into various automobiles. I was relieved that the instructors had dressed in jeans and shirts before leaving the building.

Fulfilling my other duties as security guard for the premises—which was the reason I was able to live rent-free in the loft—I checked the rest rooms to make sure no one had stowed away, tried the doors of Dorscheimer's restaurant and Buttons & Bows, the western clothing store opposite it in CHAPS's lobby, then picked up Benny's cage from the office, went thankfully up to my room, and locked the door behind me.

After making sure Benny had plenty of water and kibble, and indulging him in some cuddling and gentle head rubbing, I got myself ready for bed and lay there reading my cozy mystery that wasn't so cozy this time, trying to shut out of my mind's eye the moment when those dancers parted and all that naked flesh came into view.

CHAPTER 2

"Never again," I declared. "We'll just have to think of some other way to raise money."

Most afternoons we have a partners meeting around three o'clock. The day after the nature show, we were all seated in the office, except for Zack, who was leaning sexily against the windowsill. Zack could get a PhD in sexy leaning.

"*My* people aren't going to be nude," Savanna said with a frown.

We never used to see Savanna frown. She has this killer smile I would have thought was permanently etched on her face. She was still beautiful, of course, but the glow was gone from her perfect features. Reaching around to tuck her long black curls into a scrunchy, she looked at me pleadingly. "Bear in mind, this is *my* old high school I'm asking for, girlfriend," she said. "We were supposed to have our reunion at The Doncastle Hotel in Palo Alto, but someone goofed and booked our little group in at the same time as a big Elks convention. Every hotel of any size is filled with bodies. The Oleander Motel can provide rooms for us but they don't have a ballroom. If we don't have our twentieth reunion at CHAPS, we don't have it at all."

It is very difficult to resist someone who is not only beautiful on the outside but on the inside, too. Savanna was probably the best friend I'd ever had. I'd even agreed to be matron of honor at her wedding sometime ago, and being called a matron of anything hadn't thrilled me a whole bunch.

Savanna had attended and graduated from Alger Dix's Alternative High School in San Francisco. "Dix's Mixes," the students had called it. Its lofty aim was to graduate at-risk kids who had been written off by the local school district. That might not sound too promising, except that I'd seen a couple of photos in Savanna's apartment. The pupils had worn school uniforms, and most of the teachers looked tough as drill sergeants. I supposed that those kids who'd made it to graduation weren't too likely to turn up naked twenty years later.

"We agreed to rent CHAPS out on Monday nights," I pointed out, still resisting. "Your reunion party is planned for Saturday."

"You forgotten already how few people were here last Saturday?" Zack asked, weighing in on Savanna's side. "We'd make more from the reunion than from our regulars. Hottest August ever was—people want to be cavortin' at the beach, not in a bar."

"Nightclub," Angel corrected. Angel Cervantes is a former cowboy, one rugged hombre who looks as if he'd been carved out of copper-colored rock—which is why he does double duty as our bouncer, as well as tending bar. When he smiles, he wouldn't scare a kitten—maybe that's why he barely shows his whiter than white teeth, except on special occasions.

"Nightclub," Zack repeated dutifully.

We'd upgraded CHAPS from a tavern/dance hall to a nightclub in the most recent issue of the Yellow Pages to stop people from equating the place with some backwoods honky-tonk saloon. Having managed to get ourselves involved in a few murders, we were attempting to gloss over the negative publicity by making CHAPS as upscale as possible.

"I really want us to do this, Charlie," Savanna said, her eyes pleading as a puppy's.

I caved in with a sigh. "Tell us what you want."

She immediately launched herself into plans. Before anyone could slow her down, she'd talked Zack and Angel into putting themselves up at auction for a date. "I was going to ask you guys to do this even if we hadn't transferred the reunion to CHAPS," she said, her face wreathed with pleasure. "It's for a great cause—my favorite teacher's favorite charity—homeless kids."

She looked directly at me. "How can anyone say no to homeless kids?" she asked.

"I can," I said firmly. "I'll give you a donation, but I'm not offering my body on any auction block."

Angel didn't look too thrilled by the prospect, either, but he'd given his word and would never go back on it. Zack had no problem with the idea at all—he loves being the center of attention and I was sure he was already chomping at the bit over our agreement that if he couldn't stay celibate for six months, there was no chance of getting cozy with me. I was amazed—

and just a little nervous—that he'd stuck to his vow for all of two months.

"You goin' to put yourself up for auction?" Zack asked Savanna.

"I'm a married lady," she protested. "You can't expect me to sell myself for a date."

She sighed deeply. "Though the way Taylor is behaving, I might as well. He probably wouldn't even notice."

We all looked at her sympathetically and she shook her head and gave us a bright but unnatural-looking smile. "Miss Diaz was an incredible teacher," she said. "Still is, by all accounts. Reina Diaz. Isn't that a pretty name? She's always after me to call her Reina but I tell her I can't do it—it would be too informal."

"Reina means queen," I pointed out. "How can that be informal?"

Savanna made a face at me. "Miss Diaz is fifty years old now, but you'd never know it. She was so *dedicated*, Charlie, always looking for ways to make math and English more exciting. Everything she had she gave to the school, to the kids. She forged us into a family— wouldn't let us fail—saw talent in everyone and worked to draw it out. Remember, this was a school for kids who had problems of one kind or another. I was so pathologically shy some of my grade-school teachers suggested I was retarded, and I might never have grown beyond that if Miss Diaz hadn't brought me out of my shell. On top of all that, she dared us to throw out all our prejudices regarding color, class, gender, sexual orientation, age."

She leaned back in her swivel chair and gave me a

rueful grin. "You suppose that's why my first husband was a gay white guy twenty-five years older than me?"

Her laughter was so infectious we all joined in. I hadn't ever met Teddy Seabrook; he'd left wife, daughter, and home for his truck-driver lover before I came on the scene, but we were all familiar with the story. At least my ex had been ravishing a ravishing *female* when I caught him at it. Much as you might sympathize with other sexual orientations, you have to admit it would be tough to have your husband leave you for another guy. Some kind of blow to feminine self-esteem. Like, were you so lacking as a lover it turned him off women for *life*? The more I see of sex, or at least the results of sex, the more I think celibacy has a lot going for it. If Zack would stop giving me those zinging glances from under his eyelashes, I could probably swear off sex altogether.

There were forty people at the reunion, not counting Zack, Angel, me, and P.J., a CHAPS regular who crashed the party and was given permission to stay. It was Angel who said it was okay—which caused P.J. to go through the evening with a dazed and unbelieving, verging on starry-eyed, expression on her long and usually mournful face.

P.J., you might remember, has been on a serious manhunt ever since her divorce. It's funny how differently divorce affects people. Some, like me, don't ever want to get involved in anything too serious ever again, and others can't wait to tie themselves into another knot. P.J., whose full name was Patty Perry Jenkins, was one of the latter, so eager for commitment that every man she set her sights on sensed her hunger and backpedaled rapidly. She had targeted Angel on more than one occasion. I hadn't talked to her at length for some time, but we had bonded a couple of times and I hoped she wasn't about to get hurt again. Not that I thought Angel would deliberately hurt anyone, but not too long ago he'd been getting fairly serious about Gina Giacomini, the manager of Buttons & Bows. Angel had recently gone through considerable trauma and I didn't think he was ready to handle someone as needy as P.J.

"It's going great, don't you think?" Savanna said from behind me.

I turned and smiled at her. She was looking like her old radiant self, dressed in her favorite red western shirt and lie-down-and-suck-it-in-and-drag-that-zipper-up blue jeans, her black curls cascading down her back. Behind her, Bristow was looking lovingly down at her. Maybe they were going to make it through this miserable waiting time after all.

"Is everyone having a good time?" I asked.

Savanna waved a hand expansively at the troops lined up at the dessert table. They had already made serious inroads into the various salads and entrees Dorscheimer's had provided. "We're going to start the auction as soon as we get the floor cleared," she said.

I groaned.

"It'll be fun, Charlie, you'll see," she assured me.

Bristow snorted and smoothed the top of his completely bald head with a big hand. "The most fun will be seeing Charlie led off to the slaughter," he said.

Yes, you've guessed it. I had succumbed to Savanna's pleas and agreed to let myself be auctioned off along with the guys. I was already kicking myself. "I think I'm developing a headache," I said.

Savanna laughed.

"*La Belle Dame sans Merci*," Bristow murmured. When Bristow wasn't quoting the Bard from his stints of Shakespeare in the park—Golden Gate Park, that is—he would occasionally come up with a foreign phrase. With someone else it might have sounded pretentious, but coming from a guy whom Zack always said was a ringer for Michael Jordan, it was a charming habit.

Thaddeus (Thad) O'Connor had been volunteered by the relentless Savanna to be the auctioneer. He'd been introduced to me as the pastor of the Church of Enlightenment in San Francisco. This made me nervous. I always get nervous around religious people—I don't know why. I think I expect them to find me out—but as I've never done anything bad, I don't know what they could come up with. Some leftover problem from childhood probably. I'd gone to Sunday school at my parents' insistence. Maybe I'd filched pennies from a collection plate or something. My parents were Greek Orthodox, devout believers until the day their little plane crashed on the way to Tahoe. Which was about the time I stopped believing.

I had a feeling I'd seen Thaddeus O'Connor before, though his name didn't ring any bells and it wasn't an everyday name. One of those names people have that really fit their occupations. Makes you wonder if it was the name that influenced their choice of job.

Dark-haired and pale-faced, his features sharp, his

body lean, he was intelligent-looking in an intense, idealistic way. You could imagine his image on a saint medallion. Savanna had informed me that he was considered to be charismatic, and was the current darling of the local talk shows, having just published a self-help book for women who worry too much.

This last bit irritated me. Men who think they know better than women how women should behave always irritate me. If I wanted to worry too much, I had a right to worry. I'd felt the same way when my ex-husband, the plastic surgeon, had wanted to snip the muscle behind the dual frown lines above my nose. If I was annoyed I wanted people to know it, I'd told him, feeling annoyed.

I was even more irritated when Thad made the winning bid on a date with me. "I didn't know auctioneers were allowed to bid," I complained to Savanna when I came back to the table. "What kind of date could I possibly have with a *pastor*?"

She grinned at me. "It's for charity, Charlie. You'll have a great time with Thad, he's very entertaining when you get to know him."

"I knew this was going to be a disaster," I said.

But then Thad wrote out his check with a flourish and announced he was passing on the date. "Nothing personal, Charlie," he said into the mike. "I made the bid only as a contribution to Reina's charity. I don't date *anyone*. I'm not a priest, but I live like one— monastic and celibate."

"You and Thad have more in common than you thought," Savanna murmured next to me.

I shot her a dirty look, but she was distracted by

Reina Diaz, the teacher, who was having a sneezing fit into a large handkerchief supplied by Bristow. By the time I came back to the scene after being distracted by watching Savanna bring water to the woman, I discovered that the second highest bidder had insisted that as Thad had dropped out, his bid should stand and he should get the date. Which seemed to be just fine with everyone.

His name was Timothy Perkins, and he was a slightly built guy with a seriously lined forehead and black curly hair. Most of the people at the reunion were well-dressed, but Perkins looked like a Silicon Valley wunderkind in his T-shirt, jeans, and flannel shirt. The jeans had been washed out a few years back and they sagged over his flat butt. On the pocket of his shirt, he wore a pin made out of a piece of old computer circuit board, complete with resistors and dipswitches and capacitors. When Thad brought him over to "claim his prize," as he put it, he slapped the pin with his right hand and said, "Beam me up, Scotty, I've died and I'm on my way to Heaven."

It was hard to believe he was actually a hard-hitting, national award-winning political cartoonist, but I'd seen his stuff in the newspapers. He was good, no doubt about it.

"Call me Perky," he said, leering at me. "Everybody does."

I gave him four fingers and let him shake them. That was as close as he was going to get.

"I heard that you work out, Charlie," he said. "Maybe we should go jogging together for our date. I jog at six A.M. every day, rain or shine, right in my Noe Valley neighborhood."

"Fine with me, but not at six A.M. I don't do anything at six A.M." I was relieved he wasn't expecting some fancy date like dinner and dancing. He was at least five inches shorter than me, which is okay, nobody can help how tall or short they are, but it feels weird looking over a guy's head on the dance floor.

"I can go for that," he said. "We can have breakfast at my place after. I make a mean western omelet— loaded with habanero peppers. Positively aphrodisiacal."

He kept widening his pale eyes about as often as people usually blink. A nervous mannerism, I supposed.

"We'll see," I said warily. There were plenty of restaurants that opened for breakfast.

"I hope I didn't insult you by turning you down, Charlie," Pastor Thad said. He'd been hovering behind Perky, and had no doubt noted the sour expression on my face.

I didn't want him thinking I was worried. He might make me buy his book. "No problem," I said. "I'm not much for dating, either. Vastly overrated activity, if you ask me."

He smiled uncertainly and went back to his post on the stage. Angel was up next.

"I guess O'Connor's keeping Zack for the pièce de résistance," Bristow muttered. "Gotta get rid of the ordinary stuff before the sex symbol goes up for grabs."

Ordinary stuff!

I reached back with one booted foot, but failed to connect. His reflexes were as fast as Zack's.

P.J. wasn't going to let *anyone* outbid her now that Angel was on the block. Reina Diaz's charity was really going to benefit tonight. P.J. hung in there and was radiant as all get-out when Thad finally gave her the "going once, going twice—gone to the lady in the butterfly dress."

Thad's description was right on. P.J.'s dress-up costume of choice was a black leotard and tights with a brightly colored gauzy overskirt that fluttered around her like butterfly wings. Her idea of country-western gear. It looked a bit weird, considering her somewhat horsey face. She had a taut body, though, she'd always worked out and had recently started teaching aerobics at Dandy Carr's—the downtown Bellamy Park gym.

That gym recently sold again, by the way—it had gone through a couple of owners since I came to CHAPS, but people still called it Dandy Carr's. Zack had said the new owner was a retired sumo wrestler who had moved to Bellamy Park from Japan, but Zack was a notorious kidder. I didn't use that gym—it was too high-tech for me—but I was planning on going in sometime soon to see the new owner for myself.

P.J. and Angel were chatting animatedly. Angel seemed pleased to be won by P.J. That was a surprise to me, though I thought it was probably because he at least knew her.

Angel's a very private person, a serious person— he wouldn't have wanted to date someone he hadn't met before. It had taken a while of hanging around Buttons & Bows before he asked Gina out.

I sighed. That romance was apparently history, and, punk as she was, I liked Gina.

Bidding on Zack, as was to be expected, was brisk. The only surprising thing about it was that it was the teacher, Reina Diaz, who stayed in for the long haul and captured the main prize for an exorbitant amount of money. Judging by the eager expression on her face, I didn't think it was the thought of the homeless children that was spurring her on.

Reina was fifty years old, Savanna had said. Which did not mean she was safe with our man in black. It was always possible, of course, that she didn't want to be safe with him. I could understand that. I occasionally felt that way myself.

Zack and I, well, everyone knows by now that he makes me go whomp in my inner parts every time he puts in an appearance. Some people say that's very immature behavior on my part. I guess some people have never experienced a whomp-type attraction—the kind that affects the body and totally ignores the brain, which is trying desperately to tell the body to get over it.

I was willing to bet Thad O'Connor, with his monastic pride, hadn't run into the phenomenon. I'd been holding out for a long time now, but Zack had gradually overcome my reluctance. Though not completely. We'd come very close to "doing it," as Savanna usually referred to lovemaking, following our last adventure, but sanity had prevailed at the last minute and I'd given him an ultimatum—six months of abstinence from all women and then we'd talk.

Eyebrows slanting mischievously, he looked at me

over Reina's shoulder as he shook her hand. No, she was *holding* his hand. And gazing adoringly up at him.

"You must promise to wait for our date until after Labor Day when school starts," she was saying as Savanna hustled me over to congratulate her. "It will enhance my image enormously if the kids see their teacher going off on a date with Zack Hunter."

"It's a deal," Zack said. "Hope you won't mind ridin' in my pickup."

"How wonderfully macho," she breathed.

"It doesn't count as me datin' another woman, does it, Charlie?" Zack murmured to me as Savanna hugged Reina. "I can't let Savanna down by refusin' to follow through."

"Uh-huh," I said sourly. "I'll let you know. I haven't decided yet. We may have to start the six months over."

"I've been good," he protested. Mischief took over the green eyes. "I'm *always* good, Charlie. *Very* good. Amazingly good. Ask anyone."

"You still have four months to go," I reminded him.

He raised those slanted eyebrows of his again in the way that makes me inhale sharply. There are some women—and most men—who cannot understand that a woman can be completely and totally attracted physically to a man even though she is sensible enough to know that getting involved with him would deal a fatal blow to her self-esteem. I probably wouldn't have believed it myself until I met Zack, though when I think deeply about my past, which I try not to do, I can see I made much the same mistake with my ex-husband before he became my ex. Martina McBride sings a song I should take for my theme song: "Wrong Again."

"I'm so thrilled," Reina gushed.

"Me too," Zack said gallantly.

He probably meant it, too, I thought sourly. Reina was petite and slender and wearing a very sexy green silk jumpsuit. She was only thirteen years older than Zack—nobody would think twice about a man of fifty dating a woman of thirty-seven, or younger. Why should it be any different this way around?

She had rich brown hair that hung way past her shoulders. Straight hair. The kind I wanted to have but never would unless I took to wearing a wig. I couldn't imagine how she could keep her balance on the very high heels she was wearing.

She wasn't a beauty, you understand, but she was very pleasant to look at. My father would have called her personable. She was wearing a ring with huge diamonds that flashed fire when she moved her hand.

"That's a terrific ring," Savanna murmured. She loved flashy things. She'd said once she thought in a previous life she might have been a crow. Or a jewel thief.

"The stones are cubic zirconias," Reina said with a dismissive wave of the hand in question. "My boyfriend gave me the ring—we're going to be married soon. He couldn't afford diamonds, but he's a good man, a nice man. We'll do very well together."

She smiled up at Zack. "He's not the jealous type— you don't need to worry."

Zack looked politely puzzled. He had not ever in his expert swordsman career worried about anyone's husband or boyfriend. That had gotten him into trouble more than once, but he had obviously not considered those incidences important.

"What's your boyfriend's name?" Savanna asked Reina.

She seemed reluctant to answer, at least she hesitated, just long enough for someone else to get into the conversation.

"Those stones look real to me," a new voice said flatly.

We all looked at the man who had spoken; Savanna in a perky, tilted-head way that aroused my curiosity. He smiled intimately at her, his gaze fixed on her face in a way that excluded the rest of us, maybe didn't even see the rest of us. "Hi, Savvy," he said. "Sorry I'm late, we had a couple of problems at the store."

I'd never heard anyone call Savanna "Savvy" before.

Nor had Bristow, judging by the Spanish inquisitor's expression on his dark face. "Forrest," Savanna said softly, giving the man her right hand to hold in both of his. "I was so afraid you weren't going to make it."

Bristow made an inquiring sound deep in his throat. It sounded like a male animal grunting a challenge. Savanna introduced the two men. "Taylor Bristow, my husband," she said. "Forrest Kenyon, a very special old friend—one of my classmates of course."

Forrest Kenyon released her hand with obvious reluctance and shook Bristow's hand with a macho heartiness that didn't seem at all sincere. He was African American, like Savanna and Taylor Bristow—tall and muscular, though not as tall and muscular as Bristow. He had hair, though. Nice curly hair with a little patch of gray at each temple. Thick hair. Bristow didn't have any. Not on his head anyway. I didn't know about other parts. "I'd heard Savvy married a white man," he said brightly.

Bristow did not smile. "I guess I spent too much time in the sun," he growled.

Savanna looked at him reproachfully, then tilted her head at Forrest. "My first husband was white," she told him. "We divorced. Taylor and I were married in June."

"Guess I missed a window of opportunity there," Forrest said.

"As I recall, Savanna and Forrest were quite the item in school," Reina said archly, heaping a log or two on the fire. "Wasn't he your first ever boyfriend, Savanna?"

"That I was," Forrest said. "Number one in all things."

Savanna laughed awkwardly and launched into introductions all around. Bristow's eyes had narrowed to a glint. His negative reaction to Forrest was hovering over his head like a mushroom cloud.

"Charlie's as much a math whiz as you used to be," Savanna said to Forrest in an obvious attempt to change the subject. "She keeps our books."

Forrest looked at me without comment. He wore tinted glasses that were almost dark enough to be sunglasses. He was holding a beer bottle. He had small hands, I noticed. My rabbit preferred men with large hands. They made him feel secure. Savanna had told me once she liked men with large hands, too. "Forrest was always teacher's pet," she said now.

The fond note in her voice intimated he had been a pet of hers, as well.

Reina laughed merrily. "Every one of you was my pet," she declared. "Forrest belongs to Mensa," she told the rest of us.

He gave her a small pained smile, then turned it on me. "A math whiz, eh? Here's a riddle for you. If you count from one to one hundred, how many sevens are there?"

He must have noted my lack of enthusiasm. "Go ahead, try it, it's one of the qualifying questions for Mensa."

"I don't have enough fingers," I said, and heard Zack laugh appreciatively behind me.

"Forrest was always my brightest student," Reina said. "Never any trouble, not like some I could mention. The only reason he was sent to Dix's was because he was bored in his regular high school and kept playing hooky until his father had him transferred."

"You mentioned a store," Zack said to Forrest. "You talkin' 'bout Kenyon's Furniture in Los Altos? Got a designer there named Debbie?"

Savanna and I exchanged a glance. We had a long-standing game that had to do with what we called Zack's doll-brigade. Each member of the brigade (the women came in several shapes and sizes and colors) was assigned accessories of some kind. Flyin' Missy, for example, was a flight attendant, so she came complete with her own overnight bag and blow-dryer. Gorgeous Gertie had been equipped with satin shorts and a wrestling mat. Adorin' Lauren—well, you get the idea. "Decoratin' Debbie," I murmured. "Fabric samples?"

Savanna considered. "Bed-in-a-bag."

"One of our branches is in Los Altos," Forrest said as Savanna and I convulsed. "Debbie's one of our best," he added.

Zack nodded in apparent agreement. Best at what, I wondered.

"Anytime you need Kenyon's to decorate, all you have to do is call," Forrest said to Zack. "I believe your house is in Paragon Heights?"

Another thing about being a celebrity is that people know where you live. Zack's house had been featured in *House Beautiful*, *Better Homes and Gardens*, and *Architectural Digest*.

Zack allowed as how that was his location. Paragon Heights is the most upscale section of upscale Bellamy Park. I don't think there's a house under 10,000 square feet up there. You ever wonder what's in a house that big? I can tell you what's in Zack's. Five bedrooms, six baths, a huge kitchen, formal living and dining rooms, casual dining room with a soda fountain, and an enormous recreation room tricked out in wood paneling and white leather upholstery, featuring a large wet bar. Plus assorted nooks and crannies. And a full-size swimming pool in the backyard.

Forrest took a swig of his beer, maybe he'd noticed Bristow's smoldering eyes. "Good stuff," he said to Zack after glancing at the label. "Big body and bold hopping. Good fruity maltiness."

The beer was from one of Zack's microbrewery collections. He beamed happily. Forrest might sound like a know-it-all to me, but Zack was accepting him as a fellow connoisseur.

"So what did you mean about somethin' seemin' real?" Zack asked.

"Reina's ring," Forrest said. "Those are diamonds, not zirconias. Hobby of mine, diamonds."

Nice hobby if you can afford it, I thought.

"Well, for once you're wrong, Forrest," Reina said. "I know these are zirconias because my boyfriend said so."

Forrest shook his head. "Sorry to argue, Reina, but I'm never wrong about something like this. If your boyfriend says they are zirconias, he's lying to you."

A hot pink streak appeared on each of Reina's prominent cheekbones.

Luckily, Lonnie Tremaine and his California Rangers, one of our customers' favorite bands, and one we used regularly, chose that moment to blast into life, which effectively killed all conversation at just the right moment.

Reina stood up and walked over to a neighboring table, where she spoke to a dark-haired man. Evidently, she had asked him to dance, because he stood up at once and escorted her to the floor, where he propelled her into a rather staid two-step. "Who's that?" Savanna asked of nobody in particular.

"Kalesha's husband," Forrest said, and Savanna seemed satisfied, though still mildly puzzled.

After a moment, Savanna's frown cleared. "That's right, Kalesha told me she was married. She got married a couple months before Taylor and me."

The dark-haired man was apparently a good listener. Reina had a lot to say to him and she said it very rapidly and intently. He offered only a few words in response.

The Rangers played a variety of music to dance to. I danced a couple of numbers, then tried to disappear into the back wall. This was a night off—I didn't *have* to dance and I didn't want Timothy Perkins asking me.

I noticed that Reina was popular with the guys, especially Forrest. They danced together often. She talked to *him* intently, too. A couple of times he and she walked out to Adobe Plaza together. Ever curious, I sauntered out behind them once and saw them lighting cigarettes by the tall concrete cylinder filled with sand we'd put out for the smokers. It was a much-used spot, maybe a replacement for the old potbellied stove in the village store.

The next time Reina returned, some seriously beefy guy came over and took her hand and pulled her onto the dance floor. A second later they were charging around the floor doing the ten-step along with half a dozen other couples. The ten-step is not to be confused with the two-step. The ten-step features the guy holding the gal's hands above her head, both of them going forward around a circle. There's a lot of "heel out and up to the knee" kind of activity, with several trotting steps in between. Reina's cheeks were red before the dance was half over.

After a while, Lonnie segued into some slower and quieter numbers. Lonnie has a terrific voice, with a husky note in it that could break your heart. He's no hunk, but he has a clean-cut, freshly bathed look about him. He was recognized as a talent to watch by the Academy of Country Music last year. In my opinion, when he gets just a little better known he'll be selling out whole stadiums and we won't be able to afford him.

When Lonnie announced a brief intermission, Savanna hauled Zack and Angel and me off to introduce us to the few people we hadn't yet met. There were around forty of the classmates altogether, so their names had blurred early, but their nickname for themselves, "Dix's Mixes," sure did fit. I met Sakda, Francisca, Roberto, Jean-Pierre, Ng, Abdullah . . . .

"The melting pot in action," Savanna had told me earlier. "Black and white American, white European, Latino, Asian, Arabic—you name it."

Actually, my own high school in Sacramento, located near an Air Force base, had been just as interesting a mix. All schools should be like that.

Becky Mackinay was a Quinault, from Washington State, so we had something in common right from the start—I'd gone to Washington's U-Dub, and had stayed on in Seattle for the duration of my marriage to Rob Whittaker. Her husband hadn't been able to come with her, she said. He was home with their two-year-old son, Thomas junior.

Becky didn't work at looking "pretty" any more than I did. No makeup at all and her black hair was just dragged back off her face and fastened with a bit of narrow black ribbon wound round and round the long ponytail and tied in a knot. She had incredible cheekbones. She told me she and her husband both worked for a legal firm's Native American project, looking into land-use issues, child welfare disputes, and

Indian fishing cases. Since little Thomas's birth she'd been working mostly from home as a consultant so she could be there for her son.

Kalesha Atkins was maybe a little bit under six feet, a majestically large African-American woman in a psychedelic jersey dress. She was engaged in an argument about local politics with Dolores Valentino, a short woman with bulging muscles and eyes like those big-eyed children you see in catalogs of cheap art prints. Dolores informed us rather belligerently that she was a Mexican American—not to be called Latina or Hispanic.

"I was just saying to Kalesha and Becky that we who are called minorities will never be taken seriously until it is understood that we cannot all be lumped into one group," Dolores said to me in a voice that invited argument. "We must maintain our diversities."

I wasn't going to argue with anyone who was so obviously a serious bodybuilder, though it appeared she had a softer side—there was a valentine heart tattooed on her bare left arm. Closer examination showed that the arrow through it was dripping blood. Not so soft, after all.

"But we don't want to compete against each other," Kalesha said mildly. "There's a ton of benefits to coalition politics."

Becky gave a wicked little smile and declaimed, " 'All your strength is in your union. All your danger is in discord. Therefore be at peace henceforward, and as brothers live together.' "

"Chief Joseph?" a male voice asked. It belonged to the man Reina had asked to dance with her when the music first got under way. He had suddenly shown up between Becky and Kalesha. He was married to Kalesha, I recalled.

Becky shook her head. " 'Song of Hiawatha.' "

We all laughed, except for Dolores, who took a swig from a can of Diet Coke, then banged the can on the table, crushing it flat from top to bottom with the heel of her right hand. "African Americans and Native Americans won't be content until they take over California," she said aggressively. "This country even— maybe the world! My work involves furthering the cause of Mexican Americans." She looked at Angel as she spoke. He glanced nervously at the flattened pop can.

Becky touched my arm lightly. "Nice meeting you, Charlie," she said, then drifted away from the group.

"Dolores used to be a CPA," Savanna said. "She was another math whiz. But now she's back in school, earning a master's in sociology."

"I'm just a lowly X-ray technician," Kalesha said. "That's why I never win an argument with Dolo." There was a welcome note of humor in her contralto voice. She was a good-looking woman, with straightened hair that looked as if she'd curled it around her fingers before pinning it in place with little butterfly clips. On her it worked, just as her size did—she carried herself proudly.

"Dolores," Dolores corrected.

"Dolo has a problem with nomenclature," Kalesha said, her dark eyes glinting.

The band came back and started up with a change of rhythm. I looked up to see one of the women I'd met earlier—Francisca Gutierrez—taking up a position in front of the microphone. Evidently, she'd persuaded Lonnie to play some modernized Tejano music so she could perform. She could really belt out a song. Made my throat hurt just to listen to her.

Kalesha introduced us to her husband—Owen Jones. He was originally from Wales, she said. "First Welsh American I ever met. *Only* Welsh American I ever met," she added with a mischievous glance at Dolores. "He's very Americanized, though. I don't think he's bothered to maintain his diversities."

The man was as tall as Kalesha, but there was a lot less of him.

"Owen's an OB/GYN doctor," Kalesha offered. "That's as diverse as he gets."

Owen nodded, but didn't say anything.

"Where in Wales?" Zack asked. He was always interested in details, which was something people liked about him.

"Aberystwyth," Owen said.

"That's a great name for a town," I commented to draw him out. "Makes me want to go there."

"Watch your step, Charlie," Kalesha put in. "Owen's mine and I don't share."

She was joking, but she didn't have to worry anyway. Owen Jones wasn't at all my type, though probably any type would have been a lot better for me than the bad boys I always seemed to attract and fall for. He was a conservative-looking man, clean shaven, with dark eyes and Byronic black hair. He was wearing a sport jacket, black slacks, polished shoes, white shirt, and dark tie. He looked serious-minded. Dull. Older than Kalesha.

"Owen's not one of the old school chums," Kalesha said as if she'd read my mind. "He graduated six years earlier from a much posher school than ours. He's been in these United States since he was fourteen."

Dolores was now talking in a low voice with Angel, who was glancing from side to side as if looking for a way out. Savanna evidently noticed the same thing, she suddenly insisted he and I should teach everyone a line dance.

We chose the electric slide, which is about as simple as you can get unless you have two left feet.

I taught the basic vine, kick, rock and turn, then Angel and I gave a demonstration and walked everyone through the whole thing several times until they were able to do it to "Elvira."

All of this took up a good part of an hour. The only surprising thing was that Thad O'Connor, the pastor, picked the movements up faster than anyone, and was much more graceful about it than most. Watching him, I thought it might not have been so bad, going on a date with him. He would at least have been preferable to Timothy Perkins.

He started to say something to me as I left the floor, but I really needed to go to the rest room and pretended I didn't notice.

It was quiet in the rest room. I put a paper cover on the toilet seat, sat down, and discovered I was tired. It felt good to sit back and relax in peace for a few minutes. I even considered disappearing up to my loft, but knew I couldn't risk hurting Savanna's feelings.

I noticed abruptly that there was a pair of shoes in the adjoining stall—the handicapped stall. Shoes with feet in them, of course. I suppose it's much easier to clean rest rooms when they have these gaps at the bottoms of walls and doors. I've always thought it was interesting to look at shoes in those circumstances and wonder what the person in them looked like. When the person who belonged to the shoes emerged from the cubicle, it was often a surprise.

I knew whose feet were in *these* shoes, though—they had Reina Diaz's stiletto heels.

The feet weren't moving at all. That was unusual. Most people shuffle a little when they are on the pot. Tap their toes maybe.

Perhaps she was as tired as I was. She'd looked pooped right after that ten-step.

Maybe she was having some intestinal problem. That could be embarrassing. I should give her some privacy.

I hoisted myself up and out, washed my hands, and left the room.

Savanna stopped me as I entered the main corral. "Have you seen Miss Diaz?" she asked. "I haven't seen her in ages."

"Yes," I said. "I just saw her in the rest room."

Savanna smiled. "Maybe she's hiding out," she said as she walked away.

Sometimes I have a hunch. I've learned to pay attention. Turning on my heel, I headed back to the lobby, forcing myself not to run.

Zack was emerging from the men's room. I gestured

to him to come in the women's rest room with me. He didn't hesitate, which says a lot about him.

I called out Reina's name as soon as I entered.

There was no response.

"What's up?" Zack asked.

"Miss Diaz. Reina. I think something might be . . ." I broke off as I got up on tiptoe and tried to look over the door. It was taller than I am, so I bent down and looked under it instead. The shoes were still there. I knocked on the door. "Reina, are you okay?" I called.

I wanted her to be okay. I really did.

But she wasn't okay at all.

I saw that the moment I got down on my hands and knees and poked my head sideways under the door.

She was slumped back from a sitting position on the toilet. Her green silk jumpsuit was down around her knees. One of the reasons I would never wear a jumpsuit is that you have to take the whole thing off every time you go to the pot.

Her green panties were pulled down, too. All she had on from the knees up was a green lace bra.

Zack had stepped in next to me and was peering over the door. He made some kind of exclamation under his breath. I poked my head farther under the door. Reina's neck was at a very odd angle. Nobody could be alive with a neck at an angle like that.

CHAPTER 3

The way I saw it, I had to make sure the teacher was as dead as she looked. Without saying a word to Zack, who also seemed to have been struck dumb, I crawled under the door, reached up and checked Reina's carotid artery. Not a flutter. I noticed her hands were tightly clenched, which seemed odd. There was a piece of paper sticking out of one of them, torn around the edge.

Her eyes were open and protuberant. You don't want to know what the rest of her face looked like. There was definitely nobody home. I tried to convince myself that she might have had a heart attack and fallen backward and hit her head, but I knew damn well that wouldn't have made her head tip sideways on her neck like that.

I felt as if I'd stepped onto an elevator expecting it to go up but it had shot downward instead.

"Somebody killed her, huh?" Zack said.

I swallowed against a burning sensation in my chest. "That's what it looks like, for sure."

I slithered back under the door, stumbled into the farthest cubicle and threw up the chicken and rice Dorscheimer's had provided.

"Whoa, Charlie, you okay?" Zack called out, which was a dumb question given the circumstances.

"I'll make it," I mumbled. I waited a minute for things to settle down in my midsection, then emerged.

"Guess we'd better get Bristow on the job," Zack said as I washed my hands and rinsed my mouth.

I nodded. "I'll get him. You stay by the door and don't let anyone in."

Not bothering to dry my hands, I went shakily in search of Bristow. Savanna saw me speak to him. Something in our body language must have alerted her to trouble. She followed us out.

"It's Reina—Miss Diaz," I told her as we hurried toward the rest room.

"What is? What do you mean?" Savanna's eyes widened. "Is she sick?"

There was no way to soften the words. "She's dead."

Savanna made a little mewing sound of distress. "She had a heart attack? A stroke? She's only fifty. She seemed fine, she was dancing hard—the dance was too much for her? My God, I can't believe it. Are you sure, Charlie? Maybe she just fainted or something?"

Zack looked at her sympathetically as we entered the rest room. Bristow put a hand on her arm to quiet her. "The stall next to the far wall," I said.

He signaled us to stay near the entrance and I glanced at Savanna. Her face was ashy. I think she'd guessed this was not a natural death, but she didn't speak as Bristow peered over the top of the door just as Zack had done.

He was silent for several minutes, then muttered that his tool kit was in his car. "We have a tool kit in the cleaning crew's closet," I told him. "What do you need?"

"Screwdriver, tap hammer," he said.

I was back in no time, and Bristow removed the top and bottom hinge-pins from the left side of the cubicle door and eased himself in. I would never have thought of doing that. I had never even noticed you could get at them from the outside.

When Bristow reappeared, his mouth was set in a grim line.

"She was murdered, wasn't she?" Zack asked.

Bristow nodded. "Strangled, looks like."

Savanna's moan was more audible this time. "It's my fault," she wailed. "I brought her here, it was my idea to have the reunion here. And now she's dead."

"It probably wasn't a random killing," Bristow told her. "It could have happened wherever the reunion was held."

She shook her head, eyes welling with tears. Bristow came over, put his arms around her, and murmured gently to her as she sobbed. The burning sensation in my chest and throat didn't want to go away. After a minute or two, Bristow steered Savanna out of the rest room. Zack and I followed them out, making sure the door closed behind us. Bristow asked Zack to stand guard in the lobby and not let anyone go in or out of anywhere for any reason, then gestured me toward the office.

With his arm still around his wife's shoulders, he called Bellamy Park dispatch, then had me boot up the computer and type a notice in a large font saying the women's rest room was out of order, and another that stated the men's room was now unisex.

"Shouldn't we be telling everyone what's happened?" I asked.

"I don't want them to know we've found her until I have enough officers here to make sure nobody leaves," he said.

I stared at him, a chill turning my bones to icicles. He was saying the murderer was possibly still on the premises.

Zack chatted with me while I was taping the notices to the appropriate walls. "I remember one episode of *Prescott's Landing*, Sheriff Lazarro was called in on a strangled body. 'Strangling's a personal and up close kind of murder,' he said."

Zack often quotes from his old TV series. Occasionally he'd dig up a part of one of the plots to illustrate some theory he had about whatever crime we were involved in. Sometimes it fitted; sometimes it didn't.

"Someone had one hell of a grudge against that little lady," he was saying as Bristow and Savanna came out of the office.

Bristow nodded. "It must have been spontaneous, though—any kind of plan in mind he'd have been more likely to bring along a weapon."

"How can you be sure it was a guy?" I asked. Not that I'm for equal opportunity in murder, I was just curious.

Bristow got used to my nosiness sometime ago, though he often tells me to get over it. He usually answers my questions, all the same. "It would take strong hands to break someone's neck like that," he said. "Not too many women ..."

Savanna sobbed aloud and he broke off. "Maybe it's time we discarded that kind of thinking," he murmured after a while. "Women work out, women do jobs that were traditionally male—they are hardly the weaker sex anymore." He stopped abruptly again.

I wondered if he was thinking, as I was, of Dolores Valentino's muscles.

While we waited for the medical examiner and the crime-scene people, Bristow said he wanted me to write down exactly what I had seen and touched and done from the moment I realized something was wrong in the rest room. "ASAP," he added.

He went on to explain something he called Locard's Exchange Principle: "Any person passing through a room will unknowingly leave something there and take something away." I had an idea he was speaking so deliberately in order to calm Savanna. "Emile Locard was a French criminologist," he continued. "He conceived the principle more than half a century ago. It's still considered valid."

I looked at him. "You're telling me I shouldn't have gone under the door? But I wanted to see if there was anything I could do—if she was still alive—"

"That's always the primary duty of the first officer on the scene, Charlie. Most important thing is to check to see if the victim shows any signs of life and to give whatever aid is necessary, if it's not too late. You had the right instinct."

"But I messed up evidence?"

He inclined his head slightly to one side. "The rest-room floor might be conducive to fingerprints. Our murderer had to exit one way or another. He left the door locked, so he probably came out the way you went in. It's possible there might have been fibers, hair, or . . . ," he broke off, glancing at Savanna.

Semen? I wondered, and swallowed against the return of the burning sensation.

"You didn't touch the latch, did you?" Bristow asked.

I shook my head. "Just the floor and Reina's neck to feel for a pulse. Though I didn't think for a minute that she was alive. I'm sorry I didn't recognize it as a crime scene right away."

He studied me for a minute. "We may have to impound your clothing, Charlie, see if you picked up any traces."

Sometimes I'm not sure when Bristow is totally serious.

"We might possibly have to put a dent in your detecting career," he said sternly, then relented. "It's okay, Charlie, we just have to know what you touched so we can distinguish any of your hair and fibers from the murderer's."

Evidently, he saw the movements in the parking lot at the same time I did. There's a narrow window each side of the entryway. Still holding on to Savanna, he went out to greet the officers. Zack went with them. I went back to the office.

When I emerged, clutching my printed-out statement, the women's rest room was cordoned off with yellow crime-scene tape, but the door was open. I glimpsed someone inside with a camcorder, someone else making measurements. I recognized a very tall, slender black woman, last seen at a previous crime scene, wearing the same gray slacks and navy blazer she'd worn then. Her hair was pulled up into a twist and fastened with one of those dangerous-looking plastic claws.

It took me a minute to assign her a title and name: the county's deputy coroner, Jalena Devereau. Father's name James, mother's Elena, Bristow had told me when I first saw her.

I wandered out to the entryway to see what was going on outside. A couple of officers were writing down license plate numbers. Yellow crime-scene tape stretched around the whole tavern and parking lot. "We like to spread it around like a dog marking off his territory," Bristow had told me once.

Bristow, Savanna, and Zack were nowhere in sight.

I went into the main corral. Bristow was on the stage with a microphone. Evidently, he had just finished telling everyone what had happened to Miss Diaz. People were uttering cries of disbelief, many were crying. Pastor Thad and some others had huddled in a circle with their arms around one another's shoulders. Savanna and Becky Mackinay were hugging each other.

Savanna was still crying. Lonnie and the California Rangers were packing up their instruments and preparing to leave.

As the band descended the steps, Bristow called to them to stick around. "Nobody leaves," he said. "An officer will take your name and address and ask you a few questions, then you'll be free to go. We're going to do it alphabetically, so if your name starts with A, please get in line over there by Officer Dixon."

I noticed there were officers deployed around the room, and one stationed at each exit. It probably wasn't a random killing, Bristow had said earlier. Which meant Reina Diaz had most likely been strangled by the hands of someone attending the reunion, someone I had met, someone whose hand I had shaken. Queasiness roiled in my stomach, and for a moment I thought I was going to barf again, but I took a deep breath and held myself together.

At my side Perky—Timothy Perkins—made a sound of disgust. "How could anybody even think of killing someone in a latrine!" he muttered. "Think of the bacteria!"

I thought it might not be a bad thing if Timothy Perkins turned out to be the murderer. Anyone that callous deserved to be knocked off by the state. Besides, if he was the murderer I wouldn't have to go on a date with him.

Dolores Valentino popped up on my other side. "Did you read about that baby—that newborn baby— that was found in a toilet in Disney World a couple years ago?"

Her voice held a note of excitement. "A girl, I think it was. Her head was above the water and she was barely alive when they found her. They put her in something to get her temperature up and they were able to bring her back."

"Miss Diaz is dead," I said. "There's no doubt about that. She won't be coming back."

"You saw her?" Dolores squealed.

"I found her body," I admitted reluctantly, wishing I hadn't spoken up.

"Did you see the murderer?" Dolores's large brown eyes were fixed on my face. She was flushed, her complexion dewy with perspiration.

I looked at her hands, which were clenched in front of her. She had large hands—strong-looking.

I felt a twinge of fear. "I didn't see anyone. I certainly didn't witness the murder," I protested. "I came along well after Reina was killed. There was nothing to see."

Dolores wasn't going to let me off that easily. "Hey, listen here," she called to those nearby. "Charlie was the one who found the body. So, come on Charlie, what was she like, what was done to her?"

I had no desire to talk about how Reina Diaz had looked. "I'm forbidden to talk about it," I said, just as Bristow announced from the stage that we were not to discuss anything we might know or think we knew until the officers now present had a chance to talk to us.

Bristow brought an officer over to me and introduced us. Detective Sergeant Liz North. She had cool gray eyes and cropped brown hair.

"Liz worked for SFPD before coming out here," Bristow said. "She had one of the best case-closure records of anyone in her department."

Savanna had told me Bristow's new colleague was a woman. She'd replaced my old nemesis, Detective Sergeant Reggie Timpkin, who had been injured in the line of duty and was now working in administration.

Sergeant North asked me brusquely if we could use the office, then led the way there without waiting for an answer. Tough lady. I guess she had to be in that job.

After sitting down at my desk, she waved me to a chair, read over my statement, asked me a couple of questions, then had me sign it.

Her gaze was direct, intense, assessing, giving nothing of her own thoughts away. "You live upstairs, I understand."

I nodded. I was beginning to feel as if I'd been found guilty of something. I'd been raised to respect authority figures and it had left a mark on me.

"Was your door locked?"

"I always lock it when people are on the premises. We don't get many drunks, but occasionally . . ." I tried a woman-to-woman, you-understand-what-I'm-saying kind of smile.

She looked at me coldly.

"Are you going to search my loft?" I asked.

She let a beat go by, her gaze still examining my face for clues. "As long as it was secured at the time of the incident, I'd need to show probable cause to get a warrant, unless I thought the killer was hiding in there. You think that's likely?"

"I hope not," I said with considerable feeling.

Her face was still without expression. I decided I didn't want to alienate Detective Sergeant Liz North. "If you want to search my loft, you have my permission," I said.

"Let's do that," she said promptly.

I was a bit startled. To tell the truth, I hadn't

expected her to take me up on my offer—I'd just wanted to sound innocent.

She glanced around my apartment, something that's easy to do since it's minimally furnished. I don't want a bunch of possessions nailing me to the spot. She took a look inside the bathroom, saw Benny in his cage and stooped to poke a finger through and rub his head, which gave me cause to relax a little. "Cute bunny," she said.

Anyone who likes my rabbit can't be all bad.

"How do you like Bellamy Park?" I asked as we descended the stairs.

"Makes a nice change from the city," she said over her shoulder.

"You didn't like the city?"

She turned her head and twitched her lips in what might have been intended as a smile. "It's un-American not to like San Francisco. Everybody likes San Francisco."

She shrugged and continued on down. "The city's okay. I just happened to volunteer for duty in high-crime areas, so I didn't spend much time on the tourist track. I did vice, narcotics, rape—working toward homicide. Three years ago I made sergeant and finally got to be a detective."

"You get any static from your male colleagues?"

"You ever watch *Prime Suspect* on PBS? Helen Mirren?" We had reached the bottom of the stairs. "Some of my male colleagues will never accept women officers as equals. Doesn't matter how hard you work, how good you are, how tough you are, you're not going to change their attitude."

"You mean Bristow—"

She didn't let me finish. "Taylor Bristow is a prince among men."

She smiled wryly. "Savanna better treat him good or I might be inclined to make a move on him."

She was joking, I hoped.

Back in the main corral—God, that almost sounds like "meanwhile, back at the ranch"—people were hanging around, awaiting their turn to be questioned.

"Pastor Thad's been counseling people," Savanna told me. Her dark eyes were red-rimmed. "He reminded me of how Miss Diaz used to encourage me when I complained I could never learn everything there was to learn before I could graduate. 'Just don't bite off more than you can chew at one time,' she used to say. 'The most important time is now, the most important thing is whatever you are doing, the most important person is the person you are with. Live in the moment, and tackle one task at a time.'"

She shook her head. "I never thought when I arranged for CHAPS to host the reunion that I'd be living in *this* moment." She sighed deeply. "But what Thad said helped. He also said she'd always be with all of us, living on in us and what she did for us. I guess he's a good preacher, maybe I'll have to start going to his church."

I wondered if she was feeling the need of counseling where her marriage was concerned, but decided Miss Diaz had a point—tackle one task at a time.

The preacher in question drew up alongside about

then, just as Bristow reached us. "I'd really like to say a prayer over Reina's body," Thad said.

One thing I liked about him—he had a normal voice. You know what I mean? Certain preachers—the tele-vangelist kind, for example—get this "holier than thou," smarmy sort of voice going that turns me off altogether.

Bristow was shaking his head. "When we're through, maybe," he said.

Thad accepted the decision with a submissive nod. Wise of him. It's never a good idea to argue with Bris-tow—he's a really nice guy but he never forgets, or lets anyone else forget, who's in charge of the world.

"Reina said she had a boyfriend," I reminded Bris-tow after Thad and Savanna walked away, his arm around her shoulders. Forrest Kenyon watched them. So did Bristow, but he didn't look the way he had when Forrest was holding Savanna's hand. He just looked sad, which worried me a whole lot.

"I think you were close by when Reina mentioned her boyfriend," I said. "Didn't she say they were going to get married soon? He gave her the ring she was wearing, remember?"

Bristow nodded. "The one Mr. Kenyon was guessing the worth of."

The emphasis he gave "Mr. Kenyon" indicated a serious amount of dislike.

"I've been trying to remember if Reina was wearing that ring when I found her in the toilet cubicle," I said. "I can't bring an image of it to mind. Yet it was such a conspicuous thing I should surely have noticed it on her finger."

I closed my eyes momentarily and tried to picture the way Reina had looked. It was a minute or two before I could bring to mind where her hands had been.

She had been clutching a piece of paper. In her right hand. Both hands had been clenched tightly. No ring on the left one.

I opened my eyes and looked at Bristow, whose eyebrows had climbed to where his hairline would have been if he'd had one. I shook my head and he nodded slightly. He hadn't seen the ring, either.

Bristow turned toward the group closest to us. "Does anyone know who the teacher's boyfriend was?" he asked.

"She never mentioned a boyfriend to me," Kalesha said. Her eyes were as puffy as Savanna's. "We stayed in touch by e-mail and had lunch or dinner now and then. I don't recall any talk of a boyfriend. In fact . . ."

"Go on," Bristow said when her voice trailed off.

Kalesha shook her head. "I'm just remembering when we talked on the phone a couple weeks back, Reina was self-conscious about never having married. She was afraid people at the reunion would think she was a lesbian."

"Was she a lesbian?" Bristow asked.

"Couldn't prove it by me," Kalesha said.

"So?" another woman said in a challenging way. It was Francisca, the woman who had sung the Tejano song earlier. "Would it be so bad if she was?"

"Hey, I didn't mean anything, Francisca," Kalesha said hastily, holding her hands palm outward in a gesture of surrender. "It just occurred to me Reina might have bought that ring herself so she could pretend she was getting married."

"She wouldn't want anyone starting a rumor about her being a lesbian," a woman named Patricia-something chimed in. "Anybody got that idea, Reina'd be in trouble with the PTA right away. Even at Dix's Mixes. We might all be misfits, but we had our standards."

"You think being a lesbian is beneath the standards?" Francisca said. She had a look in her eyes that spelled danger to anyone who wanted a fight. She had an amazing amount of hair, long and really fat. It looked to me as if she had hair extensions in there, the kind you see advertised in women's magazines: "Run your fingers through it, wash it, comb it, no one will ever guess . . ." But hair *grows*, I always wanted to say. What happens then? Do you get two inches of flat hair, then this whole bush sticking out? Or do you have to have the extensions unstuck and stuck on again? One hair at a time? Or do they, shudder, *staple* it on your scalp?

Savanna had come up beside me. "Did the murderer *have* to be someone who was at the reunion?" she asked.

"Seems likely," Kalesha said.

"I don't see why," Forrest Kenyon said as he joined the group. "Anyone could have come through the front entry and ambushed Miss Diaz in the rest room, or on the way to the rest room."

Bristow looked at him without expression. I could feel hostile vibes coming from him. I wouldn't want to be the one making Taylor Bristow hostile. That's a whole lot of law enforcement officer, not just extra tall, but built. And he has this *presence*. Usually he dresses in a polo shirt and khakis, but tonight Savanna had coaxed him into a suit and tie. Whatever he was wearing, you were always aware that he was a man of substance.

"Seems far more reasonable to me that Reina would be killed by an outsider," Forrest persisted, evidently not intimidated by Bristow's grim mouth and narrowed eyes. "Everyone in this room loved Reina. Revered her."

"I believe my wife said you were the teacher's pet," Bristow said evenly.

"None of us had cause to harm her," Forrest said flatly.

"Homicide isn't always reasonable," Bristow said.

"Well, it seems to me an absolute waste of time to detain us here and—"

"Twenty," I said loudly, looking at Bristow's flaring nostrils.

Forrest's head swung my way.

"The math question you posed," I said. "I guess my brain must have been working on it. The answer's twenty. There are twenty sevens between one and one hundred."

It's disconcerting not to be able to see someone's eyes clearly. I wondered if the dark glasses were an affectation, or armor. A shadow of a smile appeared around his mouth. "That's real good, Charlie, most people say nineteen. They either forget seventy, or they forget seventy-seven has two sevens in it."

I really didn't care. But I was relieved that the tension had dropped a couple of degrees.

"People were coming into the building all evening," Angel said to Bristow. He was standing on the outer edge of the group, P.J. close by his side. Her eyes looked red, too. She hadn't known Reina at all, but neither had I, and I sure felt like bawling. Experiencing someone's sudden death is always traumatic—and when it's murder, it's frightening, too. *There, but for the grace of God. . . .*

"Dorscheimer's restaurant was open in the lobby until ten," Angel went on. "Gina's . . . Buttons & Bows was open, too. The western store. People were going outside to smoke. Miss Diaz went out to smoke several times."

We have a strictly enforced no-smoking rule inside CHAPS.

"We'll talk to everyone we can find," Bristow promised.

CHAPTER 4

CHAPS was crawling with media types for the next couple of days. A body on the potty made for great copy. Detective Sergeant Liz North told us we'd be A-OK to open on Sunday night, but we decided to give ourselves a break and hope sightseers would lose interest by Tuesday.

They didn't.

After the hordes left—we'd wanted to find ways to up our income, but this wasn't what we'd had in mind—Bristow showed up and we gathered in the main corral as we usually did when we somehow managed to get ourselves involved in police business.

This time, however, I had no intention of taking part in the inquiry—I had no reason to do so. But having met Reina, I was naturally interested in hearing how the case was proceeding. We were all off duty, so Angel served us beer or wine according to our individual tastes.

"This is a copy of the printout of a photograph Miss Diaz was clutching in her hand," Bristow said, laying a sheet of paper on the table.

"Printout?" I queried, leaning over to take a look. "From a computer?"

It was a good print, even on ordinary computer paper—a photograph of Reina Diaz at a much younger age. When Bristow had mentioned a photograph, my mind had popped up a suggestion that it might be one of Reina in the nude or in a compromising situation that might lead to blackmail and murder. But she was fully clothed and sitting in a regular studio pose, wearing a full skirt and a blouse with a round, lace-trimmed collar. She looked shy. Innocent.

"Her hair was darker then," I said, handing the photo on to Savanna.

She frowned. "Seems to me her hair was always brown. But she looks about twenty here, so that was ten years before I knew her. Maybe it's just a dark photo—though her face looks pale enough."

"I'd have thought she'd have some gray in her hair now," I said. "She was fifty, after all. Maybe she lightened her hair."

Savanna shrugged. She appeared to be getting tearful again. I put an arm around her shoulders, took the photo from her and gave it to Zack.

"Fine-lookin' gal," he commented.

"Her boyfriend must feel real bad," Angel said softly.

"He may not know she's dead, unless he read it in the newspaper or heard it on the radio or TV," Bristow said. "I can't tell him until I know who he is." He rubbed his smooth head. "Thought maybe he'd come forward after the media got hold of the story. He could just be avoiding the circus atmosphere. Sure would like to talk to him."

"Kalesha kept up with Miss Diaz," Savanna said. "I thought you were going to talk to her."

"Kalesha said she'd never heard of Miss Diaz having a boyfriend," I said.

"When did she say that?"

"When Bristow asked her. She said she thought Reina might have made up the boyfriend so people at the reunion wouldn't think she was a lesbian."

Bristow shot me a look. "Do I get a chance to say anything here, Charlie, or are you taking over the investigation? Just because you found the victim doesn't mean you are responsible for her."

I gave him a view of my totally innocent face, which seemed to worry him.

"Did you decide Kenyon was right about the stones in that ring she was wearin' bein' real diamonds?" Zack asked.

Bristow considered for a moment before deciding it was okay to reply. He always got very slow and deliberate when a case was being discussed. Mostly he stuck to a need-to-know basis. But in this case, he evidently thought it wouldn't hurt to give with some information.

"We can't make that decision until we come up with the ring," he said. "To date, it's as invisible as the boyfriend."

"It *was* stolen then?" I said. "It wasn't in her purse?"

"Interestin'," Zack commented. "Shouldn't be hard to spot if it shows up in a pawnshop."

"Far as I know, Kenyon was the only individual

who figured the ring had any value." Bristow's voice was casual, but Savanna's head came up sharply and she narrowed her eyes at him. He was looking at the photo again, though, and didn't notice.

"You talk to him about it?" Zack asked.

Bristow nodded. "Couple of times. He went into a whole rigmarole about how he was just teasing Reina by saying it was real."

"You believe him?" Zack asked. Every once in a while, Zack morphs into Sheriff Lazarro, the character he played on TV. The forehead knots, the body leans forward to show the depth of his interest, the eyes squint to show intelligence. He does it very convincingly. And sexily. He does everything sexily.

"Forrest Kenyon doth protest too much, methinks," Bristow said. Zack isn't the only one who morphs.

Sheriff Lazarro was fully engaged now. "If Kenyon did believe or had reason to believe those rocks were real, he'd be the one most likely to steal the ring, wouldn't you say?"

"Zack!" Savanna protested before Taylor Bristow could say anything. "Don't *you* start in on poor Forrest. Taylor's already paranoid about him. He's interviewed him *twice!*"

"The operative word being 'interviewed,'" Bristow pointed out. "Not interrogated, sweetheart, *interviewed*."

Savanna seemed about to argue some more, so I jumped in with a distraction, pointing at the photo that Bristow had placed on the table in front of him. "That's a good copy. Looks as if Reina might have torn the page from a pad or something. I've wondered about that, by the way."

Bristow looked at me sideways. "Surprise, surprise," he murmured. "Ms. Plato is wondering."

I ignored the sarcasm. "She hadn't been dead long when I found her, but her hand was tightly closed. Wasn't that a bit soon for rigor mortis?"

Bristow rolled his eyes ceilingward. "Charlie's been studying pathology. God help us all."

His smile took the sting out of his words. "Interesting answer to your question, Charlie. It was supplied by Ms. Devereau, our deputy coroner. Seems Miss Diaz experienced what is called a cadaveric spasm, sometimes called instantaneous rigor mortis, though it is a different process altogether. Doesn't happen often. Usually follows when there has been some kind of exertion prior to death. . . ."

Angel offered a suggestion. "She danced the ten-step."

Bristow's eyebrows rose. "Did she? I guess I wasn't watching."

"I forgot about that," I said. "Would the ten-step count as exertion?"

"I don't know, Charlie, I wouldn't think it would be enough for that result, but I'm no expert."

I was disappointed. "I thought that might set the time of death. I mean, if the ten-step could have been the cause, it would mean she was killed right after doing it."

He looked at me as if I was a particularly bright pupil. "It's a good theory, Charlie. But it's more likely that she exerted herself in the struggle before she was killed. There was considerable bruising . . ."

"The struggle?" Savanna asked, looking horrified. "You mean she was raped?"

Bristow shook his head. "There's no evidence of rape. I meant the struggle while he was strang—trying to kill her."

Savanna subsided with a deep sigh. Of relief perhaps. Murder seems much worse if the person is made to suffer some other pain or indignity beforehand.

"You were explaining . . . ," I reminded Bristow.

"Cadaveric spasm. I'm not clear on what the process is precisely, but the voluntary muscles, usually of one muscle group, contract at the moment of death, and freeze in that position."

I thought about it. "So it wouldn't be possible for someone to put that paper in her hand after she died?"

"Correct. There isn't always a cadaveric spasm, but if there is something frozen in the victim's hand, an investigator knows for sure the individual had the object in hand before death. It seems likely that the killer tried to take it out of her hand. Which would explain why the paper was torn."

"Can you get the murderer's fingerprints off the original page?" I asked.

"Doesn't seem too likely, they'd probably be smeared, but the lab is working on it."

"How about DNA?" Zack asked.

"We are most certainly trying to get a match. People do shed DNA. You can get DNA off many things. Remember the Unabomber case? They got DNA from saliva on a postage stamp. It can be picked up from a pen, keys, a telephone. Question is, what did our killer touch? Reina's neck, certainly."

Savanna made a small sound of protest. I shuddered.

"Unfortunately, it's also possible for someone to unknowingly pick up other people's DNA and leave it at a scene. Miss Diaz danced with several men." Bristow paused. "A major problem is that the state labs are having a hell of a time keeping up. Short on staff, short on money. Constant flow of stuff coming in."

He glanced at Zack. "Too bad this isn't *Prescott's Landing*—seemed to me old Sheriff Lazarro never had to wait for lab results."

Detective Sergeant Bristow was one of the thousands of people who had actually watched *Prescott's Landing*. Which was surprising in an otherwise intelligent man. I'd have thought he watched it for the entertainment of picking out egregious police-procedure errors, but when he first met Zack, there was no doubting that he was a real fan. Go figure.

Zack frowned importantly in true Lazarro fashion. "He sure had nerve, killin' her in a women's rest room with all the women that were here. People comin' and goin' like Angel said."

Bristow nodded. "He probably wasn't doing much heavy thinking. He got lucky—apparently, nobody saw him."

He paused, then went on. "But we'll get him, you can be sure of that. Whoever he is, we'll get him."

"You find out who else went out to smoke besides Reina?" I asked.

"Surely. Miss Atkins, that whole group that came from Oakland, Mr. Kenyon—"

"Forrest didn't kill her," Savanna said firmly. "Forrest adored Miss Diaz and she adored him."

"They quarreled about the ring in front of us," Bristow pointed out. "Neither one sounded too adoring then."

Savanna glared at him. She rarely gets mad, but when she does there's no mistaking it. Her whole posture, which is usually relaxed and easygoing, becomes as still and cold as an ice sculpture, and her voice takes on a clipped note.

"Forrest knows stuff."

"He's a know-it-all," Bristow said.

"He *knows* stuff," Savanna repeated. "If he said the diamonds were real, then they are real."

"Told *me* he was teasing," Bristow reminded her. "Are you saying he was lying to me?"

"I'm outta here," Angel said softly, getting to his feet. Angel looks like a tough hombre, but he's a gentle man and can't abide argument. I get uncomfortable myself, especially when the people arguing are people I care about.

"I'm sorry, Angel," Savanna said right away, obviously realizing he was upset.

He gave her an apologetic smile. "I have to be going anyway, Savanna, I have a date with P.J."

We watched him leave, stunned into silence.

"Far as I know, Angel's auction date with P.J. wasn't for tonight," Zack said. "Angel arranged to take P.J. into the city for dinner for that. Next weekend. I heard them talkin' about it."

"Then Angel must have agreed to an extra date," I said.

"You're so stubborn," Savanna said to Bristow.

Zack and I exchanged a glance. We'd evidently missed something.

"He absolutely refuses to wear a bulletproof vest," Savanna said.

I blinked. "When did that come up?"

"My wife feels like arguing with me for the sake of argument," Bristow said.

"They call that tombstone courage," Savanna said. "Going without a bulletproof vest. I call it being careless and stubborn and not caring about your family."

"Damn thing's uncomfortable," Bristow said mildly.

"So is being dead," Savanna said. She stalked over to the bar and poured herself a glass of Chardonnay, her movements still stiff and angry.

"She's worried sick about you," I murmured to Bristow.

He gave me a fond look. "I know that, Charlie," he said. He hesitated. "She's a little cranky lately. We both are."

"Four more months before you find out if you were infected," Zack said dolefully.

"We'll make it," Bristow said.

I hoped he was right.

He went over to the bar himself, ostensibly to get another beer. He put a hand on Savanna's shoulder and she looked at him with so much worry, so much love, it brought a lump to my throat.

"I guess they still aren't gettin' any sex," Zack said, fortunately in a low voice. "I'm probably goin' to get cranky myself if you don't change your mind about me bein' on probation, darlin'. Very harmful to the adult male, bein' deprived. Didn't you learn that from guys in high school? Back seat of the car?"

I ignored him. "Has anything new happened about the kid whose needle you got stuck with?" I asked Bristow as he and Savanna returned to the table.

"He's been charged with reckless endangering," he said.

"He should have been charged with attempted murder," Savanna said.

Bristow touched her arm. "He could only be charged with attempted murder if he intended me to die," he said gently.

A shudder went through Savanna's body. "He knew that needle was in his pocket."

They were both still tense. They both jumped when Bristow's pager sounded. He glanced at it and said he had to go. Zack offered to take Savanna home.

Savanna chewed on her fingernails for a few minutes after her husband left, while Zack and I sipped our wine and exchanged awkward glances. Savanna never used to have nervous habits like that. She used to be serene at all times. Marriage sure can mess up your head.

"Do you think Liz North is a lesbian?" she asked abruptly.

"I've no idea," I said.

Zack looked thoughtful. "Could be." She must not have come on to him. He'd consider that proof.

Savanna wasn't listening to either of us. "I thought maybe she was when I first met her, but now I think maybe she likes Taylor."

I remembered Liz saying Savanna needed to watch out. I sure wasn't going to pass that on.

"Jalena Devereau's a very attractive woman, don't you think?" she went on.

Major insecurity going on here.

"I think Taylor wants to prove Forrest killed Miss Diaz," she said next.

I was getting a bit dizzy with the speed with which she was segueing.

She nodded confirmation to herself, and gnawed her fingernails some more. "Taylor's going to railroad him."

"He would never do that," I said firmly.

"Normally, no, but I think he's guessed Forrest used to be in love with me. He doesn't like him, you could see that."

Well, that was true. All the same. . . .

"Would you see what you can do?" she asked, looking me in the eye for the first time.

"Do?" I echoed, feeling a rush of panic. Male/female relationships aren't exactly my forte. You may have noticed.

She had a pleading expression on her face. "You and Zack helped Angel out with his problem, and Thane Stockton when he asked you, and you worked together on Zack's situation."

"They were all in danger," I reminded her.

"Well, I'm in danger, too. And so is my husband, if he blinds himself to any suspect except Forrest, just because Forrest *likes* me. You can see how bad that would be for our marriage, and for Taylor's integrity."

"You used the present tense," I said.

"You said Forrest *likes* you," Zack repeated when she looked blank. "He still carryin' a torch?"

She sighed. "So he says. But I'm not interested in *him*. Not that way. Honestly." She looked earnestly from Zack to me. "I love Taylor, stubborn as he is lately."

"So what do you want us to do?"

Her eyes widened with surprise. "Find out who killed Reina Diaz," she said, as if that went without saying.

"Oh," I said, with a mild injection of sarcasm. "Is that all?"

"Yes," she said.

After a minute of silence, I offered the opinion that this was going to take a while and suggested we move upstairs to my loft so I could check on Benny and we could be marginally more comfortable. I say marginally because my furniture came mostly from the East Dennison Goodwill store. Not that I was all that hard up; rather, I'd stayed in my former marriage to Rob Whittaker too long because I was attached to my house and furniture. Which seems rather a shallow reason to put up with a man who constantly boffed his female patients, once he'd finished making them over into objects of beauty. Yeah, I thought it was sick, too, but I stayed on way longer than I should have. Rob was a well-known plastic surgeon, the kind Hollywood stars consulted. Did I mention that?

Zack sat on the old rocker cradling Benny in his hands; Savanna and I were on the broken-down sofa. Benny loved to hide out under the sofa, and I had an idea he was gradually removing the stuffing from the inside. It felt unreliable. I imagined a maze of tunnels throughout. The burrowing instinct has to be present even in a store-bought rabbit, wouldn't you think?

For the next hour, we chewed over that whole evening of the reunion, each of us offering up whatever memories we had. Then I asked Savanna, "Who do you think was most likely to kill Reina Diaz?"

"I'm not sure Taylor's right that it's a man," she said promptly, "but only because of what Reina said when I first talked to her about having the reunion at CHAPS. Or maybe not so much what she said as the way she said it."

She paused, her face crumpling. "Another thing she said was that she was dying to see me. *Dying* to. People say that all the time. I'm dying to go, dying to see you. They don't expect to *do* it."

I put an arm around her shoulder and she took a deep breath and blinked several times. "I admired these beautiful red roses Reina had in a crystal vase on her dining table and she said they were sent to her by a former student and she was a bit worried about it. She said she knew for sure the person was coming to the reunion, so they could have a conversation then."

She paused and looked at us expectantly. "Those are almost her exact words. You see how she avoided giving away the person's sex?"

"She didn't say who it was?" Zack asked.

"Nope."

"But it was definitely someone from your class?"

"She as good as said so." Savanna twisted her hands in her lap. "This former student had suddenly started calling her out of the blue, about five months ago, and kept on calling her and sending red roses every week. She had this really . . . arch look on her face when she talked about the whole thing."

She pulled at the fringe on her shirt, wrapping it around a finger, then letting it go. "She said she'd read some survey that said stalkers target a million women a year, and some other article that said that was how stalking often started—with calls and flowers and stuff, and it seemed very weird that a student would suddenly start communicating with her like that. She said this person had always had a crush on her even in school. She'd had to be firm with the student then and she meant to be firm now. The person would be bound to get over it soon, she said. Then she said she couldn't tell me who the person was because she didn't want me telling my husband and getting the person in trouble. She could handle it herself, she said."

She leaned back against the sofa cushions and shook her head. "Since I married Taylor nobody will tell me anything," she complained.

Zack and I exchanged a guilty look, we'd kept a few things from her for just that reason.

"Didn't you mention that Forrest was 'teacher's pet' in high school?" Zack asked.

"That was a whole other thing," she said, sounding irritated. "Miss Diaz liked Forrest because he was so smart, and she admired him because he was a daredevil. Mountain climbing, skydiving, sailing, rafting, scuba diving—anything that had an element of danger. Forrest liked her of course, just as we all did. But Forrest *loved* me."

"Have you told Taylor about someone calling Reina and sending her flowers?" I asked.

She looked horrified. "Of course not! You know who he'd suspect right away. You aren't to tell him, either." She changed her tone. "Please don't tell him."

"So you don't think it was Forrest then?" Zack asked in what was supposed to be a casual voice.

Savanna and I both looked at him.

"Okay," he said.

"So what do you say?" Savanna asked. "Will you see what you can find out?"

Zack and I exchanged a glance. How could we say no to Savanna? Okay, okay, I wasn't exactly disinterested in finding out who killed Reina. If you found a body in *your* rest room, would *you* just walk away?

Zack's eyes looked interested, too. "Okay with me," he said.

I nodded. "Me too."

CHAPTER 5

In recent years it has become customary to make a remembrance pile wherever somebody dies—at the side of a highway, next to a school, outside a convenience store. It's a nice custom, I guess, but it worried me to have complete strangers walking up with an armload of flowers and putting them next to the entryway to CHAPS. Some people even came inside as if they were going to Dorscheimer's or Buttons & Bows, and placed wreaths and teddy bears outside the women's rest room. The media hadn't spared any of the details of Reina's death. I even caught a couple of teenagers taking photos of the toilet where she had died.

Over the next few days I hung around in the lobby more than usual, keeping an eye on things in my capacity as security guard. Sometimes I wandered down in the night to make sure no one had hidden themselves away somewhere. I wasn't sleeping well anyway. Nightmares about Reina Diaz and the way she'd looked in that cubicle kept waking me, and then I couldn't get back to sleep. A lot of the time I felt anxious and nervous, which wasn't like my normal self.

I'd gone through that same set of problems a couple of times before. Post-traumatic stress syndrome, the doctor I'd consulted had told me. He'd offered me tranquilizers, but I turned them down and added a few herbal remedies to my arsenal of vitamins.

I happened to be on my self-imposed duty on the day when I saw Forrest Kenyon getting out of a BMW, with a single red rose in his hand.

It seemed as good a time as any to start working on my promise to Savanna.

I exited casually and trotted over to my Jeep Wrangler, then looked inside it as though checking on something. It was breezy out—still hot, though. The air smelled toasted. Maybe the chef at Casa Blanca was frying flour tortillas. I trotted back to CHAPS, arriving just in time to "see" Forrest placing his rose on the makeshift shrine.

We chatted for a minute about how many people had known and loved Reina—though I suspected some of the offerings were from the merely curious. Then I invited him to join me for one of Dorscheimer's wonderful turkey sandwiches.

Several female heads turned as Forrest followed me and the waiter to a booth. He was a good-looking guy. I suspected he knew that, just as he knew everything else.

"This is the sandwich?" he asked as he scanned the menu. "The one called Charlie's Turkey Sandwich?"

"They call it after me because they make it to my specifications," I told him. "They use real turkey breast and not that awful deli kind. I'm very particular about my turkey sandwich. This one includes a thin spread of Gorgonzola on one slice of multigrain bread, mayonnaise on the other, a leaf or two of romaine, and a couple of slices of onion."

"I rant about turkey myself," Forrest said with one of his little gassy smiles. "I think most of the real turkeys have been done away with. Growers nowadays produce rounded blobs of gelatinous goop that don't have any bones in them. They don't need a mate, they reproduce themselves. Hermaphroditic turkeys."

There was an element of surprise in my laughter. I hadn't noticed that he had a sense of humor, and I certainly hadn't expected to find anything in common with him. I felt quite charitable toward him all of a sudden. Anyone who joined my crusade against ersatz turkey couldn't be all bad.

"Are you married?" I asked after the flurry of serving us was over. It hadn't occurred to me to ask Savanna. I guess I figured him for an eternal bachelor, the playboy type.

"I was," he said, and I amended the image to the divorced playboy type.

"My wife died in January," he said slowly, his voice breaking slightly. He was biting his lower lip, as though to stop it from trembling.

I had obviously misjudged this guy considerably. I had to stop jumping to conclusions about people, I scolded myself, as I had done many times before. Someday I was going to learn to wait until all the evidence was in before passing judgment.

"I'm sorry," I said.

He attempted a smile that didn't quite work and busied himself grinding pepper a little too vigorously onto his mesclun salad. "She was ill for a long time," he said. "Non-Hodgkin's lymphoma."

"It must have been terrible."

He looked thoughtful. "In many ways it was of course, though she had the best of care. But cancer is nasty and messy and people suffering from it can't always be saintly about it. But we came very close together during the last year, closer and more loving than many people do in their whole lifetime. I will never forget her. Nor will I ever stop grieving."

He sighed deeply. "It doesn't matter how much you expect death, you always hope for a miracle."

Seven months ago, my brain noted. Was it possible that the death of Forrest's wife might qualify as a triggering impulse in the life of the man who might have stalked Reina, starting "about" five months ago? I wished I could see Forrest's eyes more clearly through those tinted glasses of his.

"I was . . . devastated," he went on, and the devastation was so starkly clear in his voice that I forgot to be a cold, calculating investigator and put a hand over his. He turned his hand over and squeezed mine. "Savvy says you are looking into Reina's murder," he said.

"Shoot," I said.

"You didn't want her to tell me?" He set his sandwich down on his plate and looked at me directly. "You surely don't think I killed Reina? I know Savvy's husband has cast me in the role of villain here, but that's just because he knows I used to be sweet on Savvy. As I still am. She's a hell of a woman. Always was, always will be. But you, Charlie, what did I ever do to you? You don't even know me."

"I don't suspect you," I said, though I wasn't being completely truthful. "I suspect everybody," I amended.

He summoned a laugh. "What was my motive?" he asked.

I didn't know how much Savanna had told him, and I didn't want to talk about the guy who had been calling Reina in recent months. "Something in the past maybe?" I suggested.

He shook his head. "The only thing between Reina and me was that I adored her, the way we all did, and was grateful to her for thinking—and saying—that I was brilliant, when all I was told at home was how stupid I was."

"So who would *you* put on your suspect list?" I asked. Seemed as good a question as any and would maybe get me out of the hot seat here.

He sat back, his brow furrowing above the dark glasses. "Well, Dolores was always going off like a firecracker. She and Reina used to butt heads all the time." He paused. "It's possible she had a crush on Reina. I seem to remember her fixing those big chocolate eyes of hers on Reina at all times."

"How do you think Reina would have responded to something like that?" I asked carefully.

"With sympathy, but a negative response. Reina was unmistakably heterosexual. But never judgmental. She might have tried to fix Dolo up with Francisca." His odd little grin showed up again.

"It was a long time ago, anyway," I said. "Even if Dolores did approach Reina, and Reina turned her down, I wouldn't think Dolores would wait this long to kill Reina."

"*Somebody* held a grudge a long time," he said.

"You think it *was* a revenge killing?"

"There are a lot of motives for murder, Charlie. Greed, jealousy, fear, the list is probably endless. Why not revenge? Here you have a twenty-year reunion and someone kills the teacher. Isn't it possible something happened twenty years ago that never found closure, until now?"

"What do you suppose it was?" I asked.

The waiter arrived with our sandwiches just as I posed the question, thus giving Forrest time to think up an answer. "Much as I hate to use the words, I have to admit that I don't know," he said smoothly. "I'm just proposing scenarios here. Far as I know, nothing ever went wrong between Reina and any of her students. She was a remarkable teacher and she made all of us remarkable. Why would anyone kill her for that?"

"You just said you thought it possible," I pointed out.

"Just idle thoughts, Charlie."

It seemed possible to me that he was trying to confuse me. He was succeeding.

The phone was ringing in my loft as I headed up after saying goodbye to Forrest. I caught it on the fourth ring, and immediately wished I hadn't.

"Hello, Charlie," a familiar voice said.

Rob Whittaker, my ex-husband. His voice no longer produced a tug of regret in my mind. I was over him and the havoc he'd created in my life. But being over him didn't mean I was ready to get back to being friends.

"Hi," I said cautiously.

"What's all this about you finding another body?"

I groaned. "That got out? The police said they'd try to keep my name from the media."

"They should know better than to make a promise like that. It's true then?"

"Yes, it's true."

"In the ladies' rest room?"

"The women's rest room, yes."

"Must have been tough on you," he said.

Jeez. It wasn't fair to work on me with sympathy.

"It was."

"Are you mad at me for calling?" he asked.

"No."

Maybe if I stayed monosyllabic, he'd give up on me.

"Then why are you being so . . . curt?"

He sounded hurt. Too bad. Catching him boffing Trudi the model hadn't done a whole lot for me, either.

"You call me only when a dead body shows up around here. What do you expect?" I said.

He sighed. "You're right, Charlie. I should call more often. I'm sorry."

Now look what I'd done.

"That's okay," I said.

"I was going to call you anyway. I have news."

He was going to get married. How did I feel about that? Okay, I decided. Though maybe someone should warn the intended about his tendency to stray. Not me.

"It's about Ryan."

So I'd guessed wrong. Ryan was Rob's son. Rob had two kids, Ryan and Brittany. They had made my life miserable the entire time I was married to Rob. Deliberately. They had assigned me the role of wicked stepmother and would not allow me to be anybody else.

"What?" I said.

"He's going to Stanford. He'll be down your way."

Oh, boy!

"Congratulate him for me," I said flatly.

"Maybe I should give him your phone number, just in case."

"In case what?"

"In case he needs something, gets into trouble, I don't know. Just someone he knows locally."

"Ryan does not know me," I said. "He never tried to get to know me. He was determined to hate me from the start, just as Brittany was. Why would he change now?"

"He's matured."

"Has he now?"

We talked a few more minutes in a desultory fashion. In a way I was glad he'd called. It was good to know he didn't affect me anymore. I never did say whether he could give Ryan my phone number or not. I didn't see the need. Ryan would never call me.

After hanging up the phone, I held on to the receiver a few minutes, then dialed Zack and made arrangements to get together with him and talk about our approach to the case. I could sense him shrugging on his Sheriff Lazarro persona even as we spoke.

A few minutes later, I trotted down the stairs and headed for my Wrangler.

* * *

"We need to question everybody who was at the reunion," Zack said.

We were lounging on deck chairs at the side of his pool, both of us in swimsuits, though there was a lot more material in mine than there was in his. I was trying very hard not to notice how flat his stomach was, how broad his shoulders, how slender his waist, how long and strong his legs.

I wasn't being too successful, as you can tell by that detailed description.

"That could take up a lot of time," I said.

"We could invite them all to a party at CHAPS," he said.

"You don't think they'd smell a rat?"

"We could tell them it was to make up for their reunion party gettin' called off early. We could ask questions the way we did a couple of years back."

He was referring to the time the skeleton turned up in CHAPS's flower-bed. We'd gathered all the neighbors in the main corral and conducted a mild table-hopping inquisition.

It could work, I supposed. Once in a while, Zack's ideas did pan out, much as I always hated to admit it. Also, he was very good at getting people to answer questions. I think he mesmerized them with his green eyes. He's certainly been known to do it to me.

"I have a better idea," Savanna said when we shared the plan with her and Angel following our partners' meeting. "When the committee originally floated ideas for the reunion, it was going to last a couple of days.

We were all going to take a ferry trip to Tiburon, the day after the 'get reacquainted' party. Plan was to feature lunch on Sam's Pier. But because of Reina's death . . ."

She broke off, her eyes brimming.

"The trip was canceled?" I said gently.

She nodded. After a minute, she was able to continue. "I heard from Kalesha that the committee wants to do it next Saturday, as a memorial to Reina. The funeral's Friday, if the police release Reina's body in time, so . . ." She broke off again, and Angel supplied her with a wad of tissues from the office box. As she mopped up, her eyes fixed on me.

It took me a moment. "You think we could go along on the ferry trip? I don't know, Savanna, it would be hard to come up with an acceptable excuse."

"You'd think of one, Charlie," Savanna said confidently.

"I'm not at all sure—"

Zack interrupted. "We could tell them I'm tryin' to decide if the story of the murder would make a good TV movie."

"You don't think that would sound a tad exploitative?" I asked with heavy sarcasm.

"It might seem that way, but you'd be surprised how many people love the idea of somethin' they were involved in bein' featured in a movie." He gave me the benefit of his crooked grin, the one that always provoked a response from my lower innards.

I forced myself to concentrate on his comment, remembering the last time I had a TV camera stuck in my face, and a little old lady kept jumping up and down between me and it. He was right. A surprising number of people didn't hesitate to make fools of themselves in order to get on TV. Think of all the idiotic things people do at ball games to get noticed by the cameraman.

"Angel, what do you think?" I asked.

"You and Zack are the detectives in the group," he said.

"You came up with information when we did the party after that skeleton showed up in the flower-bed," Zack reminded him.

Angel's mouth twitched, which meant he was softening to the idea. "It would be helpful if you came along," I said.

"For you, Charlie, anything."

People say that kind of thing in passing, but Angel meant it. He always means whatever he says. To me anyway. He had cause to be grateful to me—and to Zack—for looking into a serious problem he'd had very recently.

Because he was so solemn, I said, "It won't interfere with your love life with P.J., will it?"

He bestowed his rare and fleeting smile on me, but didn't protest my teasing.

He didn't answer me, either.

CHAPTER 6

Nobody seemed to mind when Zack and Angel and I joined the group on the dock at Pier 41. As long as Zack was among those present we could probably have done without the story he'd dreamed up about TV-movie possibilities. He told it anyway.

A few people who weren't part of the reunion bunch tried to surround him as we went on board, but Forrest and Thad flanked him and kept them at bay.

It was a perfect day for a cruise, sunny and summery with white puffy clouds bopping along ahead of the breeze and only a slight chop on the clear gray-green water. At least a dozen sailboats were scudding around, and a couple of windsurfers were doing enough death-defying jumps and turns to make me dizzy watching.

The huge ferryboat was crowded with tourists, so our group became scattered on the upper deck, which had row seating. Not much chance of meaningful communication, I decided.

I sat next to Kalesha Atkins and Owen Jones, her Welsh husband. Kalesha was dressed in black bicycle shorts and a bright paisley shirt open over a scooped-neck cotton top that showed off her formidable cleavage. Owen was still formal in gray slacks, white shirt, and navy blazer, but at least he wasn't wearing a tie.

Before I could launch into a discussion of the murder, Kalesha gave me an odd sort of once-over. "Lend me your cowboy hat for a minute, will you?"

I thought maybe she wanted it for protection from the wind, which was whipping around us now that we were moving along. But she held it upside down in both hands and looked into it as if it were a bowl full of something unsavory. Her eyes were half closed, her nostrils flared. "You're really suppressed sexually, Charlie," she said matter-of-factly after a few minutes.

"Somebody wrote that inside my hat?" I queried.

She laughed. Owen didn't look too amused.

"You think I'm sexually suppressed because I wear a white cowboy hat?" I asked. "I had a black one until a while back. I bought the white one because Gina in Buttons & Bows thought it looked good on me. There's nothing significant about wearing a white cowboy hat, Kalesha. Unless you count the good guys in the old movies wearing white hats while the bad guys wore black."

She rolled her eyes. "Jeez, I didn't mean to insult you, girl. I just tell it like I feel it. Holding something that belongs to someone, I sense things. It's called psychometry."

I looked at her sideways. "You see auras the way Angel does?" I asked.

She glanced with sudden interest at Angel, who was sitting farther along on the right, a row ahead of us, apparently being harangued again by Dolores Valentino. Even the back of his neck looked uncomfortable. I couldn't hear what Dolores was saying, but I could hear her voice rising and falling nonstop over the loud voices of a group of Europeans occupying the seats between us.

"Really?" Kalesha said. "I'll have to talk to him." She shook her head. "I'm not into auras, Charlie, but I am a psychic. Even as a kid, I used to know things other people didn't know—like when an accident was going to happen, or who was on the telephone when it rang. Since I've grown up I've become even more sensitive. I think it may have something to do with being around X rays all the time."

She seemed perfectly serious. "Maybe you should wear one of those lead aprons they put on patients," I said.

She looked at me blankly, then gave a half smile and touched the sleeve of my CHAPS sweatshirt. "I'm sorry if I upset you. I tend to just come out with stuff." She became suddenly animated, as though touching me had stirred up some electricity. "You're going to have a whole lot of good stuff happening around the end of the year, Charlie. It just came to me. Wow, it's amazing how much good stuff is just lying around waiting for you to pick it up. You have to watch for it, girl!"

She turned her back on Owen and looked very closely at me, making me nervous. "Everything, I mean *everything* in your life is going to come together," she said excitedly. "I'll bet you lunch on it. You're going to have this whole surge of energy that will just sweep all your problems away like a tsunami."

"I don't have any problems," I said.

She raised her shapely eyebrows. "I'd call being sexually suppressed a problem," she said firmly.

"Me too," Owen said from behind her.

"I am *not* sexually suppressed," I said. "I'm sexually uninterested."

This brought me the look of complete disbelief that such a dumb statement deserved.

"Well, whatever it is that bothers you is going to be solved by the end of the year," Kalesha said. "You can take my word for it."

I really *didn't* have any personal problems. I was healthy. I was probably too skinny, but I did *not* have an eating problem anymore. I was eating regularly and well. I had enough money to get by on. I had good friends, who cared about me. I had a pet rabbit, who depended on me. I had a place to live. What more could anyone want?

Yes, well, it does sound a bit basic, but that was the way I wanted it to be. No attachments. Attachments get broken off. That hurts.

I *was* worried about someone else's problem. Bristow would find out at the end of the year if he was a candidate for AIDS or not. But I was hardly involved in that, apart from my concern for the stress on his and Savanna's marriage.

Zack's probation would be up.

That could be a problem for me. If Zack did manage to go six months without any involvement with another woman, what would I do then? I'd made an agreement; I couldn't possibly back out after he'd served his time.

What was I thinking? He was never going to last that long.

"It seems to have to do with sex, Charlie," Kalesha said, looking at me earnestly.

It bothers me when people read my mind. At the same time, I seemed to hear my late father saying, "Forewarned is forearmed, Charlie." My father had been popping up in my mind a lot lately.

I decided to sacrifice privacy for possible information. "There's this guy," I said tentatively. "I've told him if he can stay away from other women for six months, I might consider—"

"Getting unsuppressed?"

"Something like that."

"Have you had relations with him before?"

I shook my head. "We've come close, but no, I always break it off. He's not ... I don't want any kind of commitment, I'm never going to go for that again. But I don't want to be dumped when the sun comes up, either."

She squinted at my face. "You're talking about Zack Hunter." It was a statement, not a question.

"I didn't say that."

"Came through loud and clear, psychically speaking," she said solemnly. Then she laughed. She had a great laugh, full-bodied and mischievous. "Savanna told me you and Zack had the hots for each other."

She studied my face some more. "You really haven't laid a hand on him?"

I tried for a casual shrug. "Some heavy-duty kissing, that's all."

She tilted her head to one side. "Is he a good kisser?"

I started to say "world-class" but stopped myself. "That's none of your business," I said testily. "You

surely don't need that information to make a predic-
tion."

She frowned and lowered her voice. "Tell you the
truth, Charlie, I have the hots for Zack myself. Who
wouldn't?"

I glanced around her at Owen, wondering if he'd
heard her declaration, but he had turned around to
watch the seagulls that were hovering over the stern,
looking for handouts. I remembered my father again—
he'd loved teasing me with questions when I was a
little girl—questions that were impossible to answer.
"If a bird were to get trapped inside our airplane and
fly inside it as the airplane travels from one airport to
the other, does it add to the weight of the airplane?"

He'd told me he loved the grave way I would ponder
such queries.

My eyes stung momentarily. The plane in question
had been a Cessna and it had gone down with both my
parents aboard about the time I graduated from high
school.

"Jeez, Charlie, I'm sorry if I was out of line," Kalesha
said. "I'm too clever for my own good, sometimes. I
didn't mean to upset you."

"You didn't," I said hastily. "I guess the wind blew
something into my eyes."

She looked relieved. "Well, see, about Zack, I can't
read him because of the way I react to him. So I can't
answer your question."

I gave her another sideways look. "You mean hormones get in the way of psychic vibrations?"

"You're scoffing. I don't blame you. But yeah, it's
something like that, for sure. I can't read Owen, either."

"Fortunately for Owen," Owen said flatly, having tuned in. He was certainly a man of few words.

"But even though I can't read Zack," Kalesha continued, "going on what Savanna has told me about him off and on, him and his 'doll collection' or whatever it is you call it, I'd say it's hard to believe he'd keep his fly zipped for six whole months."

"You're probably right," I said gloomily, then changed the subject. "Let's talk about Reina. If you're psychic you must have had some clues about what she was going through. There's a possibility someone was stalking her. Did you know about that?"

"Are you serious?" She had rather small eyes, I suddenly noticed. "Who?"

"We don't know. We aren't even sure she was being stalked, just that someone was sending her red roses regularly and calling her often."

"The mysterious boyfriend?"

"No, she told Savanna it was someone who would be at the reunion."

Probably I shouldn't be disseminating information, but as my father used to say, it wasn't all that easy to catch a fish if you didn't bait the hook.

I wondered why my father was so much in my mind today, and decided it was because we were on a boat—he'd loved anything to do with the water. He'd fished for striped bass on the Sacramento River and for halibut in Alaska. He was a great swimmer. Though not a big guy, he was strong. Strong enough to hold up the world, I used to think when I was little. I'd looked up to him even after I grew taller than he was.

Kalesha was frowning. "How come Reina didn't tell *me*?"

I shook my head. I was tempted to say perhaps Reina had expected Kalesha to sniff out the stalker as she was so psychic, but I do *try* to be a nice person. "When did you last see her?"

She thought for a minute, turning to look at Owen. He thought it over, too. "You had dinner with her when I was on that run up to Walnut Creek," he said.

He looked around her in my general direction. "One of my patients is a romance writer. She was doing a signing in a megabookstore and went into labor. Created quite a stir. I barely made it there in time to deliver her daughter."

So, he *could* speak in whole sentences.

"People bought a whole bunch of books, and Francisca signed them right after the baby was born," Kalesha said, then added, "You met her at the reunion. Francisca Gutierrez, the one who sang."

I remembered. The one with the hair extensions. I'd had the impression she was a lesbian. Something in her attitude when someone said Reina wasn't. And Forrest Kenyon had said something that had confirmed the impression.

Francisca could be a lesbian and still have a baby, of course. All the plumbing was still there. She'd seemed militant, though. Maybe she'd had artificial insemination.

"She writes as Francisca Bessonet," Kalesha said. "I guess she thought that sounded more euphonious. She's a good writer. Contemporary stuff. Strong women, men with brains. Great love scenes."

"I hadn't heard about her being a writer," I said. "That's interesting. Does she write heterosexual love scenes?"

"Absolutely." She flashed a glance at me. "You heard the gossip at the reunion. Yeah, supposedly she's not a lover of the male gender. But I read an article by a writer of some fairly erotic stuff who said if you did it once you could write about it forever." She had an infectious chuckle. "Maybe the baby was the result of some research."

"Did Francisca come today?" I asked. I'd remembered Savanna pointing out that Reina had not given away the sex of the person who was giving her all that attention.

Kalesha looked around briefly. "Everybody showed," she said. "Except one. But she phoned in an acceptable excuse." She nodded. "I'm close to certain Francisca's on the boat."

Owen chimed in. "She is. She has the baby in one of those things women strap on their chests."

"It's called a Baby Bjorn," Kalesha said.

Owen shrugged. "If you say so. Last I saw, she was heading straight for Zack Hunter like she had a built-in compass and he was true North."

Kalesha pursed her lips. "Maybe she's bisexual, you suppose? Zack had better watch out—she might be looking for a daddy for Maria. I wouldn't think being a single mom would be a whole lot of fun."

She paused to think. "Francisca's always been a tad on the flamboyant side. Imagine giving birth right there in the bookstore. Though they did at least manage to get her into an office. She wrote it all up in a press release while she was still in the hospital. Terrific publicity, she said. Wouldn't surprise me if she timed it that way."

She waved a hand around. "Okay, so that must have been two or three months ago that I saw Reina, but she didn't say anything to me about red roses or being stalked. She didn't say anything about having a new boyfriend, either. And she wasn't wearing that ring. Maybe all this came about since I saw her."

"Reina told Savanna the roses started coming five months ago," I said. "And I imagine the boyfriend had been around a while, considering Reina said at the reunion they were going to get married soon."

She shrugged. "I can't imagine why she didn't mention him, then. Have the police talked to him?"

"Last I heard they haven't found him yet."

We continued talking about Reina, and I asked them both the questions Zack, Savanna, Angel, and I had decided on. "Did you notice who danced with Reina the night of the reunion party?"

Kalesha remembered Reina dancing with someone called Jeffrey, and a couple of times with Forrest. "Didn't you dance with her, Owen?" she asked.

He frowned. "Did I? I'm not sure I recall . . ."

"I saw you dancing a two-step with her," I said, and the frown deepened. "She was talking a blue streak to you."

"Really? I wonder what about. I seem to have blanked the incident out."

I believed that, like I believe in fairy dust.

"Did you notice anyone being missing between the

time Reina did the ten-step and when Detective Sergeant Bristow announced she was dead?"

They both shrugged. "People were going in and out all the time," Kalesha said. "Reina herself went out a few times earlier in the evening. To smoke, I guess. She was a heavy smoker. I've given up smoking myself."

That caught my attention. "Someone said you were smoking out there."

She said something cusslike under her breath. "Yeah, well, I get tempted once in a while. I bummed one off Reina that night."

Owen frowned at her. She shrugged.

"Did you see who else she went out to smoke with?" I asked.

So far, Kalesha hadn't seemed to wonder why I was poking my nose in. Maybe her psychic sense had told her Zack and I were investigating for Savanna.

"Forrest," Owen said.

"Dolores came out about the time I left," Kalesha added, with some significance in her voice. "Made a beeline for Reina."

I looked questioningly at her, though I guessed what was coming. Forrest had made the same suggestion.

"Dolo had a crush on Reina in high school," she said.

"A lot of teenage girls go through that phase."

"Yeah, but what if she didn't come out of it? What if she was the one sending the roses, and so on?"

"Then I imagine the police will find out."

Neither Kalesha nor Owen could come up with anything else, or give specifics on who had spent time talking to Reina inside CHAPS. "Everyone," Kalesha said, then added, "You have to understand, Charlie, that *everyone* loved Reina."

"Somebody didn't. Somebody strangled her."

"I'm hoping it was some maniac who wandered in from outside just as Reina was going to the rest room."

"It's possible, I suppose, but it seems doubtful." I paused before asking the ultimate question. "If it was one of your schoolmates, who would you pick?"

She looked shocked. "I'm not going to make guesses, Charlie."

"I didn't want a guess, I just wondered if you had any psychic vibrations about the murderer."

She shook her head. "I'm probably too closely involved with all of those people."

It struck me she had more excuses than insights.

"Everyone at the reunion wanted to visit with Reina," she went on.

I looked from her to Owen. "Did you notice anything odd at all in connection with Reina and other people?"

Owen shrugged. "How would I know? I'd never met any of those people until that night, I wouldn't know what was odd or what wasn't."

"You hadn't met Reina, either?"

"No."

I caught the sudden turning of Kalesha's head as she looked at him. Saw the surprise in her expression, quickly suppressed. He'd lied. Why?

"The only thing that has seemed odd to me," Kalesha said hastily, "was Reina saying she was afraid the people at the reunion would think it odd that she hadn't married. Which I told that good-looking detective sergeant of Savanna's. I've no idea why that would worry

Reina. And if she had a boyfriend, as she told Savanna, then why would she worry about it at all?"

Just as the ferryboat docked, she had another thought. "Maybe it was Jeffrey stalking her—the big guy—the one who danced the ten-step with her."

Shortly before she died, my memory filled in.

"He probably stood on her toes as often as not. Jeffrey was a heavyweight boxer for a while. Lost quite a few matches. Ended up on the edge of dementia pugilistica."

"Which is?"

"Brain damage caused by repeated blows to the head. It was supposedly a mild case, but he's for sure even weirder than he was in school. Reina was mad at him for making her dance so fast. Got her all sweaty."

She was silent a minute and I thought she'd realized that was probably why Reina had gone to the rest room. But then she nodded and said, "Jeffrey got divorced two or three years ago. And he's the red rose type."

"How can you tell?"

She gave me a look. Oh, right, the psychic ability. "Scoff if you want to, Charlie," she said. "Then come to my house and see my scrapbooks full of cases I've worked on with police departments in this state."

She was miffed with me, obviously.

CHAPTER 7

Zack and Francisca were waiting on the dock with most of the others by the time we managed to get off the boat. Angel was just ahead of us, Dolores still talking to him. *At* him, more likely.

Francisca was standing unnecessarily close to Zack, I thought. He was looking down at the baby, or else down the neck of Francisca's flowered shirt. She had very large breasts. I supposed she was nursing. I'm all in favor of breast-feeding. I just resent the big breasts, not being so supplied myself. I don't know why it is that some women who have them say they don't want them. A couple of my amply endowed friends in college used to say they'd much rather have small breasts like mine because clothes fitted so much better.

I think they lied.

We walked en masse to the restaurant, which was a little awkward with around thirty some men and women. Why do the slowest always walk in front? Actually, the front people were Zack and Forrest, flanking Francisca. She was talking very rapidly, with lots of hand gestures and much staring up into Zack's face. Those strap-on baby-carrier thingies are very useful when you want to make graceful gestures.

No, I wasn't jealous. I'd just as soon someone would snap Zack up and save me from a fate worse than— well, I don't suppose it would be worse than death. It would probably be very good. Extremely good. But it wouldn't be good *for* me.

I was curious, though, because Zack was listening with full attention to the woman. He was of course always courteous to women. He liked women. A lot. But he was hanging on her every word, throwing in a remark once in a while, but mostly listening. Apparently Forrest wasn't saying much.

I hoped Zack remembered he was supposed to talk to several people, and hadn't forgotten the questions we were all supposed to work on.

"He's a good-looking guy, isn't he?" Kalesha said, giving me a knowing look.

"Forrest?" I said, deliberately misunderstanding. "Yes, he is. Has he always been a walking encyclopedia?"

"I wasn't talking about Forrest, and you know it," she said. "But you're right about him being a know-it-all. Yes, he always was."

"I guess he really liked Reina, huh?"

"You fingering Forrest for the stalker?"

"It was an idle question, Kalesha."

She laughed hard enough to start coughing. "Charlie, you're forgetting I can see into and through people. Nothing you've said to me since we got on that boat has been idle."

If I was the type to blush, I guess I would have

done it. But luckily we reached the restaurant about then and we were all led out onto the pier by a typically laid-back California waiter, who got us seated haphazardly. I ended up opposite Zack and Francisca, which had not been my plan. Zack, Savanna, Angel, and I were all supposed to spread out so we could talk to a range of people.

Next to me on one side was Timothy Perkins, once again wearing his circuit board pin, and on the other, Dolores. She had either lost Angel or he'd managed to escape. I caught a glimpse of him at the next table, sitting next to the ex-boxer.

Good, I thought, maybe he'd find out some more about Jeffrey. The big guy looked like a possible suspect to pass on to Bristow.

On Angel's other side was an ultra-skinny blonde woman with a nose stud and short shaggy hair. Angel's last steady had been punk, possibly he'd get along great with this waif, too.

Savanna was at the end of the same table. Forrest was next to her, I noticed. Taking advantage of Bristow not being present?

"I'll bring my portfolio over in a couple of days," Zack said to Francisca.

I blinked. That was fast, even for Zack. Francisca was beaming up at him. The baby was apparently asleep. She was really snuggled in under her mom's chin. She looked cute, but then what two-month-old doesn't?

Zack caught my speculative look. "Francisca thinks she can get me a gig as a model," he said. "What do you think, Charlie? It would be a change for me."

"What kind of model?" I asked. "Are we talking *Playgirl* centerfold here?"

"Wishful thinkin', Charlie?" Zack asked with a lift of the slanted eyebrows and a glint of the green eyes.

The waiter arrived with our orders and saved me from answering. I decided to indulge myself with a BLT, something I rarely eat, but absolutely adore.

"I write romance novels," Francisca said when the waiter got through sorting us out. "A multicultural line. I have a first-rate New York publisher, but the cover artist they use is in Monterey. His name is Piotr. He's Russian, I think—wonderfully creative and sensitive."

"Does he do clinches?" I asked, referring to the pictures of obviously enamored couples that were often featured on romance novel covers.

She smiled. "Sometimes, if the story is really hot." She looked down modestly. "Mine usually are."

"Zack would get to pose with hot female models then, I suppose? He'd like that."

Zack glinted at me again.

"I've watched some of Piotr's cover shoots," Francisca went on, talking to Zack, ignoring the rest of us. "It's a lot like making a movie. First he takes photographs, acting like a director, instructing the models playing the hero and heroine on the scene in the story. The models are dressed for their parts and they start emoting, maybe a kiss and a touch. . . ."

She paused, wetting her lips with her tongue. The baby whimpered, and moved restlessly, turning her head and opening her eyes. Francisca stroked the baby's cheek. Her chin trembled a little and her eyes fluttered shut.

"Once they get a sensual mood going, Piotr takes pictures, one after another. Later, he decides which shot he likes best and does his painting from that, putting in some kind of background that fits with the period of the story."

"Sounds like interestin' work," Zack said.

Francisca gave him a complacent smile.

"Fascinating," I said. I'll leave it to you to imagine if there was any sarcasm in my voice.

"Zack could be as successful as Fabio," Francisca said to me.

"Would he have to grow his hair long and bleach it?" I asked in my best inquiring-mind voice. "Maybe he should shave his chest. You'll have to buff up your pecs a bit," I added to Zack.

He actually wasn't at all hairy, and his pecs were as sculpted as any pecs needed to be.

I'd seen him in a swimsuit, remember, that's how I knew. *What did you think?*

"The model we are searching for has to look dark and mysterious and Spanish," Francisca said.

"I can do Spanish," Zack said, fixing a stern and haughty look on his lean face.

"Perfecto," Francisca said. "You might have to cover up the scar, though."

This was a reference to a jagged scar Zack had acquired on his cheek when a bull on the set of *Prescott's Landing* had turned out to be less tranquilized than promised.

"Though it's a very sexy scar," Francisca added.

Baby Maria woke up again and gurgled at Zack. Women of all ages adore him.

"You should be recommending Mexican Americans for such work," Dolores said.

Francisca rolled her eyes. "When the story calls for Mexican Americans, Piotr uses Mexican American models. You want to lobby someone, lobby the writers, tell them to put more Mexican Americans as main characters in their books."

"Do you do that?" Dolores asked, sounding belligerent.

"Mostly," Francisca said, with another of her smug smiles. "But this man, this hero, is pure Spanish—my heroine has gone to Spain to discover her roots, just the way I did, and this man helps her." She gave Zack a flirtatious smile. "I always write from life."

Dolores wasn't satisfied. "Why don't you ask Angel Cervantes to model for your cover?" she asked.

"Because I want Zack," Francisca said, making the double meaning plain with a flash of her dark eyes in Zack's direction.

So maybe she was bisexual, I thought.

Dolores glared at her.

"Lighten up, Dolo," Francisca said. "You look at me like that, you'll turn my milk sour, and how's my poor little Maria going to eat?"

"Dolores," Dolores said. "Not Dolo anymore. Dolores."

Francisca muttered something Spanish. It had an uncomplimentary sound to it. She turned her attention back to Zack.

Reaching in his shirt pocket, he pulled out the small

leather folder that held his business cards. He never left home without it. Extracting a card, he gave it to Francisca, who admired the thumbnail photo and tucked the card away in the diaper bag beside her chair.

"I was wondering about something, Francisca," I said. "Something about the reunion party."

She raised her eyebrows. She had beautiful bird-wing eyebrows, dark as her hair. They had to have been waxed, I thought. Her face was narrow and somewhat plain, but she had a wonderfully creamy complexion.

"Did you notice who Reina danced with?"

"I've already asked Francisca all the questions," Zack said.

I was surprised. I'd thought he was too busy admiring her bosom.

"Sorry," I said to Francisca, who smiled in a disinterested way.

I noticed that Thad the pastor was working the crowd. Once or twice a head bowed and he bowed his. I supposed he was counseling everyone.

Perky had stopped eating. He'd been stuffing himself with a huge hero sandwich, taking such enormous bites I didn't know how he got it all in his mouth, which appeared quite small.

"Nobody's asked me any questions, Charlie," he said, catching my eye, opening his eyes wide in the irritating way he had. "I was sitting behind you and Kalesha and her other half on the way over here. You were really going after them."

I must have shown some kind of worried expression.

"It's okay," he said. "I couldn't hear what you were

talking about, just the interrogatory note in your voice."

He laughed. "I was on to you anyway, Charlie. Reason I bid on you at the reunion wasn't just because I'm addicted to tall redheaded chicks. I remembered your name and you looked familiar. Took me a while to recall that I'd read about you in the newspapers and seen you on television. That time when the skeleton popped up at CHAPS. I heard afterward you had a hand in the investigation. Seems to me you got involved in some other crime since then."

I wasn't going to tell him there had been four altogether.

"You and Zack are like Starsky and Hutch, huh? Cagney and Lacey? Take one of each couple and there you are. So neither of you fooled me with your talk about coming along to see how we'd feel about Zack coming up with a story for TV."

Perky might be a geek, but he was no dummy.

I glanced at Francisca, but she was fully engaged in breast-feeding her daughter, a receiving blanket strategically draped across her chest. Zack raised his eyebrows at me. He'd evidently heard Perky. The people on either side of Zack and Francisca were engaged in conversations with those on the other side of them.

I kept my own voice low, conscious of Dolores on my right.

"We're not trying to take over from the police. They have their own investigation. We're just trying to help out, for Savanna's sake."

Perky laughed and did his eye thing again. "The Jessica Fletcher of Bellamy Park; she shall have bodies wherever she goes. Don't invite this woman anywhere! Good thing you didn't show up at the funeral yesterday, who knows what might have happened."

"I wouldn't have dreamed of going to the funeral," I said shortly, then couldn't help asking. "Did all your classmates go?"

"The entire student body since the beginning of time went," he said. "Just think of all the questions you and Zack could have asked, clues you might have overturned, red herrings you might have smelled."

A visionary gleam appeared in his pale eyes. "Hey, I might have to do a cartoon about you and Zack. Whoa, Charlie, this is exciting!"

Zack looked interested. He loved all publicity. Good or bad.

"Good grief, don't do anything of the kind," I said. "We'll sue if you do."

Perky laughed again. "I'm joking, Charlie."

Maybe so, but there was still a thoughtful look in his eyes.

I might as well see what he had to offer anyway, I decided. "Who do *you* think killed Reina?" I asked.

He didn't laugh this time. Looking around at the other diners in an extremely shifty manner, he said quietly, "I don't think it's a good idea to talk about this here, Charlie. As a matter of fact, I'm not sure you should be asking questions at all. You could be putting yourself in harm's way."

"Who would want to do me harm?" I asked, looking him right in the eye to show I wasn't afraid, which I was, actually. I've been known to take action in the face of danger, and since I took that self-defense class a while back I've felt a lot braver, but at heart I'm a dedicated coward.

"Whoever killed Reina," he came back with. "Someone put his hands around her neck and squeezed until all the life went out of her. You start poking around, maybe he'll want to do the same to you."

I stared at him. His voice had become intense—it was almost as if he was relishing the thought of my demise. Was he threatening me?

"I wouldn't want you to get hurt, Charlie," he added.

Which could be meant sincerely, or could be taken as part of the same threat.

In a louder voice, he said, "Maybe we should set up our date now."

As long as it took place in public I should be safe enough, I told myself. "Jogging was your suggestion, I believe."

"Followed by breakfast. Unless you'd prefer a night of unbridled sex?"

Under any other circumstances I'd have called the date off right then, and maybe kicked his shins, but he'd paid a large contribution to Reina's charity for this date and I could hardly waffle just because he happened to be disgusting. Besides, I wanted to find out what it was he couldn't talk about here.

"With whom?" I asked, putting an exaggeratedly puzzled note into my voice.

He sighed. "Jogging it is."

"And breakfast in a restaurant," I said.

He sighed again. "How about First Watch for breakfast—they make a great breakfast." He gave me a hopeful glance. "You wanna at least meet at my house? Six o'clock in the morning."

My expression probably answered for me. No way was I going to meet this guy in a deserted neighborhood before dawn had even cracked. "Somewhere else," I said firmly. "Somewhere public. And nine o'clock, not six."

"You're a tough person to please, Charlie Plato," he said, but his voice was resigned, as though he was used to this kind of treatment. "Luckily, I like a woman with attitude."

He ruminated for a moment. "How about the Marina Green? We could jog across the Golden Gate Bridge— you know the Green?"

"Windsurfers," I said. "Roller-bladers, kites, volleyball. People walking their dogs."

In other words, about as public a place as you could get.

The Marina Green wouldn't be crowded at nine o'clock in the morning, but there'd be people around, I felt sure. I'm no gothic heroine wandering around in somebody's attic looking for clues, just asking to be bopped on the head. I'm committed to self-preservation.

"I guess that sounds okay, but not tomorrow, I have stuff to do at CHAPS." I thought for a minute. CHAPS was usually closed on Monday nights, so I'd get to bed at a reasonable hour and be ready to brave the traffic going into The City. The City is San Francisco, of course. That's what the locals always call it. Not Frisco, please note—The City.

"We could meet at the steps that go down to the water, near where people play volleyball. Tuesday morning," I suggested. "Unless you have to be at work?"

"I work at home," he said. "I make my own hours."

He mulled the arrangements, then said, "Okay, then, that's settled." He lowered his voice again. "Better count on a chunk of time. I have a few things to tell you about."

"What things?" I asked.

"Skeletons in the closet," he said.

"What skeletons?" I asked.

"What skeletons?" Forrest demanded sharply from behind us, making us both jump and turn around.

"We're talking about the skeleton Charlie found in CHAPS's flower-bed," Perky said, thinking fast. "The earthquake popped it up."

Forrest frowned, looking important. Some people can do that. "I remember hearing about that. I thought it was just a foot."

"It started with a foot," I told him, "but there was a whole skeleton in there."

Pastor Thad appeared alongside Forrest. "We're going to have a few minutes of silent prayer for Reina's soul," he said. "I'm going to make a general announcement in a couple of minutes."

"I have to go to the bathroom," Perky said and got up and walked toward the restaurant building. It seemed rather abrupt timing, but then an urge can take you that way and he *had* been drinking beer.

"The Perk and Charlie were talking about skeletons," Forrest said. "Maybe the Perk got queasy."

"Nice lunchtime topic," Thad said, then slipped into Perky's vacated chair, leaned over and spoke close to my ear. "Sorry I let you in for that date with Perky, Charlie. He's still the bore he always was. I feel responsible."

"It's okay," I said. It wasn't, but I was beginning to think Thad might possibly be a nice guy and it seemed only fair to let him off the hook.

"I wouldn't set up a date to, well, to be alone with him, if I were you," he went on. "I don't like to speak ill of anyone, but Perky has a name for being a philanderer. He's gone through three or four wives."

"You're not serious!" I said.

"Absolutely."

I was astonished. I couldn't imagine one woman marrying the little creep, never mind three or four.

"Don't worry, Thad," Forrest chimed in from behind. "Their date is going to be in public. The Marina Green. Jogging, didn't you say, Charlie?"

How long had he been standing behind Perky and me before I noticed him, I wondered. How much had he heard? I felt very uneasy suddenly.

"I've been offering my services to anyone who needs them, Charlie," Thad went on, as Forrest finally moved away.

There was an intriguing statement. "Services?"

"Finding Reina's body must have been traumatic for you. I don't suppose it left you untouched. Perhaps we could talk about it? Analyze your thoughts about it."

I don't take kindly to interference in my thought processes. Seems to me we tend to analyze things to death nowadays.

"I don't need counseling, thank you," I said, and

felt vaguely guilty when he looked hurt. I loathe being made to feel guilty.

And then he smiled the most saintly and forgiving smile, which made me feel worse. Besides which, here was a golden opportunity to take a look at Thad's memory of the reunion.

"I would like to *talk* about it, I guess," I said, and was rewarded with an encouraging smile. "I don't feel particularly stressed about it, though. Do you?"

He ran a hand through his dark hair and smiled gently. "I'm very sad about Reina's death, Charlie, but of course, I run into many examples of man's inhumanity to man ... and woman ... in the course of my ministry."

"Yes, I suppose you do." I let a beat go by. "I expect you're a very observant person where human nature is concerned," I added in as casual a manner as I could muster.

He looked gratified.

"Did you notice anyone paying any particular attention to Reina at the reunion? Anyone dancing with her, going out to smoke with her, sitting at her table, that kind of thing?"

He frowned. "Well ... I was kept busy with the auction, you know. I didn't have a whole lot of time to watch. . . . Forrest hung out with her quite a bit, but I don't know that I . . ."

He paused, his brow clearing as if he'd suddenly remembered something.

"What?" I demanded.

"Kalesha's husband. Owen Jones. He danced with Reina and talked to her."

"Yeah, I noticed that." I was disappointed.

"Seems odd when I think about it," he said in a musing tone. "I wouldn't imagine he'd known Reina before the reunion. Yet he was right in her face, talking."

"He was with our little group for a while, during the time . . . ," I broke off.

"What time?" he asked.

A natural enough question, and I couldn't really think of a reason not to answer it. "It seems possible Reina was killed soon after she danced the ten-step. There was some slow dancing, then the band took a break. When they came back, Francisca sang, then Angel and I taught a line dance."

Thad thought for a minute. "Where did the band go on their break? I didn't notice."

"They bellied up to the bar right away," I said.

"Hmm. I guess that lets them out. I'm trying to think what I did while all of that was going on. I know I talked to several people, but it's impossible to say exactly who."

He laughed and his dark eyes sparkled, making him look much less saintly. "Sometimes I can remember whole conversations with people but have no memory of who I was talking to. Very frustrating, the tricks one's mind plays."

He thought for a minute. "I remember the band quitting for a while. And I remember Francisca singing but it wasn't a song I was familiar with. Then the lesson. That was fun, that line dance. I'm afraid I don't remember any particular person being absent from the room during that time. Sorry."

He glanced at his watch. "Speaking of time—it's moving on, Charlie. I have to go do the prayer." He gave me a thoroughly charming smile and again I half wished I was having the date with him rather than the geek. "Tell me you've forgiven me for passing you on to Timothy Perkins and I'll go do my thing," he said.

"I forgive you," I said.

A couple of minutes later, he made his announcement and everyone bowed their heads. I'm not much for praying, so I looked at the San Francisco skyline, which was beginning to get hazy in the distance, and I thought about Reina and wished her well wherever she might have ended up.

After a while Thad delivered a eulogy about how wonderful an influence Reina had been on their lives, and how they would all have been lesser people if she hadn't intervened.

"Thad always was a pain," Dolores muttered when Thad finally quit. "A seriously strange person."

"Takes one to know one," Francisca said from across the table. Her smile was possibly meant to indicate she was joking, but the expression in her eyes was cool, verging on arctic frost.

Dolores ignored her. "Church of the Enlightenment," she went on. "What kind of name is that for a church?"

"It's a nondenominational church," Francisca said. "You can't call a church after a saint if it's nondenominational. It wouldn't be right."

"Thad did this whole eulogy thing after the funeral

yesterday," Dolores said to me. "Almost the same words. It's like déjà vu. Instant replay."

Obviously, she wasn't going to take any notice of Francisca.

When Thad sat down, everybody else settled back and started chatting with one another, and the four of us were able to make our way around the people we'd missed. We used the pretext of checking on the possibilities of Zack's movie and then asked our questions.

Nobody seemed to mind the questions. But nobody provided very helpful answers. After a while, I saw Perky come back, but he didn't come near me. Not then or on the ferry. He stood against the rail at the bow, apparently watching the mauve and apricot cloud trails left behind the setting sun.

As we were lining up to get off the boat, he finally caught my eye and yelled, "I'll see you Tuesday, Charlie," which caught everyone's attention and interest.

"The auction," I explained to those around me. "I'm committed. Or maybe I should be."

There was general laughter.

"Don't forget our date, now," Perky yelled again before heading for the parking lot. No doubt about it, he wanted everyone to know I really was going on a date with him.

I nodded, trying not to look trapped.

CHAPTER 8

"What's the name of that spider that eats her mate?" Angel asked. "That's what that Dolores woman reminds me of."

We had gathered around the bar in CHAPS's main corral. It was late Sunday afternoon and we had all our chores done about an hour and a half before CHAPS was due to open. The idea of the get-together was to hash over the previous day's findings. Angel had elected to start.

"The black widow," Savanna said, eyebrows raised. "Did Dolores want to mate with you, Angel?"

A couple of streaks of red appeared on Angel's cheekbones. "Scared me to death," he admitted. "Wouldn't surprise me if she started some kind of revolution. It was like she was recruiting me. I kept getting this image of her with bandoliers across her chest."

"What color was her aura?" I asked when we stopped laughing.

He gave me a suspicious look, possibly wondering if I was teasing him, but I wasn't. I liked and was impressed by Angel's mystical bent. He'd confessed to all of us sometime ago that he'd learned how to read auras from his mother.

"Red," he said. "Not the warm red of an athlete— a harsher red, a lot of streaks of anger in it. I think she likes living on the edge. She probably had to be scraped off the top of the piano when she was a year old. By five she was probably leading a protest demonstration, waving an Uzi."

He shook his head. "I'm all for everyone getting equal rights, but I'm not going to start getting militant about it."

"Did you get the idea Dolores might have killed Reina?" I asked.

He shook his head. "I didn't get the feeling she'd killed anyone. I do think she's capable of it. Don't quote me, though, I don't want her ever getting mad at *me*."

He frowned. "I asked her the questions, and her answers all leaned in the direction of Forrest being her chief suspect." He gave Savanna an apologetic glance. "She said there were rumors Reina got it on with one of the students and she thinks it was Forrest. Reina always favored him because he was so clever, she said."

I could feel Savanna bristling on the stool beside me. She didn't want to hear anything negative about Forrest. Although I felt a little more kindly toward the know-it-all, I didn't want him driving a wedge between Bristow and Savanna—their marriage was already troubled.

"Funny she'd suspect Forrest," I said. "Forrest suggested Dolores had a crush on Reina herself."

Angel's rare but worth-waiting-for smile appeared and immediately did a disappearing act. "It would be

difficult for me to believe Dolores would want to ...
be with another woman." He hesitated, looking embarrassed. "She came on very strong to me. Said right
out she wanted to jump my bones."

"Wow!" Savanna exclaimed. "I thought she just
wanted to recruit you to her Mexican-American causes."

"That too," Angel said. He shrugged and changed
the subject. "I asked Dolores if she noticed who spent
time with Reina, who danced with her, who went out
to smoke with her, who might have been missing. She
said she went out for one cigarette with Reina. Kalesha
was just leaving. Forrest came and joined them. And
Reina danced with Kalesha's husband, Forrest, and
Jeffrey, and maybe one or two other guys, but Dolores
couldn't remember who they were."

He frowned. "That's about all I got from her." He
hesitated. "She wasn't up for the electric slide lesson."

"Nor was Forrest Kenyon," Zack said. "But," he
added, when Savanna shot a dark glance at him, "he
was among those present, sittin' at the main corral
bar, drinkin' a Red Hook."

Savanna smiled forgiveness at him.

"I asked Dolores where she was while the lesson
was going on and she said she was sitting around,
watching," Angel continued. "So I said I thought it
was funny when nobody could get the clapping right,
and she said she did, too."

"Nobody was doin' any clappin'," Zack said, looking
puzzled.

"Exactly," I said. "Which means Dolores lied and
she was possibly not even in the room, which brings

up the question—where was she?" I beamed at Angel.
"That was very clever."

He allowed himself a small smile. "Hey, you aren't
the only one reads mystery novels, Charlie."

"How did you get Dolores to not jump your bones?"
Savanna asked.

"I told her I had a steady girl."

We all looked at him.

"P.J.?" I asked, not entirely succeeding in keeping
the squeak of surprise out of my voice. I mean, sure
she'd won him for a date, and he'd possibly had an
extra date with her, and he'd invited her to stay at the
reunion, but "a steady girl"?

"P.J.'s okay," he said. "She's given up that desper-
ate attitude she used to have. She's mellow now.
Doesn't mind living alone so much."

He gave me his "flash and fade" smile again. "No,
Charlie, I don't really have a steady. I was just getting
out from under Dolores. So to speak."

He was quiet for a minute, then added, "I talked
to that guy Jeffrey, as well. All I got out of him that
was useful was he had that dance with Reina and it
pooped her out and made her cross. She told him she
was out of breath and out of shape. And he told her
she sure didn't look out of shape, never did. He thought
maybe she thought he was coming on to her. Which
he said he never would do. He'd always admired her
and was grateful to her, that was all. But it seems like
her face got pink and she excused herself to go to
the bathroom. He couldn't fix on what time it was. It
spooked him, being the last to see her alive. Except
for the murderer."

He paused. "I'm not sure Jeffrey's operating on all cylinders. He told me he's an operative for an alien venture that's planning on colonizing the Mojave desert. I thought he was razzing me at first, but he seemed real serious."

"Kalesha says he suffers from a mild form of dementia pugilistica," I offered. "He was a boxer but not too good at it, so he kept getting hit in the head."

"He was on the boxing team at school," Savanna said. "He was good. But he was always pathetic. Him and Perky."

There was a silence, then I looked at Zack.

"What?" he asked.

"You said you'd asked Francisca the questions. What were her answers? Or were you too busy admiring her ... attributes ... to listen?"

He raised his permanently slanted dark eyebrows and squinted at me. "Charlie's jealous of my relationship with Francisca," he told Savanna. "Francisca and I have this perfectly innocent business relationship. She may just launch me on a whole new career as a cover model for romance novels."

"I haven't read Francisca's novels lately," Savanna said. "I don't seem to have the time to spare since I bought into CHAPS. I used to love her books—she's really good. Which publisher is she working for now?"

"I don't believe she said. New York publisher. Multicultural line of novels."

Savanna's dark velvet eyes gleamed. "That's cool, Zack." She smiled at him. "I imagine a cover model's pay is good, and the work shouldn't be too strenuous."

"Or mind-stretching," I murmured.

"I did talk to Francisca about Reina," Zack said.

"And?" I asked.

"She said she wasn't paying that much attention to Reina. Said she liked Reina okay, but she wasn't a groupie like most of the others. She was mostly interested in the band, she said, especially the lead guy—Lonnie? He invited her to sing, she said."

"I guess he liked her, too," I said.

"I guess so." There went the eyebrows again. "Anyhow, she named Reina's dancin' partners, same as Dolores did. Kalesha's husband, Jeffrey the boxer, and Forrest. Somebody named Paul."

"Paul Matthews," Savanna suggested.

Zack shrugged.

"Did anybody talk to Forrest?" I asked.

"I did," Savanna said. "Forrest told me he danced with Reina several times because she asked him to and he was afraid to . . ." Her voice trailed off.

We all waited. "Well, he'd sensed Taylor had taken a dislike to him, so he thought it wiser not to dance with me." She paused for a minute, then blurted out, "I didn't know when I married a police officer that an old friend would be *afraid* to ask me to dance because of it."

Nobody had any comment on that.

"Forrest told me about going out to smoke with Miss Diaz," she went on. "I chided him for still smoking, and then we got off on other topics. But I know it wasn't Forrest who killed her. I *know* him."

"You *knew* him," Zack said. "People change a lot from when they were in high school. Are you the same person you were then?"

"Basically," she said, then sighed. "Oh, okay, you're right. I was painfully shy in high school, never stuck up for myself. I'm much more likely to do that now."

"Yeah, we've noticed," Zack said, making her smile.

"So, then, Forrest has probably changed, too," Zack continued. "You've no idea what he's capable of nowadays."

I thought of what Zack had told me sometime ago about *his* growing-up years. "*I've* changed," I said. "When I was in high school, and for a long time after, I was much more dependent on other people, more naive, more trusting than I am now."

"You callin' those changes improvements, darlin'?" Zack asked with mischief glinting in his green eyes.

"I am," I said firmly. "The point is if I can change for the better, and Savanna can do the same, and you ..." The glint vanished and a muscle twitched at the corner of his mouth. He never liked being reminded of his past. "Well, then," I breezed on, "it's surely possible for someone to change for the worse."

"Are we back to Forrest again?" Savanna asked, sounding aggrieved.

"I'm speaking hypothetically," I said.

"Then let's get off Forrest and talk about someone else."

"Okay." I wasn't going to argue with her. She had fire in her eyes.

"I asked Thad if he knew who the former student could be who'd been sending flowers to Miss Diaz," she said.

"Somebody sent her flowers?" Angel queried.

Savanna explained succinctly.

"Gosh, I didn't think of asking Thad that," I said when she was through. "All I did was ask if he noticed anyone paying any particular attention to Reina. He came up with Owen Jones. I suppose Owen might warrant a closer look. Did Thad know who sent the flowers?"

Savanna shook her head. "He said he'd had dinner with Reina a few weeks before the reunion and she had complained she thought she was being stalked by someone. She told him about the flowers and phone calls, just the way she told me, but she wouldn't tell him who the person was."

She was silent for a minute, her beautiful face as still as calm water. Then she nodded briskly. "You should never get Thad started on a social problem." She rolled her eyes. "He went on and on and on about stalkers. Seemed to know an awful lot about them, but I guess he'd hear such stories, being a pastor."

"What kind of stories?" I asked.

"Some woman in Idaho he'd heard of. Guy would come and lie down in front of her car regularly, begging her to kill him. He didn't want to live if he couldn't have her. After a while he was saying if he died he was taking her with him."

"We had a story on *Prescott's Landin'* had a plot like that," Zack said. "Guy kept threatenin', nobody took him seriously. He killed off half the cast in one episode."

"I remember that," Angel said. "The critics called it the bloodbath."

"It was cool," Zack said. "End of season. We were all sworn to secrecy 'bout who lived and who died until the series got under way again. There was a big fight about who would survive. None of the actors wanted to leave the show."

"Because of its high literary standards," I said, deadpan.

Zack reached over, took off my cowboy hat, ruffled my hair, and put the hat on again. I have enough trouble controlling my frizz without him making it stand on end. But what really irritated me was that it didn't look as if my nervous system was ever going to get over jumping up and rolling over and wagging its tail like an eager puppy every time this man touched me.

"What else, Savanna?" I asked, steeling myself to not look at Zack for a while. It would never do for me to soften before the six months were up. This test of Zack's staying power was crucial to any possibility of . . .

"He said California has a stalking law. But as all this person had done was send roses to Miss Diaz and call her up to talk nice to her, the courts probably wouldn't see that as a credible threat."

"Well," Angel said slowly. "There's proof of a credible threat now."

We were all silent for a moment, thinking about that, then Savanna picked up her story again. "Thad told me some statistics on stalking—like women who leave a battered spouse situation are seventy-five percent more likely to be killed if they leave than if they stay."

"Nobody battered the teacher, did they?" Angel asked.

Savanna shook her head. "I wondered myself why Thad was quoting those figures, but he usually gets to the point one way or another. Seemed like every story he told, the woman victim of a stalker couldn't rely on any help unless the guy attempted to shoot her, or stab her, or . . ."—she paused—"or strangle her."

It took her a moment to go on. Then she said, "Women do stalk men, too, he said. Women have even been known to stalk women, but mostly it's the old, old story of men after women. He said he just wished he'd paid more attention when Reina told him about it. He thought maybe she was exaggerating. Or letting him know someone found her attractive."

"But she didn't tell him who sent her the roses and so on?"

"No."

"I suppose she could have been exaggerating, or making up the story," I said. "It would go along with the story she told about getting married soon, and the ring—if she did buy it herself."

They were all frowning at me. "She might have been making up all of it so she'd seem more . . . popular," I clarified. "Someone wanted to marry her. Someone else wouldn't leave her alone."

"Not Miss Diaz—she wasn't like that," Savanna said. "If she thought she was being stalked, she probably was. And if she said she was getting married, then she was. Taylor hasn't been able to turn up the boyfriend, but that doesn't mean he doesn't exist. Miss Diaz was always a stickler for truth."

"People can say things like that—about wantin' to be truthful, or even that they *are* always truthful, but they could be lyin' all along," Zack said.

I squinted at him.

"I'm not talkin' about myself," he said cheerfully. "I never mind tellin' a lie when it's necessary to get me out of trouble."

"That's a great reassurance to us all," I said. "I'll make a note of it."

"Thad said it was much more common to be stalked by someone you'd had a relationship with than by a stranger," Savanna said.

"So it could be the missing boyfriend?" Angel asked. "He must have known she was coming to the reunion. Maybe he showed up, came into Dorscheimer's, say— kept watch and saw her come out of the main corral."

Savanna threw up her hands. "Who knows? She told me, and I guess she told Thad, that she was hoping to see the person who sent the flowers at the reunion. Or her. I mean, she didn't say if it was a him or a her. Why wouldn't she do that? Also, if it was the boyfriend and she knew it, why would she say she was going to get married to him and all that stuff about him being a good man, a nice man, and never getting jealous."

I had a sudden thought. "You know what, maybe Reina did make up the boyfriend. Maybe she thought if she talked about her boyfriend and getting married, and she flashed that ring around some, then the guy who kept sending the roses would get the idea she wasn't available and would stop his campaign."

We all thought about it. "Works for me," Savanna said at last. Zack and Angel nodded.

"You want to pass that on to Bristow?" I suggested.

"I'll pass on to him anything that will take his mind off Forrest," she said grimly.

"So what about you, Charlie?" Zack said. "We don't

have much time before the guys and gals start beatin' down the door. You were really bondin' at the restaurant with that guy Perkins—the guy who does the comics."

"Those are cartoons, Zack, political cartoons," I corrected him.

He shrugged. "Who else did you talk to?"

"Kalesha and Owen." I gave them a synopsis of the information Kalesha had given me, and told them I thought Owen Jones was hiding something.

"He said he'd never met any of the people at the reunion, not even Reina, and Kalesha looked at him funny."

"I'm not sure Taylor would accept that as proof of anything," Savanna said.

"You're probably right. But what I wondered, even without Kalesha looking at him, was, if he hadn't met Reina, how come she hopped up the second the music started and went and asked him to dance?"

Savanna looked startled. "You're right. That *was* odd. I thought so myself. I mean, there were a lot of guys there she did know. Why would she start off with a stranger?"

"She was talking to him a lot while they danced," I added. "It just seemed funny to me that she'd be that way with someone she'd just met."

There was a silence, then Savanna said, "What about Perky?"

"Now there's someone really strange," I said. I didn't get any argument from anyone. "He acted real peculiar, wouldn't talk at all about Reina at the restaurant, said he'd tell me all he knew on our date."

"Which is when?" Zack asked.

"Day after tomorrow. Tuesday. Nine A.M. We're going jogging across the Golden Gate Bridge, then on to breakfast at First Watch."

"No," Zack said.

I stared at him.

"I'm not lettin' you meet this guy alone. Are you insane, Charlie? He could be the murderer. He could be plannin' on tossin' you right off that old bridge."

Zack the protector of damsels in distress. It was a role he loved playing. But not one I was going to assign to him.

"Have you noticed the size of Timothy Perkins compared to me?" I asked.

"Granted you are tall. Granted you spend a chunk of time workin' out and are for certain in fair shape, it's still not a good idea to meet him alone. He's a possible suspect, Charlie, along with everyone who was at that reunion. We don't know yet who killed Reina, it could just as easily be Perkins. If you don't want me to go with you, then . . ."

"Yeah," Angel said. "I don't think she should go alone, either, guy probably knows by now she's looking for the killer. He wouldn't talk at the restaurant? Nobody else refused to talk. He looks to be a wiry little guy—he might be stronger than you think, Charlie."

They were ganging up on me.

"I guess you are right," I said with a sigh. "I guess it would make sense to have a buddy along."

"I'll pick you up at around seven A.M. Tuesday," Zack said.

"Wait a minute, we didn't decide who was going to go with me."

"I'm the senior partner here," Zack said. "I'm goin' with you."

"I just love it when you get macho," I cooed.

"I know you do," he said, giving me his crooked—and potent—smile.

Can't faze that man. Not ever.

CHAPTER 9

You must have heard me talk about the gym I work out in. I've said over and over to anyone who would listen—it's not fancy, it's not up-to-date, it doesn't have all that high-tech equipment that's so popular. It has a treadmill you operate with foot power, a rowing machine, a bench press, leg extension, leg press, stationary bicycle. Old stuff. Slightly rusty. I take along my own WD40 to keep the squeals down, and a spray bottle of antiseptic. I love this gym.

I may not have mentioned that the gym was actually part of a motel complex in Condor, one of Bellamy Park's neighboring towns. There was also an outdoor swimming pool that was mottled with algae. I always walked carefully around the pool. I didn't want to fall in until I made sure my shots were current.

You may have gathered this was not an upscale motel complex, and it was not in an upscale area, but the manager let me use the gym for twenty dollars a month, which amount I imagine he pocketed without informing the owner or IRS.

At 9 A.M. on Monday, I was staring in horror at a

notice on the gym door that said, "Closed for remodeling."

Two minutes later, I was banging on the door of the office. I kept banging until Banion, the inefficient manager, finally answered, looking as if he hadn't shaved, or maybe even bathed, for at least a week. He always looked like that. "Hey, Charlie," he said, moving his cigarette from one side of his mouth to the other.

"What's going on?" I demanded.

He looked blank.

"The gym. It's closed."

"Didn't cha see the sign?"

"Of course I saw the sign. Why is it there?"

"New owners, Charlie. Going to spruce the place up. New pool, new gym, new equipment."

"New equipment!" A cold chill went through me. "They're going to put in multistation stuff? Universal machines? Nautilus? That kind of stuff."

"Whole nine yards."

A thought occurred to me. "What are you doing with the old stuff? Can I buy the old stuff?" I had no idea where I'd put it, but I'd cram it into my loft somehow!

Banion was shaking his head. My heart sank.

"Stuff's already gone, Charlie."

"Gone where? Goodwill, Salvation Army? Maybe I can—"

"Gone to the dump, Charlie, garbageman and me loaded the whole lot into the garbage truck and compacted the bejesus out of it—spectacular racket." He winked. "Garbageman's a friend of mine, see."

"*Sheesh!*"

I turned away.

"I'm out of a job, ya know," he said, sounding aggrieved.

I turned back. "I didn't know. I'm sorry." I couldn't blame the owners. If I wanted to spruce a place up, I'd get rid of Banion, too.

About then, I heard my name called, and saw Zack hanging out of the window of his pickup. Every once in a while he'd join me at the gym—if Dandy Carr's was closed for some reason, or he had something on his mind he wanted to load into mine. He waved me over.

"They've closed the gym," I told him.

"Yeah?" He didn't seem devastated by the news. Actually, he sounded distracted.

I had a moment of intuition. "What's wrong?" I asked.

"Bristow wants a meet. He's at the Pancake House waiting for us."

"What happened?"

"He said to let him tell it."

I stared up at him. "That's all I know, Charlie. He called me up, told me to bring you along. You weren't home, I guessed you'd be here. You want to ride with me or take your car?"

I didn't want to leave the car in Banion's parking lot while any kind of remodeling was going on. "I'll see you there," I said.

He looked disappointed. He was sure acting as if he wanted to be with me a lot lately. Nah, he was probably just as puzzled by Bristow's summons as I was. I started toward my car, my mind tossing possibilities like a juggler's clubs until I was almost dizzy.

In a booth at the back, Bristow was eating his way through a pile of twelve grain pancakes—my favorite kind. He had a fruit plate alongside, I was glad to see. And a side of toast. Takes a lot of food to keep a big man going.

"What?" I demanded as I slid in across from him. Zack followed me in.

"Maybe you should eat first," he said.

"I'm not even thinking about food until you tell me what's up. Is Savanna okay? Jacqueline?"

"Everyone in the Bristow family is as usual, Charlie. I wanted to talk to you about Timothy Perkins."

"Phew," I said. "I was afraid something had happened."

"It has," he said gravely, setting down his fork. "Mr. Perkins has been shot."

I stared at him, utterly dumbfounded.

"He was shot in the back yesterday morning whilst jogging not far from his house. Single bullet."

I clasped my hands on the table. "Perky told me he lived in Noe Valley."

"That is correct."

"Is he, did he—"

"He's dead, Charlie."

I put my head down on my hands. Zack rubbed my back gently.

"Coffee all around," I heard Bristow say.

After a minute, I dragged myself upright. "Do you know who shot him?" I asked.

He shook his head. "It was a drive-by shooting."

"You think it was a coincidence?" I wasn't going to believe that. In my opinion, Perky's death had definitely taken Reina's murder out of the random-killing possibility. There had to be a connection.

"It's highly unlikely." He resumed eating, chewing thoughtfully before speaking again. "I didn't hear about it until this morning early, when I went to the station. I immediately drove to the Mission station and talked to the detectives involved. They were thinking Perkins was probably killed by someone he did a cartoon about. Some of those cartoons of his were very pointed, close to libelous, I would think. He got various individuals very agitated on a regular basis."

"Did you tell them about our murder?"

He looked at me.

"Sorry," I said. "My mouth doesn't always wait for my brain to boot up."

"I've noticed."

The coffee arrived in a large thermal pitcher. Zack poured a cup and passed it to me. It felt good going down, warming.

"I can't believe he's dead," I said at last.

"We were going to meet him tomorrow at the Marina Green," Zack said.

"So my wife told me," Bristow said.

My wife. Not Savanna. That didn't sound too good, but my mind was too preoccupied to think it through.

"Charlie had set up the date he won at the auction," Zack was explaining. "I said I'd go with her, just in case . . ." He sighed heavily. "I guess he wasn't the murderer."

I felt a huge pang of guilt. I'd thought it would be a good thing if Perky turned out to be the murderer because then I wouldn't have to go on the date with him. *Be careful what you wish for—you may get it.*

"You going to order anything?" Bristow asked.

I shook my head, both hands holding on to the coffee mug, but then Zack ordered a toasted bagel and I thought that might be a helpful thing to eat and changed my mind.

"Did anybody see anything?" I asked.

"So far the good guys are batting zero on the neighborhood canvas. One individual let her dog out and thought she heard a shot as she did, but decided it must be a car backfiring. People still seem to think that, but in these days of fuel injection, unless it's an old car, it's not going to do that. The woman actually did see a car—a large car. Unfortunately, she did not have her glasses on yet, so couldn't see the make or the license number."

He sighed. "It's a choice neighborhood. Houses have been very nicely refurbished. Good restaurants. Considered safe. At least it was. People knew Mr. Perkins. Anyone who was up that early saw him jog. Time your watch by him, they said."

He took my cup from my hands and poured me another cup of coffee. "According to the detectives, Mr. Perkins had made a few enemies in the neighborhood. He reported anyone who let a dog out without a leash, yelled at kids on bicycles or roller blades if they rode on the sidewalk. Let somebody so much as lean against a eucalyptus tree and he was all over them."

"He wasn't a charmer, that's for sure," I said, remembering what Perky had said when Bristow announced where Reina had been killed. *Think of the bacteria.*

Bristow winced when I told him this.

"Savanna said you talked to Perky for quite a while at the lunch in Tiburon," he said.

"Mostly setting up the date. He wouldn't talk about Reina, acted really cagey about it, looking around to see if anyone was listening. But after we set up the date, he did say something about talking to me about skeletons in the closet. A couple of people—"

Bristow looked at me sharply, but luckily, the bagels arrived and I was able to pretend that was why I'd stopped speaking.

Once I had my bagel spread with Neufchâtel, I started in about Perky almost appearing to be threatening me, or at least warning me. I shouldn't be answering questions, putting myself in harm's way, and so on.

Bristow listened patiently but when I was done, he looked me right in the eye and said, "A couple of people did what, Charlie?"

Oh, well, I had to tell him now. I took a sip of coffee. "A couple of people overheard him talking about skeletons. He passed it off as being something to do with that skeleton that turned up in our flower-bed. He was convincing, I think."

"Who overheard?" he pressed.

I sighed. "Thad O'Connor," I said.

"And?"

"Forrest Kenyon."

He looked pleased.

"Now look, Bristow," I said. "That does not prove Forrest had anything to do with Perky's death."

"You're smitten with Kenyon, too, are you?" he asked.

"No way," I said. "I don't even like the man, though I feel sorry for him. His wife died a few months ago, you know. He was devastated, he told me. And I believed him."

He nodded but made no comment. Savanna was right, he was going to get Forrest if he possibly could pin anything on him.

"Skeletons in the closet would indicate something that happened in the past. Something involving Reina," I said.

"Sounds possible."

"Something else," I said as he rose to go.

He looked down at me.

"At the reunion party, before Reina was killed, Perky told me he always went jogging at six A.M. in his neighborhood. He wasn't talking in a particularly quiet voice."

Bristow sat back down. "Who was close enough to hear?"

"Not Forrest," I said. "He turned up a little while later, when Reina was showing off her ring. He'd been delayed."

Bristow inclined his head.

I closed my eyes the better to think, then opened

them again. "I've no idea." I squinted, hoping that would help. "You were there."

"I didn't hear the statement about jogging. Maybe nobody else did, either."

He wasn't going to bother about any possible evidence that didn't include Forrest's presence.

"I don't remember who was at the tables next to us," I said. "Maybe you could ask Savanna."

"I'll do that."

He stood up again, shook hands with Zack and with me, then took his leave, several heads turning to watch him go. He had such *presence*.

So far no one had noticed Zack. That was unusual. He was wearing his shades, and he'd kept his cowboy hat on. "That's where a cowboy hat belongs—on the head of a cowboy," he'd said once.

"What do we do now?" he asked as the door closed behind Bristow.

I shook my head. "I don't know if I want to stay involved, Zack. If I hadn't poked around on that ferry asking questions, Perky might still be alive."

"Come on, Charlie. You don't know that. And we were all asking questions. Any one of us might have stirred something up."

I felt better. That was a possibility. Or maybe Perky's death *had* been a coincidence. No. I didn't believe that.

"Give me an overnight and I'll try to come up with some ideas," I said, adding as a look of extreme interest entered those wicked green eyes, "I did not mean that literally."

He started to lean forward and I gave him a push. "Let's go, I have work to do at CHAPS."

One thing about Zack, he would never keep a woman locked in a booth against her will. Too many willing women were standing in line waiting to jump in my place.

CHAPTER 10

At this time we were conducting line-dancing lessons at CHAPS every night but Monday. We hadn't been sure that would increase attendance, but it had—dramatically. Especially since the weather had cooled down considerably. Once people get exposed to country dancing, line dancing especially, they love it. Men can show off their precise turns and jumps and look macho doing it, women love it because they don't have to have a partner in order to join in—and everybody's happy with the fact it doesn't matter how old you are, you are welcome.

We had a bunch of regulars at all times. Students from the University, lawyers and doctors from San Francisco, tech-heads from Silicon Valley, local people aged twenty-one to eighty who just happened to like country music. Depending on the season, there'd usually be a smattering of tourists mixed in.

The idea came to me in the middle of teaching a new line dance called the starbright. I've noticed I get more ideas when my mind is completely occupied than when it's lying fallow.

The starbright is a dance Angel and I choreographed ourselves because we wanted something to go with LeAnn Rimes's "I Want To Be A Cowboy's Sweetheart."

"Okay, everybody," I said into the mike, to get things started. "Let's all come forward here, or the people at the back are going to run out of room."

I walked them through the dance several times. Some people catch on fast, some are a bit slower, some you just flat give up on. But everybody's in a good mood, it's a great workout and there's a whole lot of laughing going on, especially when you say something like "Hitch the left foot over the right, do a half swivel and a hitch turn and a right, left, right." Half the dancers will hitch the right foot over the left and there's no way they can recover.

We'd made starbright to fit into the intermediate range and we had a few beginners who had to get some special instruction from Angel, which they didn't seem to mind a bit.

And then, just as everything was going real good and I was about to say, " are we ready for the music?"— the idea came into my head as though it had been shot there with an arrow.

What about the classmate who didn't go on the ferry trip?

Well, sure, once I thought of it, I wondered why on earth I hadn't thought of it before, but remember there had been a lot going on since that fateful—and fatal— night when Reina Diaz was murdered. As far as Bristow had been able to find out, there were still no clues to Perky's killer. And that trail was getting colder as time passed.

I realized my dancers were waiting, most of them watching me with arms folded, grins on their faces.

"Where are you, Charlie?" Angel called from the other side of the dance floor.

"Sorry, I was thinking about that part everyone's having trouble with, trying to work out a way to make it simpler."

"We've got it now," the man right in front of me said.

I smiled at the middle-aged Asian man who had started coming to CHAPS several weeks ago. He was a terrific couples dancer, could usually find himself half a dozen partners on any given night, and he'd throw them all over the floor, but he was a klutz when it came to line dancing. If *he* was ready . . .

"Okay," I said. "Let's give it a shot."

I signaled Sundancer Brown in the deejay booth and he started LeAnn on her way to her cowboy. That young woman sure could yodel! When I was a kid, I wanted to be able to yodel, never could manage it.

To my surprise, Zack came alongside and did the dance with us. He was always a crowd pleaser and seemed to be able to perform any dance perfectly. He rarely got involved in the lessons, though—he wasn't even always present.

After a few false starts, everyone suddenly caught the rhythm and we melded into a group. It never ceases to amaze me that you can start out with a bunch of people going off in all directions, and then quite suddenly, there they are, coordinated, moving easily through the steps as though they'd been trained on Broadway, stomping at the same moment, clapping on the same beat. Feeling fine. Smiling at each other like they were best friends all their lives.

I grabbed Zack at the break, told him to get hold of Savanna, who was waitressing in the little corral, ran out to the office for a notepad and pen, and dashed back to join my partners at a table, way at the back of the club.

"Somebody didn't go on the ferry trip," I said to Savanna. "Kalesha said the person had an acceptable excuse. But she didn't mention a name. What if the missing person was the murderer? What if the missing person decided not to risk showing up at any more get-togethers?"

"It's a thought," Savanna said.

Zack nodded wisely, returning instantly to his Sheriff Lazarro role.

"I hadn't realized *anyone* missed the trip to Tiburon," Savanna said. She leaned back, gathering her thick curls in her hands and lifting them off the back of her neck. Every move this woman made was graceful. I should study her more.

"Becky Mackinay wasn't there," she finally said with an air of surprise. "You met her at the reunion. I sure can't see her as the murderer, Charlie."

I remembered Becky, of course. A Native American woman with a sweet smile. A consultant on Indian affairs. I didn't think she would be as militant as Dolores Valentino.

Becky and her husband and son lived in a small house in Mountain View. Zack and I drove there on Saturday afternoon. There were two vehicles parked in the driveway. A dark green van and a hot pink automobile. Zack made male admiration noises and we both stopped to look at the car. "It's a Karmann Ghia," he said with reverence in his voice. Men are funny about cars. Even though Zack didn't want to drive anything but a pickup, he could still rhapsodize about certain automobiles.

I had to admit I'd never seen a car quite like it. How many times do you see a car that is hot pink? It had beautiful lines and was in perfect condition. The upholstery inside was gray with bands of hot pink.

"You suppose it's his or hers?" I asked. Call me sexist, but I couldn't imagine a man owning a hot pink car, though Zack was sure admiring it.

"It would have to be hers," he said flatly. Which of course made me feel contrary. Why shouldn't a man own a hot pink car if he wanted to?

A car says a lot about its owner, I think. Whoever this car belonged to, the person obviously liked a touch of luxury—and color—in his or her life.

With a grin Zack indicated a sticker in the rear window: "Yield to the Princess."

"Hers," he said.

Nobody answered the doorbell, and after a few minutes we walked around the side of the house. Becky was on her hands and knees weeding the garden at the back. The air was perfumed with her flowers. There were roses of all colors, big daisies, salvia, lobelia, geraniums. Bougainvillea cascaded over a brick side wall. A magnolia tree with dinner-plate-size white blossoms shaded the small area. Palm trees stood guard between Becky's fenced lot and the one behind her.

I always admire beautiful gardens, especially the kind like Becky's that look riotous, yet are really part of a careful plan. Plant groupings look so much more attractive than flower borders planted in stiff straight rows. But I wouldn't have any idea how to achieve such a result.

Becky stood up and wiped her hands on her jeans, then shook hands with us.

"That's a great car in your driveway," Zack said.

Her face lit up. "That's my baby. Isn't she wonderful? I saw a Karmann Ghia when I was a teenager and fell in love. I wanted one in the worst way. Soon as I thought I could afford it, I did a bunch of research, looking for a used one, and Tom found her by surfing the Web. The color was a bonus! You should see inside the trunk—it's an air-cooled engine and even the air duct is hot pink. Did you notice the sticker? A friend gave me that—said it suited the car and my driving!"

She laughed, then gestured toward the house. "It's time I had a break, and I imagine you came here for a purpose. Why don't we go in and say hi to Tom and have some tea."

Tom was of average height, sturdy, dark-haired, and studious-looking. He was in a small very neat study, working at a computer, making some kind of spreadsheets, judging by the display on the monitor.

"Nice to meet you," he said courteously, standing to shake our hands. "Becky mentioned you both after the reunion. You own CHAPS, right? Becky and I visited your Web site."

I'd finished creating the Web site a couple of months

ago: http://members.aol.com/chapsclub. You could go there.

Tom draped an arm casually around his wife's shoulders. "That reunion sure turned into a disaster. Reina was a lovely woman. I can't feature anyone wanting to kill her."

"You went to Dix's, too?" I asked.

He shook his head. "I'm from Oklahoma originally. Went to school there, then came here to Stanford. Becky and I met in Sacramento at a demonstration." He looked fondly at his wife, tightening his arm around her shoulders. "Becky does a great protest, gets everyone organized."

He and Becky both laughed. "Becky's had Reina at the house a few times," Tom added, at the same time casting a wistful glance back at the computer monitor.

"Don't let us interrupt you," I said. "We just want to ask Becky a few questions."

"We're going to have some tea," Becky told him. "I'll bring you a cup."

"Thanks, honey," he said, already taking his seat.

There was a nice feeling between those two, I thought. A comfortable, appreciative atmosphere. Rob and I had experienced that during the first years of our marriage, especially when we had worked together on the house we had both loved. Working together toward a common goal brings out the best in people. But our relationship had become tattered and strained between the fifth and sixth year, through no fault of my own.

Correction. It takes two to make a marriage; two to break one. I'm not putting all the blame on myself, but something Rob had needed he evidently hadn't been able to find in me. So he'd looked elsewhere. Boy, had he looked elsewhere!

The Mackinays' living room was furnished with comfortable sofas and chairs, beautifully cared-for tables and attractive lamps. There was a playpen with a large assortment of toys near the picture windows that looked out on the garden.

As Becky poured and brought in the tea, I remembered she was a Quinault, from Washington State. My ex and I had spent several weekends at Quinault Lodge, and Becky and I discussed the beauty of the rain forest for a few minutes before I brought Reina up.

"I thought maybe Reina was the reason you came," she said.

We were interrupted by something that sounded like a baby crying and Becky stood up abruptly and went to open a door in the hallway. I was expecting to see two-year-old Thomas junior, but instead, three very large, very furry cats emerged, stretching and complaining.

Becky apologized to each one individually for having left them alone for so long, then introduced them to us. "These are my girls: Marmalade, Magic, and Snowball. I can only let them out while Thomas is sleeping, or in his playpen. He's going through a tail-pulling phase."

I pressed back in my chair, trying to disappear. But there were three of them and three of us, and as soon as Becky sat down, they chose laps.

I hadn't been around cats in a long time, I reminded

myself. Maybe I was no longer allergic to their dander. Snowball had chosen to leap onto my lap. She was, as her name implies, all white, with blue eyes that were even more vivid than mine. She was marching around in a circle on my lap, trying to find a soft spot to settle on.

Zack was making a big fuss over the black-and-white furball that had chosen him for a partner. Becky beamed at him over the top of the marmalade-colored cat she was stroking. He beamed back. Evidently, he liked cats. I hadn't known that. It was also obvious he liked the look of Becky. That was not such a surprise.

"I'm still in a state of shock over Reina's murder," Becky said, apparently not noticing I was sitting as stiff as a board, trying to keep my nose as far away from Snowball as possible.

"I heard about Perky, too," she went on. "Kalesha called me and then I saw the story on TV. Have the police turned up any clues?"

"A few," Zack said, looking earnest. "Nothin' they are willin' to release publicly yet."

"Do they think the two murders are connected?"

Zack shrugged. I didn't feel a need to comment.

It was a struggle to sit up, reach over Snowball, who was now kneading my abdomen, and set my full cup and saucer on the coffee table, but I managed it. At the same time, I got a hand behind the cat's posterior and tried to discreetly push her off my lap, but she sat down hard on my hand, pinning it to my leg.

"I'm sorry I missed the ferry trip," Becky said, looking directly at me just as I was about to give Snowball another shove. I tried to look innocent. "I was taking care of a friend's newborn baby while she was getting day care set up." She hesitated. "To tell you the truth, I could possibly have got out of it, but I didn't think it was right to be going off like that in a kind of celebration when Reina was dead. Not that I'm being critical of the others," she hastened to add. "It just didn't seem right for me."

"Tell us about you and Reina," Zack said smoothly.

I flashed him a "well-done" look, which he apparently didn't notice. He was concentrating on Becky. Like a good detective should? Or because he was interested?

I slid a hand under Snowball's bottom, ready to evict her as soon as nobody was looking.

Becky sat back in her overstuffed recliner and looked at the ceiling for a few minutes. Marmalade had stretched out from Becky's chest almost to her toes. The cat on my lap was curled in a purring ball.

So far, I seemed to be okay. I tried to relax.

"To do that I'd have to start with how things were for me as a kid," Becky said. She paused again before going on. "My mother was that clichéd Indian woman— a single mother on welfare, an alcoholic, a hopeless kind of woman. She couldn't seem to grab hold of life. Mostly she just drifted through it."

There was a deep sadness in her eyes. "I've no idea who my father was. Mom was only fifteen when she had me. Evidently, she drifted into and out of relationships without paying much heed, or noting mundane details like name and description. So anyway, when I was fourteen, I left the reservation and hitched my way south until I got to San Francisco and turned up on my mother's cousin's Victorian doorstep. She said I could sleep in the tower bedroom for a while, but I'd have to go to school."

Zack was nodding wisely. An aunt had rescued him when he was a teenager and I could tell he was relating. Becky was sensing his empathy and responding to it. She hadn't even looked my way in a while. Which was just as well given my feelings of antipathy toward her cat. It wasn't that I didn't like cats. At a distance. It was just that close up, they used to make me itch. A lot. A condition I kept expecting to occur.

Gently setting the marmalade cat on the floor, Becky poured more tea for Zack and herself, noted that my cup was still full, then opened up a container of chocolate chip cookies and set them on the coffee table in front of Zack. "Cousin Dorrie got me registered in high school and I went for a while, but I wasn't doing any better than I had in Washington. I really didn't care one way or the other. I played hooky a lot, went to the beach, went fishing, that was a lot more fun. But then I was sent to an alternative school. Alger Dix's School."

"How old were you then?" Zack asked.

"Fifteen." She laughed. "When I look back at that period in my life I see myself as the princess in the tower—totally self-involved—cut off from everybody. I guess that's why I like the sticker my friend gave me for my car. My aunt's house was Victorian, but she didn't clutter up the interior the way the Victorians did. It was about as minimalist as you could get, which was the way my mother's place had always been. I always thought I didn't care about having stuff, but about the time I went to Dix's, I'd grown out of being satisfied with the bare essentials. I wanted comfort. Reina Diaz rescued me, she brought me down from my tower, put me on an accelerated program so I could graduate with everyone else my age. She also let me live rent-free in the cozy mother-in-law apartment over her garage, until I went to college on scholarships she helped me get."

The marmalade cat had wandered over and was looking up at me as though deciding if my lap was big enough for double occupancy. I gave her the evil eye while Becky was sipping her tea, her eyelids lowered.

"So you were only at Dix's for three years?" Zack said.

She nodded. "All the people who were at the reunion were there at the same time, though."

I decided it was time for me to jump in. "What were they like?" I asked. "Were you surprised at how any of them turned out?"

She smiled vaguely at me as though she'd forgotten I was there, then shook her head. "I have a theory that people don't change that much as they grow older—they just become more set in the ways they developed early. Thad, for example."

"Dolores said he was a pain in school."

"Well, I wouldn't say that, but then there's a lot Dolores says that I wouldn't say." She and Zack both laughed and made eye contact. Were those pheromones I could smell in the air?

"Thad was always a righteous boy," Becky said after a brief silence. "A good boy. He never played hooky, never got into fights, always behaved very properly.

Had great manners. Always respectful. I wasn't surprised at all when I heard he'd been ordained as a minister."

She paused to think. "I was always a bit afraid of Dolo, to tell you the truth. Once, when she was mad at one of the teachers, she tried to get me to join some gang she was organizing. She wanted to take control of the classroom, just to prove she could. I turned her down but she convinced a few others. But then they got into a big fight among themselves, and Dolo never did get to be queen for a day."

She laughed. "Perky—now, he was another one who was always in a tussle with someone. He had a hostile nature and from what I saw of his cartoons and the way he talked at the reunion, he hadn't sweetened up one bit. I'm sorry he's dead, though. Underneath his caustic manner, I think he was quite a good person."

She surprised me by looking directly at me. "Do you think he knew something and was killed for it?"

"It's possible," I said. I was going to say more but I could feel a horrendous sneeze building up in the back of my nose. I stuck my tongue up in the roof of my mouth—sometimes that helped prevent a sneeze from erupting.

Becky was silent for a moment, then she said, "Perky used to be obsessive-compulsive. Always washing his hands, cleaning his teeth—in class he was constantly rearranging his desk, counting everything in it. He even counted stuff on his plate in the cafeteria. And he collected stuff, not the way other people did— not like philatelists and people who collect commemorative spoons—Perky kept junk—like ferry tickets and timetables, newspapers, catalogs that came in the mail, candy wrappers, cereal boxes. Reina and I went to check on him a couple of times when he didn't show up for school. He and his folks lived in this teensy little apartment and he had a bedroom that was stuffed wall to wall with that kind of junk. Unbelievable. He told me at the reunion that he'd kept on collecting after he had his own place, but quite recently he'd started seeing a psychiatrist and was in the process of cleaning the stuff out. I was glad to hear it. I can only imagine how much junk he'd acquired in the last twenty years."

She went on to talk about some of the other people who had been at the reunion. How most of them seemed to be average people getting through life the best way they knew. We asked her the questions we'd asked everyone else, but she didn't come up with anything new.

"Someone suggested Francisca Gutierrez was a lesbian," Zack said. "But she brought a baby along on the Tiburon trip."

Becky smiled. "Maria? I went to see Francisca just before the reunion. Such a cute baby." She looked over at the empty playpen with a fond look on her face. "I do love babies."

She laughed. "Sorry, Tom and I are trying for another child. I get carried away." She frowned. "Where was I? Oh, sure—Francisca told me she seduced some guy she met at a writers conference, some editor. She wanted a baby and that seemed the easiest way to get one. She didn't tell the guy that he got her pregnant. He was married anyway." She rolled her eyes. "Francisca always did carve her own path through life."

My sneeze exploded like a clap of thunder, scaring the cat right out of my lap and back into the room down the hall she had come out of. Marmalade skittered back across the room to Becky, who heaved her onto her lap and petted her. Zack's cat stood up on his lap and yowled.

"I'm allergic to cat dander," I said apologetically to Becky's startled eyes, then promptly sneezed again.

"Well, for heaven's sake, Charlie, why didn't you say so?" Standing up, holding Marmalade, she scooped Magic out of Zack's lap and took both cats down the hall to join their sister. Those were heavy cats. She was stronger than she looked.

Zack laughed. "That was some powerful sneeze," he said.

I made a face at him. And sneezed.

As soon as Becky reappeared, a happy little voice called out "Mommy get Thomas," and she went back into the hall and showed up some minutes later carrying a very cute little dark-haired boy dressed in minuscule jeans and a T-shirt with Winnie the Pooh on it. He was a miniature image of his father.

"Say 'how do you do,' Thomas," Becky instructed.

He looked from me to Zack with alert black eyes. "Hi," he said.

Becky carried him over to the playpen and popped him into it. He immediately got down on his knees and started playing with a little car, pushing it across the playpen pad, saying "voom, voom." Guys and cars. Must be in the genes.

Becky brought me a box of tissues and I did my best to blow my nose delicately. Feeling embarrassed, I went back to questioning her as soon as she sat down. "What did you think of Forrest when you were in school?"

"Forrest was always terrific," she said, though without much enthusiasm. "He always had money, he'd treat everyone quite often. Buy them lunch. He was born with a silver spoon and a silver tongue." She hesitated. "Problem was, he always came off like the lord of the manor. Put a few people's backs up, but he was definitely a decent person."

I was beginning to get the idea that Becky found good in everyone.

"Forrest really, really liked Savanna," she went on. "We were all surprised he and Savanna didn't get together after school. We always wondered if something might have happened."

"Like what?" I said immediately.

She shrugged and looked vague. "Well, you know how those crushes in high school go. Sometimes they work, sometimes they don't. Forrest's father was a controlling type, maybe he had something to say."

"How was Forrest with Reina?" I asked.

For the first time, Becky looked wary. I could sense her backing off a bit. "Forrest was just like the rest of us," she said. "He loved her. We all did. She was wonderful to us and with us." She hesitated and a faraway expression appeared in her dark eyes. "There wasn't anything *wrong* with the way any of us felt about Reina, if that's what you mean."

She glanced at a clock on the mantelpiece. "I should be getting Thomas his bottle."

It was apparent to me that she mainly wanted to quit talking. I wondered what protective response my question about Forrest had triggered. Maybe she was just upset with me because of my cat problem.

Thomas climbed to his feet and hung over the playpen rail when we stood up. "Bye, bye," he said politely and held out his right hand, obviously expecting us to shake it. Which we did.

He seemed a very nice little boy. I checked for the presence of any maternal yearnings in my brain, but didn't detect any. They were either still dormant or dead.

"Nice little kid," Zack said as we drove back to Bellamy Park. "I'd sure like to have one like that."

I looked at him in surprise. "You don't think a child would cramp your style?"

His sideways glance was mischievous. "My style's already cramped."

I'd walked into that one. Best not to comment, I decided.

"Nice Momma, too," Zack added. "Seemed real forthcomin'."

"You didn't notice she suddenly clammed up on us?"

He shook his head. "She probably just got tired of answerin' questions." He shot me a sideways glance. "Or else she was afraid you'd sneeze her house down."

"Very funny."

I found myself thinking about what Becky had said about her early living conditions. The word minimalist had struck a chord with me. It surely described the way I lived in my loft. When I'd finally left Rob, I'd sworn I'd never get attached to "things" again. I'd realized how they could trap you and tie you down.

It had seemed a mature attitude to me when I drove away from our Tudor house on Puget Sound, but after sitting in Becky's comfortable living room, it began to seem rather childish.

After Zack dropped me off at CHAPS, and I'd fed Benny and myself and clipped Benny's nails, a job we both hate, I looked around my loft with my eyes wide open. Boring and shabby. No doubt about it. Maybe I was in danger of becoming the same. Maybe if I changed my surroundings, that might effect a change in me.

My investment in CHAPS had not taken all the money my parents had left me. My Scottish mother had taught me to be thrifty. Actually the remainder of the money had increased tremendously in the mutual fund I'd stuck it in. Maybe I could use some of the interest to buy new stuff.

I knew just where I could go to look.

CHAPTER 11

It was Monday morning before I could get out of CHAPS again. Throwing my credit cards and wallet and cell phone into my backpack, I set off for Kenyon's Furniture Store in Los Altos.

The cell phone was the one Zack had given me sometime ago, by the way. He'd finally got it reprogrammed for me so I wasn't receiving daily calls from his old female friends. I hadn't yet told him that when they asked who I was I'd said I was his wife, Buffy. Ha!

The furniture was arranged very cunningly in little rooms set off by screens or bookshelves or plants so you could get some idea of what would go well together.

The first sofa I saw that I liked was over six feet long and had large faded, abstract flowers all over it in shades of blue and gray. Wouldn't show dirt, I thought. I might want to get nicer stuff than I had, but I still wanted it to be practical. There was a big chair that matched the sofa. It had a large ottoman that turned it into a cozy-looking chaise.

I was trying it out when a young woman came walking toward me with much clicking of high heels on the hardwood floor. "One hundred percent goose-down-filled," she said.

"Mmm," I responded.

"This cotton-sateen cover is very long-wearing."

I don't like sales talk. I like to go in a store, look around, decide what I like, decide if I can afford it, and if I can afford it, buy it. I had no interest in hearing how many feathers each cushion contained or whether it was hypoallergenic.

"Is Mr. Kenyon around?" I asked. "Forrest Kenyon."

"He's in the office, yes, but . . ."

"Would you tell him Charlie Plato's here, please?"

"Well, I suppose. . . ."

She marched off. While her back was to me I turned over the label on the sofa. Eighteen hundred dollars. *Sheesh!* My thrift store sofa had cost me $150.

And looked it.

I sighed.

"Hey, Charlie!" Forrest came striding over to me, tinted glasses gleaming, teeth flashing. I wasn't sure if it was all a front, but decided to accept his apparent friendliness at face value.

"I'm thinking of refurnishing my loft," I told him, which made him look even happier. He sat down on the sofa and stroked it tenderly as if it was one of Becky's cats.

"You can't do better than this set," he said. "It's extremely well made, guaranteed not to fade, certainly very comfortable."

"And very expensive, too," I commented.

"Not when you consider how long it would last, how

much comfort and pleasure you'd get out of it," he said. Salesman talk.

He looked down and away and up again. "How's Savvy doing?"

"She's just fine," I said, which probably wasn't strictly true, considering Bristow's attitude.

"You still investigating?"

"Off and on." I sat up as straight as I could on the cloud otherwise known as a chair. "That reminds me," I said, as if I'd just thought of it, and hadn't chosen this particular store for any other reason than to look at the goods. "Savanna said at the reunion that you were teacher's pet. What exactly did she mean by that?"

He looked uncomfortable even though he was sitting on a cloud, too. Then he shrugged. "Reina thought I had a good brain. She encouraged me to excel. She continually challenged me to do better, to work harder. She'd let me, and others, keep redoing a paper or essay or whatever until it deserved an A. And she looked at us as more than just students. . . ."

His voice trailed off.

"What?" I asked.

"She cared," he said. "She cared about every single one of us, not just in our class, but all the students she taught through all the years. She cared. She let us know how important we were to her. She cried at every graduation. She loved us."

He paused, then added, "Whoever killed her had to be out of his mind. In my opinion, it had to be a woman. All the guys adored her."

"Did she ever say anything to you about someone maybe stalking her?"

His head came up in surprise. "Reina? She said someone was stalking her? Who? When?"

"Savanna didn't tell you?"

"No."

That was interesting.

"In the five months before Reina was killed, some former student sent her flowers every week, called her often."

I still couldn't see his eyes clearly behind those tinted glasses, but something closed down in his face— the set of his chin, the corners of his mouth. Something had struck a chord.

"You call that stalking?" he said. "It sounds more like courting." Something had closed down in the voice, too.

"Courting's often a prelude to stalking. Especially if the *courtee* doesn't want to be courted."

I badly wanted to come right out and ask him if he'd ever sent flowers to Reina, but I suddenly realized the young woman who had first greeted me was nowhere in sight, and there were no other customers in the store. All of a sudden I felt vulnerable, though I had no idea why I should. Monday morning was probably not a big furniture shopping time for most people. All the same, it was probably a good idea to be a little cautious.

"Do you have any idea who might have behaved toward Reina in that way?" I asked instead.

He stood up. "It could have been anyone who ever met her. How would I know?"

He looked vaguely around. "Let me know if you decide on some furniture, Charlie. I'll be happy to advise on size and accessories, et cetera."

"I'm probably going to think about it for a while," I said. "I hadn't realized how expensive furniture could be."

He nodded, then turned abruptly and walked back to his office.

Something I'd said had gotten under his skin.

But what?

I was halfway back to CHAPS when I impulsively decided to go take a look at Dandy Carr's gym and its new owner. I'd avoided it for quite a while, because of memories I didn't want to dwell on. It wasn't my kind of gym anyway—too high-tech, too twenty-first century—too polished and mirrored and metallic and state-of-the-art.

But I needed to work out regularly and it didn't look as if I'd be going back to my usual gym even after it was remodeled, so I took a right on San Pablo Avenue and headed for the parking lot behind Dandy Carr's.

It was still before lunchtime and the place was almost deserted. I was wearing a western shirt and wrangler jeans, so I was hardly dressed for a workout. I told the attractive young woman at the front desk I wasn't a member, but I was thinking of joining and I'd like to look around a bit. I didn't mention I'd been there a couple of times before. "Whatever," she said with a big smile.

A short time later, I was studying a chart on the wall that purported to explain one of the machines and not getting very far with it. I might have to stick with a treadmill and get some free weights for my loft, I thought.

"Anything I can help you with?" a pleasant male voice said behind me.

I turned around.

He was big. Imposing. Not taller than me, but carrying a lot of weight. Three hundred pounds wrapped in navy blue sweats with the Dandy Carr logo on the jacket. He was definitely Asian. I liked his face on sight. Though he had a lot more face than I was used to seeing, it was a cheerful face with lively dark eyes and smooth skin. His hair was cut short.

"You must be the new owner," I said.

He inclined his head. "Fred Nishida."

"Fred?"

He laughed, his double chin wobbling. "My parents are Japanese, but they wanted me to be an all-American boy."

"You *sound* like an all-American boy," I said.

"I was raised in this country," he responded. "Right here in Bellamy Park, as a matter of fact. Went to school here."

I suddenly remembered my manners. "My name's Charlie Plato."

"From CHAPS?" He seemed delighted. "Yeah, I know the owner, Zack Hunter, he works out here. He's mentioned you a few times."

I was curious to know what Zack might have said, but could hardly ask. "Did Zack tell you I'm a partner in CHAPS?" I asked.

He frowned and said, "Oh, I expect he did." I was

quite sure he was just being polite. Zack did own half of CHAPS, but people always took it for granted he was the sole owner.

"I think he told me you used some . . . other gym, in Condor."

"I expect he told you it was retro, too. I have to tell you, Mr. Nishida . . ."

"Fred."

"Okay, Fred it is." We shook hands. He had big hands. Benny would like him. "I have to tell you that I like retro in a gym. I'm a bit intimidated by all this equipment and all the bodybuilders who come here."

"But you shouldn't be. You look in terrific shape." He poked a finger at my right biceps and grinned. "Much better shape than me!" He laughed again. "I'm working on it, though. With a lot of prodding from my wife."

"I understand you were a sumo wrestler."

"Long story," he said and indicated a couple of bench presses nearby. We sat. "When I was sixteen," he said, "I was a bit of a rebel, getting into trouble at school, playing hooky, and the usual, so on and so forth. My parents sent me to Tokyo to live with my grandparents for a while. I spoke Japanese, so no problem, but it was hard for me at first, being an outsider. My grandfather was crazy about sumo wrestling, so he took me and I went mad for it, too. I felt absolutely compelled to do it. Before I knew it, I was living and training with other rookie *rikishi*. I felt real lucky to have the opportunity. And it made my grandfather proud. My parents too. All was forgiven. It's damn hard work, but you're treated like royalty once you get known.

Girls love sumo wrestlers. I liked girls. It was an ideal situation. I was very happy."

We both laughed.

"Why did you quit?" I asked.

"Most sumo retire in their midthirties. I developed over-the-top blood pressure, and borderline diabetes. Well, you know, sumo eat twenty thousand calories a day. My peak weight was three hundred and ninety-five pounds. I'm comparatively skinny now. And still going down. Strict diet. Enforced by the local diet-police officer, also known as Sachiko, my wife." The fondness in his voice took any possible complaint out of his statement.

He gave me an amused look and said, "I heard you and Zack work on murder cases sometimes."

"You mean Zack gave me credit? That's a first."

He looked puzzled.

"Zack told you we worked *together*?"

His face cleared. "Oh, I see. No, Zack didn't tell me about the murder cases. That was Pastor Thad."

"Thad O'Connor!" I knew there had to be a reason I'd decided to drop in here. "He works out here, too?"

"Occasionally. But I know him mostly through my wife. Sachiko goes to his church." The fond note was back, and his eyes were bright when he spoke his wife's name.

"You don't?"

"I'm a backslider," he said cheerfully. "Tell the truth, Charlie, I got so marinated in the tradition and culture and spirituality of sumo I haven't wanted to look at anything else."

"I wonder why Thad would tell you about Zack and

me." I was interested in learning about sumo traditions, but right now it was the other topic I wanted to explore.

He shrugged his massive shoulders. "Television was on, something about that teacher who was murdered at CHAPS. Thad was here. He told me she was his teacher, and talked about the reunion, and that led to you and Zack helping the police."

"Well, I wouldn't put it that way," I said. "Nor would Detective Sergeant Bristow. I guess he works out here, too?"

He nodded.

"You have a woman member named Dolores Valentino?" I asked on a sudden urge. "Looks like a serious bodybuilder. Hispanic. Mexican American," I corrected, remembering Dolo's preference.

He shook his head. "Name's not familiar."

I shrugged. "Zack and I are just a pair of amateurs. We feel responsible because of the murder happening at CHAPS. What else did Thad tell you? What do you think of him?"

He laughed. "Is this how you do your detecting, Charlie? Snapping out questions? He didn't say anything more except that he honored the teacher and was sad when she was killed. And worried about who might have killed her. That it might have been one of his classmates, someone he knew."

"And the second part of the question?"

"Sachiko insists he's a great preacher and counselor. She thinks very highly of him."

"And you?"

"I like him okay. We talk. He's very interested in sumo, went up to Vancouver, B.C., for the big tournament that was held there. Told me he used to live up that way."

"Really?" I was trying to think of any more questions I could ask. "He told me he was monkish, celibate," I said.

He blinked and raised an eyebrow.

"You had to be there," I said. "I wasn't making a move on him, believe me. Is that true, do you think, that he lives more like a priest?"

He was talking before I finished the sentence. "Sachiko says many women in the congregation would like to be more than friends with Pastor Thad—they act like sumo groupies, she says. But she also says he shows no interest, which proves he is a truly good person."

His dark eyes glinted. "My wife did not approve of girls flinging themselves at me when I was a *rikishi*. Me, I didn't think it was all that bad."

He had a great laugh, full-bodied. "Pastor Thad said he thought it was dangerous for civilians to mix themselves in police work," he added. "I don't think he approved of your involvement, Charlie. He seemed concerned for you."

"Pastor Thad wrote the book about women worrying," I said. "Sounds to me like he's a worrier himself. I'll take my chances."

"You let me know if you need a bodyguard, Charlie. My nickname in Japan was 'the immovable one.' I put myself in front of you, nobody can get to you. I also learned to glare good. Sumo wrestlers get very good at glaring."

He demonstrated, staring me down so icily I felt chills down my spine.

"I'll bear that in mind," I said. I stood up. "Come out to CHAPS sometime, bring your wife."

"I just might do that. Sachiko likes nightlife, complains she doesn't get enough. She likes to dance." He smiled. "I like watching her dance. You going to become a member here?"

"Going to sign up right now," I said.

I liked Fred Nishida a lot, I decided. I had an idea Dandy Carr's was going to flourish under his care.

I drove home to my loft, feeling much more cheerful than when I left Kenyon's Furniture Store. It had felt good to talk to someone who had no connection with the murders.

Zack, Savanna, and Angel came over in the evening to discuss the schedule for the rest of the week. We brought all the boards up to date with upcoming events, then Angel and Savanna left and Zack lingered.

"How about a beer?" he asked.

"Okay," I said.

The green eyes brightened. "Here or upstairs?"

The man was incorrigible. "Here, Zack. Right here. With all the lights on. You still have until December to prove yourself."

"Have a jolly Charlie Christmas," he crooned as he opened a couple of beers and set them on the bar.

While we sipped beer and nibbled on some crackers and cheese, I told Zack about the conversation I'd had with Fred Nishida.

"You're going to use the gym? Great," he said.

"I guess Fred really was a sumo wrestler. He's big enough, for sure."

"He rose to the rank of *makushita*—seventh of about eleven rankin's."

"How come he doesn't have the topknot?"

"It's called a *chonmage*—very ancient style, he told me."

Zack was always interested in the details about a person. Sometimes I thought it was because he figured he might one day be called upon to play a character like that. He'd hardly be cast as a sumo wrestler, though.

"Evidently, when a sumo wrestler retires, there is a special haircuttin' ceremony," Zack explained, then added, "Wait until you meet his wife, Sachiko. She's a pistol. Full of energy. Tiny little woman. Puts me in mind of a hummin'bird."

I told him about going to see Forrest Kenyon.

"You're buyin' furniture!" he exclaimed. "You're thinkin' of settlin' down?"

"Furniture can be moved," I pointed out. "And I haven't made up my mind yet."

He had a couple of swallows of beer, then set the bottle down and squinted at it for a minute or two. "You have an ulterior motive goin' to look at furniture, Charlie? You think Forrest might be the killer? That would break Savanna's heart. She seems mighty fond of the dude."

"I'm not casting anyone in the role of killer yet," I said. I filled him in on the conversation I'd had with Forrest. "There was definitely *something* that struck home when I talked about the flowers and phone calls."

"Might be an idea for Taylor Bristow to check on

some of these people's telephone bills, see who called Reina," Zack said. "I remember once on *Prescott's Landin'*—"

"That's a great idea," I interrupted. "Why don't you suggest it to him?"

"You think he'd take that kindly, comin' from me?"

"You're Sheriff Lazarro. Of course he'd listen."

He nodded thoughtfully. Sometimes I'm incorrigible, too.

We finished our beer and Zack left without protest, which surprised me. But then, not ten minutes later, just as I was tucking Benny into his cage for the night, the doorbell extension in my loft did its horrendous *"Aroogah!"* and made Benny and me both jump out of our skins.

I jogged down the stairs to the dark lobby and peered through one of the glass panels that flanked the entryway. Zack peered back at me.

"I already told you no," I said after I got the dead bolts open.

"My battery's dead," he said. "You got any jumper cables around here?"

"Sorry," I said. "I probably should have, but I don't."

His grin was pure mischief. "Seems like I should maybe stay the night, then call the dealer in the mornin'?"

"No way," I said. "I'll let you look up the number for a cab in the office."

"You're so cruel, Charlie."

"Uh-huh," I agreed.

It took only a couple of minutes for the cab to arrive. I watched it leave the parking lot—making sure Zack was really going. He was being suspiciously good-natured about this test period. Did that mean he was serious about getting a passing grade—or that he was just pretending to be celibate and having a laugh at my expense?

As I closed the door, it occurred to me that if Angel or Savanna or even Bristow came around early for any reason, they were going to be very intrigued by Zack's pickup being in the parking lot not too far from my Wrangler.

CHAPTER 12

I hate when people tell me about their dreams. Especially if there are a lot of confusing details. Dreams never mean anything anyway—or if they do, who wants to figure out why people were sounding their horns at you because you were driving in your Wrangler with your hair soaking wet?

I'd gone to sleep lying on the sofa watching a videotape I'd made of a rerun of *Law & Order*. I hadn't even changed into one of the long T-shirts I wear as nightshirts. When the tape ended, I'd thought vaguely that I should find the bootjack and take my boots off, but I'd trotted off into the arms of Morpheus before the thought could produce any action. This was not unusual for me—TV is my narcotic.

So there I was dreaming this truly stupid dream, and all of a sudden something went *"Faaawooof!"* and my eyes opened right up because I knew instantly that sound had nothing to do with the dream. Disoriented, I glanced at the clock. Two o'clock in the morning. At the same moment, I heard an urgent beeping sound that sounded something like a truck backing up outside, yet not quite.

In the next instant, I realized with horror that the sound was coming from CHAPS's smoke detectors. All those emergency hormones that gave our ancestors the speed and endurance to escape primitive dangers flowed into my bloodstream with the speed of light. Unfortunately, they bypassed my brain. The first thing I did was to yank the fire extinguisher off the kitchen wall and fling open my loft door. Only then did it occur to me that you were supposed to feel the door first to make sure it wasn't hot. It was too late for that now. Not only was the downstairs level full of smoke, it was rolling up the stairs toward me.

My next impulse was to run down the stairs and see what was going on, but fortunately, some small part of my brain kicked in and decided the better part of valor was to retreat.

After closing the loft door, I grabbed a couple of towels from the bathroom and rammed them into the gap under the door, grabbed Benny's cage and carried it over to the window, then threw myself onto the floor so I could drag out the chain ladder that was stored under the bed.

After what seemed an age, I managed to get the ladder straightened out, after which I wrestled open the slider window on the back side of the building, punched out the screen and hooked the ladder in place.

During all of this, my mind was producing images of my body being incinerated to charcoal while my fingers and thumbs got in each other's way. But as I started to climb over the windowsill with Benny's cage in hand, those images were replaced by one of me trying to climb down a swaying chain ladder with that bulky cage in one hand. How could I keep Benny from rattling around in it?

Setting down the cage, I grabbed Benny out of it, tucked him inside my shirt, and threw the cage down to the ground. By now I was huffing and snorting like a grampus, whatever that is. My father used all those weird expressions in English, Latin, or Greek, sometimes French, and they were stuck in my head without any translations.

I couldn't see any smoke coming out of the building on the parking-lot side, but the smoke detectors were sounding off relentlessly, spurring me on.

Just as I was about to swing a leg over the windowsill again, I spied my cowboy hat and my backpack on the nearby table; I jammed one on my head, then threw the other down to the ground. As soon as I let go of the backpack, I remembered the cell phone that was in there. I could only hope it wouldn't break. I took a swift look around, but decided there wasn't anything else worth risking a delay for. One of the advantages of a minimalist lifestyle.

I'm fairly agile, but let me tell you, I'd never make a cat burglar. It took me a long time to get down to the ground. Well, several minutes anyway. Cowboy boots are not your usual choice for such activities, and I was losing circulation in my hands from gripping the chains so tightly. But hey, I was lucky I'd gone to sleep with my clothes on. Maybe I was psychic like Kalesha.

Terra firma never felt so good. My legs were wobbling like cooked pasta, but I was able to grab my backpack and Benny's cage, which looked considerably dented, and stagger to the edge of the parking lot.

Poor little Benny had gone totally still and stiff and
felt like a lumpy inanimate object inside my shirt. Rab-
bits do that when they are threatened. Benny had done
it a couple of times before, scaring me senseless when
I thought he was dead. I could feel his heart beating
as I put him into his cage, so I was sure he was okay this
time, just as he had been on those previous occasions.

Now that Benny and I were safe, I had a strong
urge to fall apart or throw up or something equally
useless, but I made myself get the cell phone out of
the backpack. It seemed okay—the bag was padded.
I dialed 9-1-1. "Charlotte Plato," I told the dispatcher.
That ought to show what mental shape I was in—I
never call myself Charlotte. Maybe I wanted dispatch
to know I was a helpless female.

The dispatcher was very calm, very cool. Which was
just as well, because as soon as I tried to tell her what
was going on, I started sobbing. I somehow managed
to answer all her questions, assuring her there was
nobody left in the building. I can usually keep my head
in a crisis, but the minute I try to talk about it to
someone, out come the tears. Maybe my tear ducts are
connected to my voice box. It's maddening because it's
a sign of weakness, in my opinion, though I decided
most people would be shaken up after climbing down
a ladder to escape a fire.

The fire engines arrived lickety-split, sirens blaring,
lights flashing. Picking up Benny's cage, I went forward
to let whoever was in charge see me. One of the guys
trotted over to find out if I was the one who'd called
in the fire and to check that I was sure nobody was in
the building.

It's amazing how efficiently firefighters work—within seconds they were kicking down the front entry door and entering the building, manhandling hoses without once getting in each other's way. In no time, another couple of firefighters had a huge hose sending up a curtain of water between CHAPS and the Plaza Bank next door. You can see why that would be a priority.

After a patch of time that seemed endless, the firefighters who had gone into CHAPS backed out again, and I got the impression they hadn't been able to contain the fire.

I trotted well out of the way, toting Benny along, and called Zack, Angel, and Savanna. It was astonishing to me that I could talk at all when my whole body was shaking in reaction, and my throat felt as tight as if someone was trying to strangle me.

Without ever meaning to, I'd come to think of that tavern—sorry, nightclub—as home. My partners were my family. That was my whole life going up in front of me. It was obvious already that the fire was well involved. Smoke was coming out under the roof, where it joined the eaves, then sucking back in and coming out again.

Detective Sergeant Bristow arrived with Savanna. A couple of patrol officers showed up around the same time. Savanna and I hugged hard, which started me crying again. She joined in. Bristow went off to confer with someone in the command post. Between sobs I explained to Savanna what had happened. "But how did it start?" Savanna asked, which was something I hadn't gotten around to worrying about. I could only shake my head.

Angel arrived, looking stunned as his gaze went beyond us to all the activity going on around our building. Just as he joined us, the ladder truck dropped a couple of firefighters on the roof and they chopped a hole above where Buttons & Bows and Dorscheimer's were located. Almost immediately, black smoke and flames shot upward through the hole as if it was a chimney.

Zack turned up at that moment, in a cab—his pickup was still in CHAPS's parking lot next to my Wrangler. Looking as stunned as Angel, he came straight to me and cupped my face in his hands.

"Are you okay?" he asked, looking right into my eyes. "Charlie, when I think what might have happened if you hadn't woken up. . . ." His voice was shaky.

"I did wake up and I'm fine," I told him.

He continued to look at me deeply. I felt my eyes burn, and attempted a laugh that didn't quite make it. "Emotionally, I'm a wreck," I added.

Which comment made me start crying again. Zack put his arms around me and pulled me in to his shoulder. The macho guy comforting the damsel in distress. One of the roles he always played to perfection on *Prescott's Landing*. I'm here to tell you it felt very comforting all the same.

Moments later, the wind changed and started blowing smoke in our direction, and a van from one of the TV stations drove into the parking lot. To avoid both, we went down to the corner and around the buildings to the plaza.

The residents of the Granada apartment complex were either hanging out of their windows, or hanging out at the edge of the plaza, some in robes and slippers, others with coats over pajamas. Soon after we joined them, P.J. came over with one of those quilts with snap fasteners and handed it to me. I hadn't even realized how chilled I was. I set Benny's cage down on the ground and clutched the quilt around me, noticing as I did that one of the patrol officers who'd arrived with Bristow was now mingling with the crowd. Was he there for crowd control, or was he looking for possible suspects? I wondered.

Zack crouched down to check on Benny. "Looks like he's shivering," he said.

"I'll take him to my apartment," P.J. volunteered.

Angel went with her to carry the cage, muttering something about being unable to watch.

"You're welcome to stay with me, Charlie, until you get squared away," P.J. said over her shoulder.

Friends are sure a comfort during an emergency. I didn't feel so sick anymore, but I still had this cold sense of dread that life as I knew it was over.

Next on the scene was Sundancer Brown, our slightly demented deejay. "I heard about the fire on my police radio," he said, staring at the scene in front of us.

He was listening to a police radio at two o'clock in the morning?

"You *own* a police radio?" Savanna said.

He shrugged as if to say, doesn't everybody?

"I should have called you," I said. "I'm sorry, I wasn't thinking too straight."

He looked at me owlishly through the thick lenses of his glasses. His wispy hair was standing straight up, which it often did. "You were inside?" he asked.

I nodded, swallowed hard, and dragged a used tissue out of my jeans pocket so I could blow my nose again.

"Benny okay?" he asked.

I didn't normally think of Sundancer as huggable, but that question made him eligible. I restrained myself. "He's fine," I said.

He smirked at me. In a way he reminded me of Perky. Probably because they were both geeks.

"Looks like we're going to join the ranks of the unemployed," I said.

"No problemo," he said, sticking his hands in the front pocket of his parka.

"Well, it's a hell of a problemo for the rest of us," I said.

He looked vaguely apologetic. "Sorry, Charlie, didn't think. It's just I've been wanting some time to work on mixing my own tapes."

Quite frequently I didn't understand what Sundancer was talking about.

"You want to do what?" Zack asked.

I wasn't alone in my ignorance.

"Take samples of sounds and music and make my own mixes," Sundancer said, speaking loudly, as if that made it any clearer. "Electronic music."

"Oh," I said, which could be taken for understanding, awe, or incomprehension. A very useful syllable.

About the time Sundancer drifted off with a "See ya later, guys," Bristow tracked us down and gestured us away from the crowd.

"How come you weren't in your nightgown?" he asked me.

Savanna looked at him questioningly. I wasn't sure myself if that was a personal question or an official one. I explained about going to sleep watching TV. Bristow seemed okay with my answer.

"It looks like arson," he said after a minute or two in which we watched the activity around CHAPS. "Nobody's saying anything official until the investigation is over, but there are some obvious burn patterns and there was definitely some kind of accelerant involved."

Arson.

The thought hadn't even crossed my mind. If I'd wondered about the cause at all, I would have thought the electrical wiring was maybe defective. I'd read somewhere that was the major cause of accidental structural fires. The building was old and I had no idea how close to code it adhered.

Arson.

"Someone deliberately set this fire!" I said.

My voice sounded as bleak as Zack's did as he said, "Somebody wanted to burn us out?"

"Funny thing, though," Bristow said. "Apparently, there was no sign of forced entry. Arsonist maybe had a key?"

"Only the four of us have keys, apart from the cleanin' crew," Zack said. "Cleanin' crew is reputable—I checked them out thoroughly."

Bristow nodded. "I'll make sure they're looked into all the same." He thought for a second. "Individual might have come in earlier and stayed inside after you locked up."

That comment hit me right in the pit of my stomach. While I was dozing in front of the TV set, someone might have been lurking down below me, waiting for the area to close down for the night.

"I told the fire department there was nobody in that building but me. But I suppose it's possible the arsonist was in there. Maybe he's still in there." I thought for a minute. "Only Zack's pickup and my Wrangler were in the parking lot when I locked up."

I then had to explain about Zack's battery dying, making sure to let Bristow and Savanna know he'd gone home in a cab. "I suppose if someone did come into the building earlier, like when we were having our business meeting or working on the indoor marquee, they could have parked on one of the side streets," I added.

Bristow nodded.

"Why would anyone want to set fire to CHAPS?" I asked.

Bristow shrugged. "Usual motives are spite or revenge; vandalism—just because it's there; pyromania—someone gets their jollies watching something burn. Sometimes there's a profit motive."

"Nobody's going to make a profit out of burning CHAPS down," I said. "How could they?"

His eyes seemed hooded. "Well, Charlie, that motive comes into play when an owner decides he wants out of business and he can make more on insurance than he can on selling out."

He looked at Zack. "You have a good policy on CHAPS?"

"The best," Zack said.

"When was it last updated?"

These were not idle questions, you understand. Bristow was definitely on duty.

Zack squinted. "I bought it two, two and a half years ago, haven't changed it since."

"Good," Bristow said.

It took me a minute, but I figured that was a better answer than Zack saying he'd increased the value of the policy a week ago. I supposed it was natural we'd be among the suspects, but I really didn't think Bristow could seriously believe . . .

"We love CHAPS," I said. "Every one of us loves it."

Zack put his arm back around my shoulders. There was quite a lot of light in the plaza, even though the flames had died down. There was half a moon and streetlights all around. Zack looked pale. I thought I probably did, too.

"So who d'you think might have torched it?" Bristow asked. "One of your wannabe cowboys or girls, maybe? Anyone get mad at the management recently?"

Savanna shook her head and shivered. The night air was chilly. Savanna was wearing a black leather jacket that provided more glamour than warmth. I realized my own soft as butter leather jacket was now lost to me and felt a twinge. You see, that's what happens when you get attached to things!

I offered Savanna part of my quilt, but she declined and snuggled closer to her husband instead, which was a good thing to see, considering how they'd been acting lately.

"I can't think of anyone," I said. "Most of the people who come to CHAPS are regulars. They come for a good time and that's what they get."

"They love CHAPS as much as we do," Savanna finished staunchly, then looked miserable. "What are we going to do?"

"Let's not worry about it tonight," Zack said.

"There's a lot of water going in there," I said.

"I called the insurance company on the way over," Zack said. "Someone should be here any minute."

The insurance adjuster had shown up in record time when we had our earthquake damage. Celebrities like Zack seem to get faster service than ordinary mortals.

The firefighters continued to go about their business with a minimum of fuss, and eventually the fire was determined to be completely out. Our beautiful old building was nothing but an adobe skeleton. But danger to the bank and the rest of Adobe Plaza had been averted.

The insurance adjuster arrived, camera in hand, and after I filled him in on what had happened, Zack went off with him on a walk-around.

"You wanna come home with me?" Zack asked me when he returned.

"You're welcome to stay with us," Savanna said, and Bristow nodded in agreement. "I'll be here a while," he said. "You two go ahead and I'll get a ride home later."

"P.J. took Benny in. I'll stay with her," I said. I felt around in my backpack and came up with my car keys. "Take my Wrangler," I told Zack. A thought occurred to me. "If whoever did this saw your pickup and my Wrangler in the parking lot last night, he'd think we were both inside the building." I felt chilled to the bone again in spite of the quilt. "If he knew us, that is. And knew what we drove, and maybe knew I lived up there."

"Don't go jumping to conclusions," Bristow said. "Wait until the investigation's complete." He paused, then looked from me to Zack. "You been asking more questions about Reina Diaz?"

Zack shook his head and I stopped myself just in time from telling Bristow I'd visited Forrest Kenyon that very morning. Because surely Forrest wouldn't have . . .

Suddenly overcome by weariness, I arranged to meet Zack and Savanna in the morning at Casa Blanca—the Mexican restaurant on the other side of Adobe Plaza. Jorge and Maria had recently started opening up for breakfast.

"I'll call the Robinsons and the Dorscheimers," Zack said.

The Robinsons owned Buttons & Bows, but rarely showed up, leaving everything to Gina Giacomini, the manager. I hadn't even thought about Buttons & Bows and Dorscheimer's, the concessions in CHAPS's lobby. I was too exhausted and upset to go look at the inside of the building, but it was clear there wasn't much left.

"I'll let Angel know about our breakfast meeting," I said, and trailed off in the direction of the Granada apartment complex.

CHAPTER 13

It's hardly surprising that I didn't sleep too well for what little was left of the night. I don't suppose my partners or anyone in the area did. But P.J. had done her best to make me comfortable and I was able to rest at least. Angel slept on her living-room sofa, saying he wanted to be available early the next day. I wondered if he'd slept there before. My question was answered when he went into the hall, opened a closet door and came back with a pillow and a blanket.

It took me a couple of days to realize Benny and I had been lucky. What if I'd just thought that *"Faaa-wooof"* sound was part of my dream? What if whoever set the fire had disabled the smoke detectors? That was one of the first things the investigators had looked for. Disabled detectors and sprinklers were often a red flag pointing at the owner or owners. Because they usually wanted to make sure the entire structure was destroyed.

I was put through the grill because I'd had my clothes on and because I was supposedly the only person in the building—and nobody had broken in. Zack was similarly suspect because his pickup had been left in the parking lot, and he'd kept the insurance papers and an inventory of CHAPS's contents in his bank safety-deposit box. "Where else would you keep important documents?" he'd asked.

He was able to convince the investigators he'd put them in there two years ago. It took me longer to convince them I'd gone to sleep in front of the TV with my clothes on. Apparently, nobody innocent ever did that.

The investigation took several days. Angel and Savanna were questioned, the neighborhood canvassed, the debris sifted. We weren't allowed into CHAPS until the investigators were through. Some of the collected material was sent to an ATF laboratory in Walnut Creek for more study.

The conclusion: Definitely arson, the fire had been set in four separate places. The accelerant was some kind of alcohol mix.

One other benefit of having a celebrity on board was that the media concentrated on Zack and left the rest of us pretty much alone. One morbid reporter wrote that perhaps the fire had been a blessing, and might have cleansed the building of the evil that had caused previous deaths connected with CHAPS. When I got over being amazed at this one, I teased Zack about it, asking if he'd been overdramatizing again, or borrowing one of *Prescott's Landing*'s more bizarre plots, but he solemnly swore he'd had nothing to do with it and didn't believe in evil spirits, even though he had been caught up in an exorcism in one episode.

The neighbors came up trumps, supplying me with

temporary clothing and making me soup and casseroles and bread. P.J. had gone shopping for Benny's critter litter and his favorite veggie-flavored bunny bites. She'd even thought to buy nail clippers for him. And she spent almost a whole afternoon straightening out his cage while he romped around her living room, apparently unaffected by the whole experience.

Finally the four of us were allowed to go look at what was left of CHAPS. Which was very little. What was there was hopelessly charred and blistered and scorched. Not to mention the water damage. Zack managed to rescue his wine and microbrewery beer collections from the cabinets they'd been stored in. The main corral bar was strangely intact. So was the stage. Everything in the office was in ashes, the computer wrecked. The loft was . . . gone.

A week after the fire, we met at Casa Blanca, which had turned into our unofficial headquarters. Jorge had even given us exclusive use of his small party room for as long as we needed it. We were joined by the owners of Buttons & Bows, Amy and Stan Robinson, and Rick Dorscheimer and his wife, Tilly.

To my amazement, after very little discussion, the decision was unanimous: the insurance coverage was good; the three businesses had been going concerns; we would build again.

The depression and numbness that had hung over me for a week suddenly lifted a little. My life wasn't over, after all.

"Maybe that fire was an act of God," I said into the

happier atmosphere. "I was thinking of buying new furniture. Maybe I wasn't supposed to do that."

"You'll have to buy it now," Savanna said. "I suppose you'll go shopping at Goodwill again?"

"Maybe not this time," I said.

It hit me that I hadn't told anyone but Zack about my visit to Forrest Kenyon's furniture store. It still didn't seem a good idea to share that information. Savanna would be very suspicious of my motives if she heard I'd gone there. And if I broached the subject with Bristow, he'd think I was suspicious of Forrest and possibly add that to his own convictions about the man.

Zack was looking at me, probably having similar thoughts. I shook my head slightly at him and he nodded. He was getting good at reading my mind. All the same, I thought, I was going to have to tell Bristow about my conversations with Forrest Kenyon. If he found out any other way, I'd be in deep trouble. And in any case, I *did* have my doubts about Forrest. And the fire had been started hours after I went to talk to him.

"You going to keep bunkin' in with P.J.?" Zack asked. "You know you're more than welcome to use one of my guest rooms, darlin'. There are beds to spare."

His smile was wicked.

Everyone looked at me with great interest. Especially Rick Dorscheimer. Evidently, the others weren't all that surprised that Zack would invite me to be his houseguest. But they were still waiting for my response.

"Yeah, Charlie," Angel added. "You're interfering with my social life."

Whoa! For Angel that was a major declaration.

He realized it in the next moment and those telling crimson streaks appeared on his high cheekbones.

"Social life, or love life?" Savanna asked in a teasing voice.

Angel looked at her.

"Actually, it's none of my business," Savanna said, holding up her hands in surrender, but smiling broadly. It was good to see her smile.

The short exchange had taken the attention off me, but once Angel refused to be drawn out any further, it returned to its original focus.

"That's very kind of you, Zack," I said sweetly. "Actually, I've talked to the manager at the Granada about renting an apartment. He has a vacancy, said he'd hold it until we decided what we were going to do. It's expensive, but then so is everything else in Bellamy Park. Now that we've decided to rebuild CHAPS, it will work out fine for me to be just across Adobe Plaza, where I can keep an eye on things. P.J. said she could lend me her futon."

Zack gave me his lopsided smile, which had a disappointed edge to it. "You're always so practical, darlin'," he drawled.

I grinned back at him, and for a moment our eyes held. Since the fire, whenever that happened a whole world of feeling was conveyed between the two of us. Sometimes I even regretted making Zack vow to be celibate for six months. Maybe life was too short and uncertain for so much delayed gratification.

"We going to build exactly the same as before?" Rick Dorscheimer asked, breaking the tension. "I know we have to do it in adobe to fit the rest of the plaza, but I'd like to have an external door on the side of the building, as well as the one off the lobby."

Everyone started talking at once, but eventually calm prevailed and it was agreed there was nothing wrong with the original design, given a few additions, such as Rick's doors and more rest rooms for CHAPS.

"Yeah, Charlie, we'll rebuild your loft for you," Zack said without my asking.

The discussion went on for another hour, then the Dorscheimers and the Robinsons left.

"You and Zack going to keep on looking for whoever killed Miss Diaz?" Savanna asked.

"You'd better believe it," I said.

"We sure are," Zack said at the same time.

We looked at each other. "He made it personal," I said, and Zack nodded.

"We aren't just doing you a favor or trying to exonerate Forrest Kenyon anymore," I said to Savanna. "I'm not about to believe some crazed arsonist just wandered in on a whim and torched CHAPS. The fire had to be the work of the murderer. He killed Reina; he killed Perky, possibly to stop him talking to me; if he knew I was living at CHAPS, he tried to kill me, and probably thought he was also killing Zack."

Savanna nodded solemnly. We were silent for a moment, then Zack said he was starving and that lightened the atmosphere. As long as we were right there in a restaurant, we decided we might as well eat.

We were about halfway through when Detective

Sergeant Bristow dropped in to say hi and elected to stay for lunch, too.

I raised my eyebrows at Zack and he nodded, reading my mind again.

I waited until Bristow's enchiladas had been served, then asked him if anyone had turned up any clues to the identity of the arsonist.

He shook his head. "Apparently, he wasn't trapped by the fire. No traces of human remains showed up. Unfortunately, none of the neighbors saw anything or anyone suspicious before or during the fire."

He glanced at Savanna. "We've talked to everyone who was at the reunion. Everyone has a different idea of who might have killed Reina Diaz. Nobody knows anything about anyone starting a fire, or talking about starting a fire."

He paused. "It's possible of course that the fire had nothing to do with the murder of Reina Diaz. Just as it's possible that Timothy Perkins's death had nothing to do with it, either. All three events *could* be separately motivated and carried out. But experience has taught me not to put much stock in coincidence."

I took a deep breath. "Did you talk to Forrest Kenyon recently?" I asked.

Savanna's head came up.

"I talked to everyone," Bristow said. "Why pick on him particularly?"

"Yes, Charlie," Savanna said, sounding very terse. "I'd like to know that, too."

"I'm not picking on him," I said, not even trying to hide my exasperation. "I just think we have to look at everything and everyone very suspiciously. This whole thing has gone beyond people's friendships and histories and personalities. We need to find out who committed the murders and set the fire. Nothing else is important."

"Well said, Charlie," Bristow said, his eyes glinting. Savanna glared at him.

I told about Forrest bringing the single rose to Reina's remembrance pile, and our subsequent conversation, making sure to include what Forrest had said about his late wife, mainly for Bristow's benefit. Judging by his thoughtful expression, he took it in sympathetically, as I meant him to.

"You think there was something significant in him bringing a rose?" he asked.

I looked at Savanna.

For a minute or so she met my gaze stubbornly, then she sighed. "I guess you're right, Charlie," she said wearily. "There's something I haven't told you," she said to her husband. "Before the reunion, I went to see Miss Diaz at her house, to set the event up, remember?"

He nodded.

"She had these red roses in a vase on the table. She told me she was receiving a bouquet like that every week from a former student. She was worried about it. She said the person was coming to the reunion, so they could have a conversation then."

"Did she say exactly why she was worried?" Bristow asked. His voice was far too even, but he was evidently going to wait until all the evidence was in before jumping on Savanna.

"She said this person had called her out of the blue,

five months earlier, and kept on calling her. And the flowers started arriving at the same time, and kept coming every week. Miss Diaz had read some article about how stalkers often started by being complimentary and affectionate."

She paused and took a long drink of water. Bristow waited patiently, but he'd stopped eating.

"This person?" he echoed finally.

"I'm not holding the gender back," Savanna said stiffly. "That was the way Miss Diaz said it to me. She said she couldn't tell me who it was because she didn't want me telling my husband and getting the person in trouble, when she wasn't yet sure there was a problem. She could handle it, she said."

Bristow had his elbows on the table, and had steepled his fingers. His expression was impossible to read, but there were very angry vibrations coming out of him. Angel was looking at him, his dark eyes wide with alarm. I wondered what color Bristow's aura was.

"Have you kept any other information from me?" he asked ominously.

Savanna shook her head. "I didn't like the way you were determined to pin the murder on Forrest," she said.

Bristow's eyes were hooded. He turned his stern gaze on me. "You knew about the stalking, Charlie?"

I gulped and confessed that Savanna had told me early on. I also admitted I'd gone to the furniture store to look at furniture and to question Forrest.

That brought me a sorrowful look from Savanna.

I told Bristow everything Forrest had said, and

included his sudden discomfort when I mentioned the possibility that someone had been stalking Reina.

"But you've got to remember," I added hastily, "none of this was anything Forrest had kept back from you. All we have is what Reina told Savanna, and my subjective impressions of Forrest's reaction. There was never any doubt in my mind that he loved his wife and was still mourning her."

Savanna looked at me gratefully.

Bristow still looked stern. "A couple of people mentioned this stalking possibility to me," he said. "I take it they got that idea from you? You'd talked about it to them?"

"I suppose," I said uneasily.

"I may have said something about it, too," Zack said.

I appreciated his coming to my defense.

"Thad said Miss Diaz told *him* about the stalker, too," Savanna said abruptly. "Did he tell you?"

"He did indeed. Mr. O'Connor has been most open and helpful all along, as have most of your other classmates." His glance stated, *"Except for my wife and her associates."*

Angel spoke up. "Dolores Valentino said there was a rumor around the school that Reina got it on for—" He stopped himself, then continued, "That Reina had an affair with a student. Dolores thought it might have been Forrest."

"Forrest said it might have been Dolores," I reminded him. "And Kalesha thought Dolores might have had a crush on Reina in school."

Bristow sighed. "If I may paraphrase old Will, 'Each

conscience hath a thousand several tongues, and every tongue brings in a several tale, and every tale condemns another for a villain.' "

"Seems to me it might be a good idea to check local florists. And maybe some telephone records," Zack said. I hadn't noticed that he'd acquired his wise Sheriff Lazarro expression, but there it was. His voice had deepened, too. He'd morphed again.

"I might even have thought of that," Bristow said, which was the closest he'd ever come to telling Zack he wasn't all that dumb.

CHAPTER 14

You may have noted that Bristow hadn't said that we should quit messing around in police business. Don't feel bad if you missed it, it took me a night to realize it and to decide what to do next. No, I didn't come up with anything brilliant, I just decided we should start over. And for some unknown reason, the person who popped into my mind was Owen Jones. I still had the feeling he'd known more than he was saying. It might not be a bad idea, I thought, to talk to him without Kalesha present.

I think I would probably have gone on investigating the murders without the fire that destroyed CHAPS—I'd never liked quitting a job while it was half done, but as I'd told my partners, the arson had made it personal. I was now absolutely determined to get whoever was responsible.

It was Zack's idea that we surprise Owen Jones in his office. Apparently, surprises had been very important on *Prescott's Landing*. The writers had constantly come up with new ones. The surprise to me was that people watched the program at all, but I refrained from blurting that out. Zack knew my opinion of his TV show by now—and why should he care anyway when so many thousands loved it?

I called Dr. Jones's clinic and made an appointment for a GYN checkup. The plan was that while I was filling out insurance forms or whatever, Zack would engage the staff in conversation and find out how Owen rated in their opinion.

Three women in colorful smocks and white pants were huddled together over the curving counter that divided the office space from the waiting room, all three staring at a computer screen, while one of them tapped frantically on the keyboard. "It's not there, either," she wailed finally.

It was a couple of minutes before one of the women looked up. "Sorry," she said, handing me a clipboard with forms attached. "We're having a problem here this morning. Our office manager had a family emergency and had to leave town and we can't find some documents we need."

Her gaze drifted beyond me to Zack. Her eyes widened. "Wow!" she said, when she got her breath back. "Aren't you Sheriff Lazarro from *Prescott's Landing?*"

Zack smilingly allowed that he was guilty as charged.

The two other women jerked upright and looked equally stunned.

I took the forms over to a seat in the waiting room to fill out, one ear taking in the breathless comments of the women on the other side of the desk.

By the time I got that done, Zack had posed a few questions. It was to be expected that the women weren't going to say anything too negative about the doctor—he paid their salaries, after all. But I looked up each time they answered, thinking I could judge by their body language if they were telling the truth.

"The best," one of them said firmly, her eyes shining. "Our patients swear by him," another said. "So do we," said the third.

After I handed over the clipboard I mooched around the area, studying pictures that according to their captions were all of Wales: Aberystwyth Seafront, Beaumaris Castle, a mountain resort named Betws-y-Coed, and so on. Other photographs depicted groups of men singing, groups of women with naturally beautiful complexions, all wearing tall black hats, not unlike top hats, but with a rim of pleated white fabric underneath. There was an impressive flag hanging in one corner of the waiting room—a red dragon on a green-and-white field—and a model of a harp on a side table.

Obviously, the doctor was proud of his natal country, even though he'd left it more than thirty years before.

I saw when I went to the rest room to fill up the usual little jar that there were pictures of newborn babies all over the walls in the hall. There were also thank-you cards by the ton, and if the ones I looked at were a fair sample, the patients were all extremely grateful for Dr. Jones's wonderful care.

I managed to persuade the nurse that I would prefer to talk to the doctor before taking all my clothes off. That was fine with her, she said, quite a few patients preferred to stay dressed through the initial discussion. "Would your husband like to accompany you?" she asked.

"Husband" stepped forward with alacrity.

Owen Jones was, of course, completely taken aback by our sudden appearance in his office. "You're here for a routine checkup?" he asked, peering into my new chart, which so far contained only my weight and blood pressure.

"I'm afraid we practiced a little deception on your office staff," I admitted. "We really wanted to talk to you in private about Reina Diaz."

He sat back in his leather chair. He was dressed as formally as before in slacks and shirt and tie, but instead of a sport coat he had on a starched white coat. He looked very dashing in a poetic way. I could imagine some of his patients getting somewhat lustful about him. Outside of the delivery room, of course. "You didn't get enough out of me on the ferry?" he asked without a trace of humor.

"We're startin' a second round," Zack said.

"Because of the fire?"

"You heard about that?" Zack asked suspiciously.

"Difficult not to. Pictures all over the newspapers, stories on television. Too bad. You have my sympathy. You going to rebuild?"

"We are," Zack said.

"Well, I fail to see how I can be helpful. And I am very busy. . . ."

"Just give us a couple of minutes," I said.

He looked at me without any particular expression. "And your official standing is?"

"Zero," I confessed. "Savanna asked us to help out because she was afraid her old friend Forrest was looking like a suspect and she doesn't believe he is."

"Can't say I cared much for Forrest," Owen said.

"He still deserves justice," I murmured.

Owen sighed and closed my chart and squared it up on his desk. "I really don't see any reason why I should talk to either of you."

"Well, it might prevent you having to talk to Detective Sergeant Taylor Bristow," Zack said, which he had no business saying. We couldn't guarantee something like that.

Owen looked at him with great suspicion as though his thoughts were similar to mine. Standing abruptly, he went over to the watercooler near the door and filled a Styrofoam cup with water. As he carried it back to his desk, I noticed that it was trembling slightly.

"I've already talked to both detectives," he said. "I had nothing valuable to offer. I didn't know Reina; I didn't know any of the people at the reunion; I certainly didn't have any ideas about who killed her."

"But you were there and you met her," I said.

He inclined his head, lifted the Styrofoam cup and sipped some of the water. There was still a slight tremor in his fingers, and he set the cup down very carefully when he was through.

"I'd heard about Reina from Kalesha, of course, but I didn't meet her until the night of the reunion and we exchanged no more than a few words."

"That was when you danced with her?" I said.

"Yes, that's right. We did dance. Yes. She asked me to dance. I don't know why. It surprised me."

Funny, he hadn't looked surprised.

"We didn't talk much," he went on. "I enjoy dancing,

but I like to concentrate on the music, the rhythms, the experience itself."

Sure, I thought.

Evasive sort, our Doctor Owen Jones. "Seemed to me Reina had a lot to say to you," I said.

Owen squinted at his ceiling. "I suppose she did. People do tend to corner doctors, you know. I can hardly go anywhere without someone saying, 'Say, Doc, what do you know about arthritis?' Or angina. Whatever. One of my colleagues got so tired of it, he started telling people to take their clothes off and he'd take a look at them."

His laughter sounded forced. "I'm afraid if I tried that, some sweet young thing would actually do it."

Sounded like camouflage to me. Evidently Zack was having the same reaction. "So what did Reina want advice on?" he asked.

Owen shrugged. "I didn't mean *she* needed advice. I really don't recall *what* she was talking about." His smile was as false as his laughter had been. "My short term memory is really shot, I'm afraid."

"You could try *Ginkgo biloba*," I suggested, not without sarcasm.

He glanced at his watch. "I really am very busy today, Charlie. My office manager had to fly up to Spokane to collect the baby she's adopting. She received the call last night, so we are all at sixes and sevens and—"

"Maybe I could help out?" I said. "I happen to be unemployed at the moment."

I hadn't meant to say anything of the sort, but my brain had produced an image of the computer in the front office and me taking a look at whatever might be inside it—like something about Reina Diaz.

Owen was looking at me blankly.

"I used to be office manager for my ex-husband, Rob Whittaker. You may have heard of him? The plastic surgeon. Seattle."

"I don't think . . ." He was looking extremely nervous again. "Thanks . . . thank you for the offer, Charlie, but I really, I don't think, I have a temp on order already." He looked at his wristwatch again. "I take it you don't really want a checkup?"

I nodded. I guessed we weren't going to get much more out of him, anyway. I don't know why I'd thought we might. And he still seemed nervous, fingering the pens in a pen holder on his desk, opening and closing the chart the nurse had begun for me.

He looked relieved when I stood up.

Was he really just worried about getting behind in his schedule? As we walked down the hall to the door, I noticed there were a few patients waiting.

"We're going to get blasted by Bristow for interfering again," I said to Zack as we settled ourselves in his pickup.

He gave me a sideways glance. "You think the doc's going to tell on us? I wouldn't think he'd want to."

"We're going to have to tell Bristow we went to see him. Didn't you see how nervous he was?"

"Nervous?"

"His hands were shaking, Zack. Innocent people's hands don't shake."

"Maybe he had a hangover," Zack said. "Maybe he's

sick. Maybe he has some medical problem that's makin' his hands shake."

He had a point. I still thought we should mention him to Bristow.

I settled back in my seat and thought about Owen Jones. I really couldn't see how he could be a major player in this particular scenario, but I was curious about him just the same.

"You want to come over for barbecue Saturday?" Zack asked.

My eyes had drifted closed. Ever since the fire I'd found myself getting sleepy occasionally in the daytime. It was as if either experiencing the fire, or the fire itself, had sapped some of my energy.

I sighed. "I don't think that's a good idea," I said.

"Even if I invite Bristow and Savanna? And Angel?"

"In that case, I'd be delighted to accept." I never eat barbecue as a rule. But I'd been living mostly on sandwiches and salads, as I hadn't bought any pans yet. Something cooked sounded good.

"Around five o'clock, then. We can have a couple of beers beforehand."

I turned my head to look at him. "You won't forget the part about inviting the others, will you?"

He gave me a sideways grin. "You aren't too big on trusting me, Charlie darlin'."

"That's true."

We both laughed.

"I'm thinkin' seriously about takin' that job," Zack said after a few minutes.

"What job?" I asked, sitting up straight. What on earth was he talking about? The job with Dr. Jones

I'd just got turned down for? I hadn't really wanted a
job. The insurance company had agreed to pay my rent
for the duration, and eventually there would be money
to replace my clothing and dishes, et cetera. But Zack
couldn't possibly do that job!

"The job Francisca looked into for me," Zack
explained. "Seems like her publisher is interested in
welcomin' me into the stable."

Light dawned. "You mean the cover model thing?"
He nodded.

"You don't think that would be a bit of a comedown
after starring in a major television series?"

Zack didn't always recognize sarcasm when it
should have bit him on the nose. "I don't think so,
Charlie," he said seriously. "It's sorta like comparin'
apples and oranges. But I've been thinkin' . . ."

His voice trailed away and I wasn't sure he had
anything more to say on the subject, but I waited to
be sure.

"Cher said somethin' a while back that I memo-
rized," he said finally. "She said, 'Some years I'm the
coolest thing that ever happened, and then the next
year everyone's so over me and I'm just so past my
sell date.' I think about that a lot. It happens."

He paused. "Do I want to keep goin' down that same
old road?" he asked, apparently rhetorically. "You only
get so far when things aren't goin' well for you, and
you start feelin' like a failure, and the sharks sense it
like blood in the water. I don't want to go on until I
reach that stage. I'd rather get off the bus under my
own steam and have people wishin' I'd stayed on, than
have to be pushed off at the terminal."

There were a few mixed metaphors in there, but I was getting the picture and I could see how devastating that prospect would be for someone who had been picked by major tabloids as "Sexiest Man of the Year," not too long ago. Every once in a while, I forgot that Zack wasn't as conceited as he sometimes appeared. A speech like the one he'd just made reminded me that he was also vulnerable—endearingly so.

"I still photograph okay," Zack continued, sounding plaintive. "Probably will, for a while yet."

"You photograph beautifully," I said. With sincerity, I might add. The camera really loved this man. Tilt his cowboy hat forward at just the right sexy angle, say something to make his sensuous mouth turn up at the corners and his eyebrows slant over his nose and his green eyes gleam. Add his lean but muscular body into the picture and you had something very, very special. Something that made my particular set of hormones toss themselves up in the air like electrically charged confetti.

Romance novels sold extremely well, I knew. I suspected that no matter how attractive the cover models might be, readers still wanted a good story on the inside, but Zack on the cover would not be likely to *harm* sales.

"Francisca will be pleased," I said. Without being snarky. Honestly.

He looked at me just the same. "Francisca likes women best, Charlie," he said.

"She told you so?"

"She told me so."

"Why? Did you make a pass at her?"

He gave a long-suffering sigh that lost some of his effect when his smug smile was taken into account. "You have to get over this jealousy, Charlie darlin'. It's most unbecomin'."

"I am not jealous," I said firmly. "Just curious."

He laughed. "That I believe," he said.

I called Bristow's apartment around six P.M. Savanna answered and said he'd just left for Dandy Carr's gym. "You find something out, Charlie?" she asked.

"No, I just had something to tell Bristow, that's all."

"You want him to call you back?" Savanna asked.

I thought about it. "Maybe I'll catch him at the gym."

"You're working out at Dandy Carr's now?"

"I signed up a couple of days ago."

I had a sinking sensation whenever I allowed myself to think of all that I'd lost in the last couple of weeks—my gym, my job, my home, all my clothes, my furniture, shabby as it was.

The best way to get rid of a sinking sensation, I'd discovered long ago, was to do something.

I had to borrow sweats from P.J. I'd done some clothes shopping at the western store in Condor, but I hadn't got around to buying gym clothes yet. To tell the truth, the fire had left me feeling apathetic about everything. Apart from finding out who did it, that is. Quite suddenly I remembered Kalesha telling me on the ferry, "You're going to have this whole surge of energy that will just sweep all your problems away like a tsunami."

I guessed Kalesha wasn't a very good psychic, after all. The fire had swept away a lot of stuff, but my problems had multiplied.

The only pair of P.J.'s sweats that came close to fitting me were green, which made me look like an extra-long green bean. They were a bit short in the crotch, but, hey, what's a little discomfort between friends?

"Good-looking sneakers," Bristow commented when I showed up on the treadmill next to his.

I'd stopped off at the mall to buy a pair of Easy Spirits, which I'd noticed in the morning paper were on sale. They had only blue and white in my size. Luckily, I never did like being color coordinated.

It took me a couple of minutes to set my chosen program—the Alpine hike—and figure out how to get the machine to start. One of the disadvantages to this high-tech equipment. At my old gym, all I had to do was push in the green key and start trotting.

"I was going to call you tonight," Bristow said, his long legs pumping like pistons. "Department had a call from some guy in Washington State, inquiring about you. Sheila fielded the call. Dr. Rob Whittaker, she told me. I seem to remember that being the name of your ex-husband."

I gaped at him. "Rob called the police station?"

"This afternoon. He said he'd suddenly lost track of you and was worried about you. He'd called CHAPS and was told the phone had been disconnected."

"I haven't put a phone in the apartment yet. I've

been using the cell phone Zack gave me." I shook my head. "I hadn't even thought about Rob calling me. He checks up on me from time to time. God knows why."

"Maybe he still loves you, Charlie."

"Yeah, sure, like he loved all those other women."

He grimaced slightly and I figured Savanna had filled him in on Rob's extracurricular activities with his famous patients.

"So what did Sheila tell him?" I asked. I'd met Sheila a couple of times, first when the earthquake came to town, and another time when I was looking for Bristow.

"She told him about the fire burning down CHAPS and that we'd ask you to call him, but it was up to you. She didn't have a number for you, so I said I'd let you know."

"I guess I'll talk to him soon then." I hoped it didn't have anything to do with Ryan. I'd managed to put Rob's news about him being at Stanford out of my mind.

We both slogged along for a couple of minutes, while I tried to think up an opening. "Are you here at the same time as me by accident, or design?" Bristow asked.

He knows me.

"I have a confession to make," I admitted. I may have sounded a little short on breath. I was climbing a computerized mountain.

"You want me to Mirandize you first?" Bristow asked. "Some of the courts haven't been allowing confessions to be admitted in evidence if they came before the suspect was—"

"Not that kind of confession," I said flatly, though

I knew he was joking. His amber eyes were alive with mischief.

"Zack and I went to see Owen Jones," I went on.

"The doctor? Isn't he an obstetrician? Let me guess—you're preggers and Zack's the happy daddy?"

I gave him a look and he laughed. "Okay, Charlie, I'm listening."

"Owen tried to tell us he hadn't even met Reina before the reunion," I said. "But I always thought it was strange that if she didn't know him she'd jump up and ask him for a dance the minute the music came on. Then she kept talking away to him. It was like she'd just been waiting for a chance to talk to him."

I repeated verbatim the conversation Zack and I had had with Owen. "I had the impression our doctor friend was nervous about something and at the same time attempting to cover something up."

I almost slipped as the treadmill program changed to a downhill slope. This thing required concentration. I glanced over at Bristow's program. It looked as if he was doing straight laps. That's probably what I should have started out with.

"Well, it's for certain that anything that was going on in Reina Diaz's life at that time could be significant," Bristow said. "What made you think the doctor was nervous?"

I explained about Owen's trembling fingers.

"Could be a hangover," Bristow said.

He and Zack thought alike. Hangovers must be a guy thing.

"I'll take another look at the doctor," he said. He pulled off the towel that was draped loosely around his neck and mopped his bald head with it. His treadmill was slowing down. A minute later, it stopped and he stepped off.

"You planning on terrorizing anyone else this week, Charlie?" he queried with a grin.

As long as he was smiling, he was obviously not put out by my continuing to look into things. I've thought from time to time that he quite appreciated my doing so. I could go charging in without having to worry about the Miranda warning and not letting someone confess anything before I had all the proper legalities in place. As for Zack, well, people sometimes told him stuff they wouldn't have told me, and definitely wouldn't have told the police. Especially if they'd seen Zack in his role as the all-wise, compassionate and totally trustworthy Sheriff Lazarro.

"I don't have anyone in mind at the moment," I said, which wasn't strictly true. I was definitely planning on returning to Kenyon's Furniture Store. To look at furniture.

Okay, okay! *And* to see if I could pry anything else out of Forrest Kenyon.

"I made a discovery myself," Bristow said, looking at me with a tight-lipped grin that didn't quite seem genuine.

I waited. I was going uphill again.

"Forrest Kenyon ordered roses from Tessler's four times in recent months. Stopped recently."

"They were delivered to Reina Diaz?"

"That's an affirmative."

"He sent them every week?"

"Not from Tessler's, but he could have used more than one florist."

Stupidly, I switched off the treadmill without moving my feet to the side rails. I came close to doing a nosedive. "What did Forrest have to say about it?" I demanded when I'd recovered my balance.

"Nothing so far. He's out of town. Some trade show in New York, supposedly."

I stared at him. "When did he leave?"

"The day after your fire."

"You think there's some connection?"

"I never think until I have some evidence to think about, Charlie."

"You sure he's in New York?"

"He's there all right. I just wonder if he really needed to go." He paused. "Nobody seems to know when he's coming home. There was some talk around his store employees of him doing a little sightseeing. Yeah, sure. While he's ferrying over to the Statue of Liberty, I'll check his phone records. It'd be a toll call from Los Altos to Reina Diaz's house in San Francisco."

"Have you told Savanna?"

His grin turned rueful. "Not yet. I'm waiting to see."

"You really do think he's the murderer?"

He looked away, his eyelids hooded. "I'll decide that when the evidence is all in."

CHAPTER 15

Zack's house, you may remember, is up in Paragon Hills, the ritziest area of upscale Bellamy Park, where flowers are brighter, grass is definitely greener, the trees shadier, the sky bluer.

The house was a very large, airy, spacious red-roofed one-story Spanish-style adobe house built around a central courtyard that featured planters full of flowers, a full-size swimming pool and hot tub.

I rode up with Angel in his truck. That way I figured I wouldn't be tempted to stay behind after everyone else left. I was always on guard against temptation where Zack was concerned. I know, I know—everyone else thinks I'm crazy, too. People I know—including my other partners, and P.J., with whom I'd had some long and intimate conversations recently—could not understand why I didn't just do it with Zack and get on with my life.

Sometimes I didn't understand it myself. But my instincts kept telling me to hold out.

Zack, as you might expect, had a truly magnificent barbecue setup. While we sat around on chaises in the shade, sipping beer, he busied himself with marinating chicken, which he'd chosen for my benefit, he said, knowing I didn't go for red meat. Then he opened a beer for himself and joined us, looking scrumptious in cutoffs and a tank, which is about what the rest of us were wearing—except Savanna who had on a bandanna print blouse that was tied in a knot under her breasts and left nothing to the imagination. We all looked rather strange, to tell the truth. All except Bristow, that is. He had on walking shorts and a polo shirt, which wasn't so different from his usual uniform of the day. The rest of us were used to seeing one another in western clothing. But it was a hot day, and we weren't on duty at CHAPS. We wouldn't be on duty at CHAPS for a long time.

You'd expect someone as dark-haired as Zack to be fairly hairy all over, but his skin was tan and smooth. I'd thought at one time he might have himself waxed, but I'd seen him in a swimsuit enough times to decide his appearance was all natural.

Angel dropped the first bombshell of the evening, right after Zack sat down. "Unless you all need me, I'm going to move to Salinas until CHAPS is up and operating again. Miguel offered me a job, and I do need to work."

Angel's brother was a bull rider and a partner in a company that provided rodeos with bucking horses and bulls. It was this company Angel would be working for.

Though I would miss him, I thought it would be good for him to get away for a while. The burning of CHAPS had really affected him, coming as it did on the heels of a trauma he'd gone through some months previously. "You will come back?" I asked anxiously.

He smiled at me. "Unless a bull kicks me in the head, Charlie, I'll be here the minute you call to say I'm needed. It's only just over eighty-five miles here to there. You can come on down and visit. Miguel would be thrilled to see you."

"We could *all* drive down," Zack said, and everyone looked at him, including me. "Make a day of it," he added lamely.

"Sure, Zack," Savanna said. "Nothing to do with you not trusting Miguel around Charlie."

Zack grinned ruefully. "Maybe I don't trust Charlie around Miguel."

I'd liked Miguel when he was in the area a few months ago, but there was something a little dangerous around his edges that had persuaded me not to get involved. I could usually find excuses not to get involved with a man. Though I was running out of them where Zack was concerned.

We chewed over Angel's decision for a while. None of us wanted him to go away, but when a guy needs a job and his brother offers him one, you can't offer a whole lot of argument.

We did make him promise he'd come up from time to time to see how CHAPS was coming along.

About the time Zack served another beer all around, Bristow decided to take over the floor. "I could a tale unfold," he said. You'll remember his penchant for quoting Shakespeare, I expect. He was looking pretty cocky all of a sudden. Forrest, I thought, with a feeling of dread. Savanna was looking worriedly at him, too.

"I spent some time yesterday with Dr. Owen Jones," he said.

Savanna and I both breathed out.

"Official time?" Zack queried.

"An interview at the station, yes. A voluntary visit. He just showed up and asked for me by name. Imagine that."

"You're not saying Kalesha's husband murdered Miss Diaz!" Savanna said, her eyes wide.

"As far as I know at this time Dr. Jones had nothing whatsoever to do with Reina's death," Bristow said solemnly. "However, our two heroes here—" He paused to salute first Zack, then me, with his beer bottle, before going on. "Our two heroes visited him earlier in the week and scared him into coming forward." Setting down his beer on the table next to his chaise, he took off his sunglasses, picked up a napkin, and polished the lenses with great care. "A most interesting story," he added.

"You'd better be about to tell this story," I threatened when he paused again and took his time over a long swallow of beer.

"The pool is close by," Zack added.

Bristow grinned. "Our man became concerned that he had somehow become a suspect. He had decided, he said, that it was okay to break doctor-patient privilege after the patient was dead. Reina would not be hurt by it now."

"Reina was Owen's patient!" I exclaimed. "She had a gynecological problem?"

"This is strictly between us. Not to be revealed to anyone else, okay?"

We all nodded, rapt.

"Dr. Jones was Reina's obstetrician," Bristow said.

We gazed at him in awed silence.

"Recently?" Savanna asked finally, her voice cracking.

Bristow shook his head. "Almost twenty years ago."

"Reina had a baby almost twenty years ago," I said, more to convince myself than to repeat the obvious. I looked at Bristow. "Owen Jones delivered it?"

"Affirmative." He put his sunglasses back on and leaned back in his chaise.

"According to Dr. Jones, backed up by Reina Diaz's medical records, which he brought along with him, Reina gave the baby up for adoption. She was determined to do it from the start, he said. She didn't want an abortion, her religion forbade it, but she didn't want the baby, either. She didn't even want to see it after it was born. She called the baby 'it,' Dr. Jones said. 'It' was a healthy baby girl. Full-term."

"Did Owen know who the father was?"

"He says not."

"Did he know who adopted the baby?"

"Again, his answer was negative. An agency took care of the details. He was not involved. Reina didn't want to know who the adoptive parents were."

"How could anyone just give a baby away?" Angel protested. Angel had lost his parents earlier than he should have, just as I had. It makes you more appreciative of the meaning of family.

Savanna shook her head. "This doesn't sound like Miss Diaz at all. She was always so warm, so loving."

"Evidently, she didn't love this baby," her husband

said. "I was surprised myself, but not too—I learned a long time ago that there's no knowing what any individual will do if driven to it. I learned not to judge, either. We none of us know what we might be capable of."

"Well, I couldn't give away a baby," Savanna said firmly.

"I know that," Bristow said, looking at her fondly.

"Dr. Jones didn't see Reina again until the night of the reunion," he continued. "When Kalesha had a slight medical problem Reina recommended him to her, and that was the only contact otherwise."

"What kind of problem?" Savanna asked.

"He wouldn't say, and as Kalesha was his patient and his wife, I couldn't force him to." He paused. "However, he did turn quite red—always a problem for white folk—and I had a strong suspicion we were talking about an abortion."

"Wow!" I said.

"So then Owen and Kalesha became friends and eventually, more than friends. Evidently, it was Owen who persuaded Kalesha to get out of the dead-end job she had in some kind of convenience store, and into radiology."

We were all subdued after these revelations. Reina's baby was something to think about. Maybe that baby, twenty years old now, had come to Bellamy Park, snuck into CHAPS, and killed the mother who had given her away.

Hardly seemed likely. Would she even know who her mother was?

"Did Reina ever hear who adopted the baby, do you

suppose?" I asked later. By that time we were eating Zack's spectacularly seasoned chicken and accompanying roasted veggies and Caesar salad at the French bistro setup that took the place of most people's picnic tables and chairs.

Bristow shrugged. "It's a little difficult to ask her. We did go through all her personal papers at the time of her death—there was nothing revealing in there."

"Did Owen tell Kalesha about it?"

"He says not. He's very strong on the doctor/patient privilege, would not have told anyone about the baby if Reina hadn't died. He thought possibly it might be a clue. He was also afraid he might have become a suspect for some reason, so he wanted to lay what few cards he had upon the table."

"You think it's true that he didn't see Reina during that twenty-year period?" Zack asked. He was sitting next to Bristow at the oval table.

"I have no evidence to say he did," Bristow said. "He and Kalesha were married in a private civil ceremony, and then had another ceremony in Wales with Owen's family, so there was no question of inviting Reina or any of the old school pals to the wedding."

He grinned at Zack. "You didn't happen to have a plot like this one on *Prescott's Landing*, did you, old buddy?"

Zack started to consider, then realized Bristow was teasing, and punched his shoulder.

"Did Dr. Jones explain what Reina was talking to him about so intently while they danced?" I asked.

Bristow frowned. "He said she wanted to be sure

he hadn't told anyone about that baby," he said. "He assured her he hadn't told a soul." He paused.

"Seems as though there's something about that baby—" He quit that line of reasoning. "Did you call your ex back?" he asked, which brought me a look from Zack.

"Yes, thank you."

Bristow's eyebrows climbed. "That's it? You pump me for information and I ask a simple question and that's all I get?"

"Rob had heard about the fire. He just wanted to make sure I was okay."

"What's it to him?" Zack asked, giving me his squinting-in-a-dust-storm look.

This was the second time Zack had made jealous noises this evening. He'd never done that before. I wasn't sure if this was a good sign or not. "Rob worries about me," I said. "He doesn't think I'm capable of taking care of myself. Evidently, his son, Ryan, had tried to call me and was told my phone number was no longer in service. So that worried Rob."

I'd already told Zack about Ryan coming to Stanford and that I was hoping he'd leave me alone, so he accepted that and settled back in his seat.

But the thought entered my head, as it had a few times in recent months that it was entirely possible that Zack was coming to care for me, as distinct from lust or pride or whatever it was that had caused him to come on to me.

Why pride? Women didn't resist Zack. Women fell all over themselves to get close to Zack. A celebrity gets used to that type of reaction. He comes to expect it. Maybe when he doesn't get it, he thinks his manhood is in jeopardy.

Zack's personality and habitual responses did owe a lot to testosterone, so pride was possible as a motivation. It could explain why he was hanging in there as if he'd laid siege to a castle and wasn't about to retreat until the occupant surrendered.

CHAPTER 16

Monday morning seemed like a good time to go looking at furniture again. Of course there were furniture stores in Bellamy Park and in most of the towns on the peninsula, but somehow Kenyon's in Los Altos seemed like the best place to go. That so-comfortable sofa kept calling to me.

I really didn't expect Forrest Kenyon to be on the premises again. Honestly! Bristow had intimated nobody knew when he was expected back. But there he was, coming toward me with his hands out as if he was happy to greet an old friend. He clasped both of mine warmly. "Charlie, I'm so sorry about CHAPS. That was a marvelous old building. And I understand you lived there."

That was interesting, that he'd known I lived there. Not too many people knew that. I took pains to keep it from our clientele in case some cowboy wannabe took it into his head to get too friendly some night when he'd imbibed too freely.

And there'd been no reason to announce it at the reunion, or later.

He must have noticed the inquiring look on my face.

He let go of my hands. "Ah, Tara told me she'd read in the *Chronicle* that you lived above the nightclub," he said, gesturing in the direction of the young woman who had talked to me briefly on my first visit.

Okay, so much for suspicion. I wished newspapers wouldn't be quite so keen on reporting all the facts, though I supposed it didn't much matter now. It would be a little difficult for someone to "break and enter" a building that was no longer there. By the time CHAPS was rebuilt—six months was the quote, though I thought it could probably be doubled—surely, nobody would remember the *Chronicle* story.

"I heard you were out of town," I said.

"New York," Forrest said enthusiastically. "I love that city. You'll think I'm crazy but I love hiking up Fifth Avenue from the Village to Central Park. All those people walking shoulder to shoulder. So much energy."

He was much more likeable when he was enthused like this. "Don't suppose I'd want to live there, though," he added. "Los Altos suits me just fine."

Los Altos would suit me fine, too, if I could afford it.

"I've rented an apartment," I said. "As you can imagine, I *really* need some furniture now. I'm still interested in that sofa. And the chair. You happen to have a cheaper version?"

"Well, Charlie, cheaper wouldn't be the same, would it, now? That sofa's stuffed with down. You don't get real down without paying for it." He laughed. "We just might be able to work out a deal, though. Any friend of Savvy's is welcome to negotiate!"

He led the way over to the sofa in question and gestured me down onto it, which was a smart sales move. It was the most marvelous experience, sitting down on that sofa. I was getting kinks in all my parts from sleeping on P.J.'s futon.

"I could possibly sleep on this sofa temporarily, and get a proper bed later," I murmured.

"Oh, Charlie, didn't you know? That was dumb of me, I apologize. It *is* a bed—a sofa bed." He gestured me to my feet, lifted off the sofa cushions, and demonstrated the easiest, smoothest mechanism I'd ever seen. He was watching my face. "How about twenty percent off?" he asked.

"On the chair and ottoman, too?" I queried quickly.

He sighed a salesman's "my goodness, aren't you a good bargainer?" sigh. "Done," he said, and slid the bed back into place again.

I helped put the cushions back on and sat down again. It felt so good! I hoped it was rabbitproof. I bent myself in half, lifted the skirt, and saw that the frame came very close to the floor. I doubted Benny could do the limbo. There was a good chance he wouldn't be able to gut this sofa, as long as I didn't turn him loose when the bed was open.

"What else will you need?" Forrest asked.

"That's it for now," I said. "That's a huge decision I just made. I won't be capable of any more for some time to come."

"But you'll need occasional tables, lamps, dining chairs, a dining table—"

I held up a hand to stop the list midflow. "I figured

I'd get some orange crates or apple boxes or something for now," I said.

He winced, then laughed again and sat down in my new chair, first moving the ottoman out of the way, smiling at me as if we were old friends now. "I'm afraid we don't have any orange crates in stock right now."

He paused, then blurted out, "I talked to Detective Sergeant Bristow again earlier this morning."

I was mildly disappointed. I'd been thinking I could possibly make points by being the one to tell Bristow that Forrest was back in town.

I waited.

"I was the guy who sent roses to Reina," he said. He darted a glance at me. "I think you'd guessed that, hadn't you?"

I made a sound that could have meant agreement or denial. He sat forward, his hands hanging loosely between his knees. He was wearing a beautiful suit. Definitely designer. Maybe he'd bought it in New York.

"I was always very fond of Reina," he went on. "After my wife passed on, I felt terribly lonely. I guess I got lonesome for the good old days, and that meant Reina. So I'd call her every once in a while and we'd talk. But she seemed to still see me as one of the students, not as a man to be taken seriously."

He sighed, took off his glasses and mopped at his eyes with a spotless white handkerchief he'd taken from his inside jacket pocket.

"I'm okay," he said, when he caught me looking. "My eyes give me fits a lot of the time. I've an allergy to dust, which is difficult to avoid. That's why I wear the shades—my eyes are often red. I don't want people thinking I'm a drinker."

He put the glasses back on and sighed. "I'd hoped seeing Reina at the reunion would make a difference, but then she announced to one and all that she had a boyfriend who was going to marry her and I realized how foolishly I'd been behaving."

He gave me a look that was fraught with intensity. "I told Sergeant Bristow and I'm telling you, Charlie, that I never pressured Reina in any way. I'm not even sure what it was I wanted from her, just some recognition that I was alive and I was a man, I think. Certainly, I thought of us as friends. Why she'd tell Savvy that she was afraid I was stalking her—well, that *someone* was stalking her, I don't know. For one thing, I did not send roses every week. I sent them perhaps three, maybe four times in all. And of course, I had absolutely *nothing* to do with her death."

He sounded genuine. But then how many murderers would say, "Well, sure I stalked her and when she wouldn't have anything to do with me, I did away with her."

I mean, they might do that after being questioned by police and seeing that a strong case could be mounted against them—especially if they thought it would help their side to seem to cooperate, or they were aiming to plea-bargain. But they wouldn't come right out with it to just anyone.

"Nobody seems to know anything about this boyfriend Reina's supposed to have had," I said after a brief painful silence. "Bristow hasn't been able to find him. Of course, if you don't have a name or description it gets tricky sending out an APB. There's a strong opinion among some of the classmates, and I think I subscribe to it, that Reina made up the boyfriend and bought the ring herself. Some think it was to misdirect the stalker and perhaps persuade him or her to stop."

Actually, as far as I knew, I was the only one to come up with that theory.

"But there *wasn't* a stalker," he said, sounding exasperated.

Says you, I thought.

"Look, Charlie," he said. "If I had been stalking Reina, why would she dance with me, go out and have a couple of smokes with me, talk to me? Besides, it's ridiculous to think she made up the boyfriend. He's real, all right. I had no idea Sergeant Bristow was trying to find him. He didn't mention him to me. I could have told him exactly where he is. He owns a small hotel in The City."

"How do you know that?" I demanded.

"Reina told me. The night of the reunion. While we were dancing. After we'd had that silly quarrel about the ring. She was cross with me because I'd told everyone they were real diamonds. She didn't want anyone to know—she was afraid of the ring being stolen."

"Did you tell Bristow that?"

"About the ring being a real quadrillion? Yes, sure. It was stupid of me to say otherwise earlier. I panicked, I guess."

"But you didn't tell him about the boyfriend?"

"I didn't know he didn't know."

This was going to earn me seriously major points.

"What's the name of the hotel?" I asked.

"Hotel Ainslee." He frowned. "Hang on, I'll come up with the street it's on."

"I know where it is," I said. "It's the one with the funny roof and too many window boxes. It looks French."

He nodded.

"I've gone by there several times on the way to Macy's," I told him.

"Guy's name is Donald Ainslee," he said. "The hotel's been in the family for two or three generations." His mouth tightened at the corners. "You want to tell Sergeant Bristow for me, Charlie? I don't really want to get in his clutches again. That man really has it in for me."

"He's a great guy," I said. "I think he's a bit blinded by jealousy right now, but he'd never go too far with his suspicions without some kind of proof. He's a fair man."

"I hope you're right." He didn't look convinced.

He stood up. "Okay, Charlie," he said. "Give Tara your new address and we can deliver the furniture. How's Wednesday suit you?"

I nodded.

"How do you want to pay for it—you want us to set up an account for you?"

I shook my head. "I'll write you a check. I don't do time payments."

He handed me over to Tara and went up the stairs to the upper story.

I couldn't wait to get back to my bare little apartment and call Bristow. I didn't want to try and track him down with the cell phone while I was driving. I think that's dangerous, the way people do that.

But when I did call, he wasn't around.

"Got some excitement over by Flood Creek Bridge," Sheila said. "This crazy old drunk who comes in here crying wolf once or twice a week, telling us about some crime never took place, bodies stacked up in deserted buildings, blood on the side of a tree, people fighting in some apartment building—man, we get a lot of that kind of stuff from him when the moon is full! Have to check it out, of course. You never can tell. So an hour ago here comes Old Yellow—we call him that because he's so jaundiced—telling about how some big fight went down in the shanty town down there and a couple of guys were hacking each other up with knives. And what do you know, it turned out to be true. So that's where our entire force is right now, Charlie."

"I hope none of this involved my friend Rory," I said.

You might remember Rory. He took a major role in one of my earlier adventures. The guy who lived in a packing case under that same bridge. Liked good cigars. Lived with Thane Stockton in his mansion for a while, then got homesick for his packing case. I hadn't seen him in a while, and, of course, he came immediately to mind.

"Roderick Effington the third, you mean?"

"The very same."

"Nah, he followed Old Yellow in about five minutes later and confirmed the story. That's how come we knew it was for real. He sure is a hoot, that old guy. Effington. All reports—it sounds like a real mess down

there. Four or five old guys involved by the time our
guys got there. Three of them dead. Seems like somebody stole somebody's food cache. Newcomer. Individual it was stolen from went around accusing everyone."

I might have guessed it was a newcomer causing
the trouble. Normally the homeless population in Flood
Creek—which dried up years ago, by the way—kept
very low profiles. In return, the police let them be.

I grieved for the men who had died. When existence
was that basic, it seemed even more tragic when that
little bit of a life was violently taken away.

After I hung up, I put a cassette of the Dixie Chicks
on the Sony Walkman I'd bought a couple of days
earlier, along with two very small speakers. I'd had
a considerable collection of favorite cassettes in the
Wrangler—Doug Stone, Mark Chesnutt, Tracy Byrd,
Trisha Yearwood, and Patty Loveless—and had moved
them into the apartment. Singing along with Natalie
to "You Were Mine," I fixed lunch and ate it at the
card table P.J. had loaned me. The two folding chairs
that came with it weren't comfortable, but they were
certainly useful. I had to keep Benny from sharpening
his teeth on the bottom bars, though.

When I was done, I brushed Benny down with one
of those specially made mittens that has rubber nubs
on it to pick up loose hair. It was a necessary ritual
that we both found soothing, unlike the dreaded nail-
clipping ordeal.

By the time I was through with the brushing, and
the glove bristled with brown hairs, Benny was totally
relaxed, practically boneless. I put him gently in his
cage and watched him wiggle into the cardboard box

he used as a bed. A moment later, his head appeared in the arch-shaped opening I'd cut in the box when I gave it to him. His eyes were already closing.

I went into the kitchen and glanced at the stove clock. Two P.M. If a person was to drive into The City right away, she could probably avoid the worst of the traffic going in. And could always hang around The City for a while to miss the worst of it coming back.

I want to explain something here. I'm a very independent-minded woman. You may have gathered that. However, I'm no dummy. I wasn't about to go to The City, to this small hotel Forrest Kenyon had told me about, without someone at least knowing I was going there, and perhaps even accompanying me.

We still didn't know who had killed Reina Diaz or Timothy Perkins. For all I knew, Donald Ainslee could be a maniac who went around knocking off anyone who displeased him.

I'm mentioning all this so you won't think I'm some weak-kneed chick who's scared of her own shadow. Which, if the sun was in the wrong direction, I could be. Why should you think this? Because the first thing I did—after deciding I couldn't possibly wait until Bristow was free again before finding out what kind of guy Donald Ainslee was, and what exactly had gone on between him and Reina Diaz—was to call Zack Hunter and ask him to go with me.

Which he agreed to do.

The hotel wasn't as charming as the bed-and-breakfast Savanna and Bristow had honeymooned in, but it was very stylish, tailored and businesslike, rather than whimsical and Victorian. I imagined it was used mainly by businesspeople from out of town, something that was confirmed for me by the owner when the receptionist summoned him for me.

"Most of our rooms are singles," he said, looking from Zack to me. "They are comfortable, but for a couple—"

"We aren't a couple," I said firmly.

"Not yet," Zack murmured.

I didn't even bother to glare at him. "We wanted to ask you a couple of questions," I said.

"You're reporters?" he asked, then took another look at Zack. "Hey, I know who you are. You did that *Prescott's Landing* show on TV. The sheriff."

Zack nodded modestly. Don't let that modesty fool you, though, he loved being recognized.

"My ex-wife thought you were the sexiest man in the world," Ainslee went on.

I remembered hearing that Paul Newman resented his image as a sex symbol. Our man in black relished his. If Ainslee's ex-wife had been on the premises, he'd have signed anything she wanted him to sign, bare flesh included.

Donald Ainslee appeared to be around sixty, a solid person—not thin, not fat, just sturdy-looking, dressed in a gray suit, white shirt, red tie. He looked like an everyday businessman himself. Maybe that came from hanging around business types all the time. The most notable thing about him was his extremely melancholy expression. It would have seemed more suitable on an undertaker's face.

He invited us into his office and sat us down side

by side on a black leather sofa. "What can I do for you?" he asked.

"We understand you were engaged to Reina Diaz," Zack said before I could get a question formed.

I usually try to work into an interview slowly, by degrees. Zack prefers the straightforward approach that was always used by Sheriff Lazarro. It has a certain shock value. Sometimes it works; often it doesn't.

"Where the hell did you get that idea?" Ainslee demanded, looking stunned.

Zack looked at me. He does that when he gets stuck.

"Reina told us she was engaged. A friend of hers, a guy, said you were the man," I said.

"Where the hell did *he* get that idea?" Ainslee said.

"From Reina, he said."

Ainslee shook his head.

There was a pause while Zack and I regrouped. "It isn't true?" Zack asked.

Ainslee stood up and walked over to a file cabinet in the corner, where he picked up a framed photo and brought it over for us to see.

It was a picture of a woman—a fiftyish, plain, dumpy, dowdy woman. Her grayish hair was held back in three or four places by old-fashioned bobby pins. No makeup. Tight lips.

"There was this guy," Ainslee said in a tired way as he sat down again. "Sales rep. Used to come around every three months or so. Started showing up more and more regularly. I didn't think anything of it, just that he must be really hustling. Turned out he was after Julie."

He indicated the photo. I placed it on the desk and

gave him my inquiring look. "My wife," he said. "She ran off with the sales rep a year ago."

"I'm sorry," I said.

Zack muttered something. Probably some fellow feeling for the sales rep. He'd possibly run off with a few wives himself in his heyday.

Ainslee moved his head from side to side, slowly, as though he was testing out a crick in his neck. "Never could understand it," he said.

Zack and I exchanged a glance.

"Why would anyone want to run off with Julie?" Ainslee asked. "I mean, look at her. Why would he?"

I gave myself a brief talking-to. This was no time to pop off on the surface appearance of people not being their most important attribute. I was looking for information, not argument. Besides, sometimes I doubt that judging by looks is as bad as it's made out to be. I think by the time people reach forty or so, most of them have the face they've made for themselves with their habitual expressions and lifestyles. Ainslee's wife looked as if she'd deliberately tried to look unattractive. Maybe so Ainslee would leave her alone. It would be interesting to see what she looked like now.

After another minute or two of silence, Zack moved a little in his seat. "So did you *know* Reina?" he asked.

"I met her right after Julie took off," Ainslee said, sitting up straight. "I met her in a store in Ghiradelli Square. She was looking for a glass thing with a wick, the kind you fill with lamp oil and then you put it in the neck of an empty wine bottle. Makes an interesting light for the dinner table. I was looking for a gift for my mother—bought her a mirrored angelfish with three bubbles ascending. She didn't like it. I hung it in my private bathroom."

He paused, looking even gloomier than before, then went on. "Reina and I got talking. I took her to lunch at that big restaurant that looks out on the water there."

"McCormick and Kuleto's," Zack supplied. He knew everywhere there was to take a date.

"Did you date regularly after that?" I asked.

He nodded. "Once a week or so. Until a couple months ago. She called me up and told me something had happened that had upset her and she thought it best to stop seeing me for a while."

A couple of months ago. A month before Reina was murdered.

"I suppose she didn't tell you what had happened?"

"No, and I didn't ask. I always figure if someone doesn't tell you something it's because they don't want you to know."

He looked directly at me. "We never were . . . intimate. I got out of the habit of that with Julie a long time ago. She didn't care for sex much, and I lost interest after a few years. What else could I do? Reina didn't seem to want . . . that, anyway. And we certainly were never engaged. Once was enough, as far as I was concerned."

"She had a ring she said you gave her."

He shook his head. "I don't know anything about a ring."

"It was very flashy," Zack said.

"I can't imagine Reina wearing something flashy," Ainslee said. "She was a classy lady."

Zack nodded. "Maybe flashy was the wrong word. It was a great-looking ring—a quadrillion. She said the stones were cubic zirconias, but the guy who said you were her fiancé was supposedly an expert on such things. *He* said they were diamonds."

Ainslee sighed. "Well, whatever they were doesn't make much difference to me, it's not something I gave her or saw her wear, or ever heard of before this minute."

"Why would she say she was engaged to you?" I asked.

He looked irritated. "How would I know? I haven't seen her from that day to this. Why don't you ask *her*?"

Zack and I looked at each other again. Probably I looked as appalled as he did.

"You haven't heard?" I exclaimed. "How can it be possible you haven't heard? It was in all the media."

Ainslee looked puzzled.

I swallowed hard, then let out a long breath. "Reina Diaz is dead," I said as gently as I could.

His face showed shock. "My goodness, that's most unexpected. She seemed like a very healthy woman to me." He turned his head away for a minute and blinked several times. "I'm sorry she's dead," he said. "I liked her very much."

"She was murdered," Zack said, cutting to the chase as always. "Strangled by person or persons unknown."

Sheriff Lazarro had sneaked in when I wasn't looking and repossessed my partner. He might have given Ainslee time to recover from the first shock before administering the second.

Ainslee looked as if someone had punched him in the midriff. "When?" he asked faintly.

I calculated mentally. "About five weeks ago. Middle of August."

He nodded. "That explains why I didn't hear anything. I took Mom on an Alaskan cruise. Marvelous scenery. And the food was out of . . ." His voice trailed away. "I don't often get time to read the newspapers or watch television. This place keeps me busy. And having been gone a couple of weeks . . . you said she was strangled? That poor woman. She was such a very nice woman. Charming. A pleasure to be with. She had the best posture!"

He was silent for a couple of minutes. I shot a glance at Zack, hoping he'd interpret it as a message to hold off for a while.

"Did the police catch whoever did it?" Ainslee asked.

"Not so far," I said. "There are several suspects." As briefly as I could, I summarized the details surrounding Reina's death, leaving the potty out of it. "It might not be a bad idea for you to contact the detective in charge of the case," I suggested when I was done. "Detective Sergeant Taylor Bristow of Bellamy Park Police Department. He's been trying to find you."

I rooted around in my jeans pocket and came up with one of my own cards, useless now, though once we rebuilt, they'd be good again. After jotting down Bellamy Park PD's nonemergency number, and my own cell number, I handed it to him. "The address on here isn't any good," I told him, but didn't tell him why. He'd taken in enough for one day.

The bleak feeling came over me again, but I pushed

it away. CHAPS was gone, but it would be rebuilt.
There was nothing to get teary-eyed about. I was lucky.
I had a roof over my head. I was alive.

Ainslee picked up a small box from his desk and
gave me one of his business cards in return.

"I'll call the detective," he promised.

"I'll tell him to expect your call," I said, just in case
he needed a little extra persuasion.

CHAPTER 17

I called the station as soon as Zack dropped me off at the Granada complex. Bristow wasn't available. I called his apartment and got Savanna, who said he was still busy with the mess over at Flood Creek.

I gave her Ainslee's name and number to pass on, and told her some of what he'd said.

"I had high hopes of the boyfriend," she said mournfully. "I really hoped it would turn out he was the one who killed Miss Diaz. So it wouldn't be anyone I knew."

So it wouldn't be Forrest, she meant.

"There's always a chance Ainslee's lying," I said. "If he is, Bristow will get it out of him."

"How did you find out about him?" Savanna asked.

Darn, I was hoping she wouldn't ask that. "Someone told me his name," I said.

"Protecting your sources, are you?"

"Tell Bristow I'll be happy to answer any questions," I said.

"Sure, Charlie." She sounded disgruntled. I had an idea she'd guessed it was Forrest who had put me on Ainslee's trail.

* * *

We had put the few things we'd managed to rescue from CHAPS's remains in storage, and the little that was left was due to be bulldozed the next day, Tuesday. That was something I had no desire to see or hear. I thought of going shopping for some dishes and pans, maybe knives and forks and spoons, too. So far I'd made do with the few things P.J. had loaned me, but I couldn't go on like that for as long as it would take to get CHAPS restored.

Shopping is not something I do willingly, and there wasn't anyone there to coerce me, so I decided instead to risk another sneezing attack. One thing about having an apartment with only a futon and a rabbit cage in it, there's not much in the way of chores once you've washed your cereal bowl and coffee mug.

After I cleaned out Benny's cage, I played tag with him—something that was a lot easier to do in an empty apartment, though Benny did seem to keep looking for a sofa to chew on. I kept the living-room door closed on the futon so I wouldn't have to replace it.

As soon as I had Benny settled in again, I left. Machinery had already filled up a good chunk of what had been CHAPS's parking lot, I saw as I drove by it.

This time I hadn't called Zack to go with me. Not because he and Becky had gotten along so well, honestly, but because I thought I might get her to talk more when she wasn't so distracted.

The hot pink Karmann Ghia was still parked in the driveway, shining, obviously newly waxed. The van was missing. I surmised that Tom was at work.

Becky was in her garden again. The sun was hot and she was wearing a long cotton dress of the kind you see in homespun country catalogs, and a straw hat with a frayed brim. Thomas junior was wearing a similar hat, digging happily next to his mother with a small spade. "Hi," he said. "Thomas weed."

"Good for you," I said.

Becky didn't seem displeased to see me. But she did look beyond me. "Zack didn't come with you this time?"

"I didn't invite him," I said.

"He's a very attractive man," she said, her glance measuring me, though not offensively.

"Uh-huh."

"This is a very nosy question," she said, "but are you and he ..." She paused delicately.

"Yes," I said. Well, she might just be nosy, and I could relate to that. And she might have been going to ask if we were friends, which we certainly were. I didn't think she was the type to stray—she and Tom, as I had noted earlier, seemed totally comfortable together, and she'd talked about them having another child. But you could never be sure about anyone, so just in case—okay, okay, I was warning her off. I might not be completely convinced I was going to risk getting involved, but until the six months was up I wasn't going to risk any trespassing, either.

She seemed to take my terse statement in good part. "Take a seat, Charlie," she said, indicating a bench beneath a trellised arch that was garlanded with big pink roses. "I'll get us some iced tea. It's probably best if you stay out here, don't you think? Away from the cats. Or is it too warm for you? I know you redheads have to watch out for old Sol."

"I'll be fine," I said. I was wearing my cowboy hat and a long-sleeved shirt and jeans; the trellis and the magnolia tree offered plenty of shade. Plus I never left home without slathering sunblock on.

"Keep an eye on Thomas, will you?" she said, and off she went into the house, leaving me to sit tensely watching the toddler, wondering what I was supposed to do if he did something he shouldn't, or if I even would recognize he was doing something he shouldn't. Thomas continued to dig with intense concentration without paying any attention to me, putting dirt in a brightly colored little bucket, patting it down, then turning the bucket upside down so that the dirt emerged in a potpie shape. He then flattened his creation with the spade and began patiently loading it into the bucket again. I thought of one of the Greek mythology stories my father used to tell me about Sisyphus, who was punished for his evil ways by being condemned forever to roll a boulder up to the top of a hill, and do it over and over when it rolled back down.

"I've been wanting to talk to you, Charlie," Becky said when she returned carrying a tray with two tall glasses and a baby bottle on it. Ice clinked against the frosted glasses, making me feel cool and refreshed before I even took a sip.

As Becky set the tray on a tree stump that had been sanded smooth and sealed, I thought of my Scottish mother. She had never taken to iced tea. Tea was meant to be served hot, she had always insisted. First you scalded the pot with boiling water. A brown pot was best. Then you measured in the loose tea—a teaspoon for each person and one for the pot. Bring the water to a rolling boil and pour it onto the tea. Put a knitted cozy over the pot to keep it warm while the tea steeps, then pour it out through a strainer into delicate cups.

Oddly enough, after all this insistence on proper preparation, she had added sugar and milk, which seemed also to be part of the British tea culture.

My father had always laughed at her, but she'd drunk her hot tea several times a day all the years of their life together.

I still felt a wrenching sensation whenever I thought of the two of them, though I had been barely eighteen when they died.

I realized Becky was looking at me questioningly. She'd settled herself in an Adirondack chair next to the stump. Thomas was on her lap, slumped in a very relaxed way against her, sucking vigorously on his bottle. Becky's black hair was loose around her face today, making her look hardly old enough to be his mother.

"Sorry, I was thinking about my mother," I said. "She loved tea."

She nodded and looked wistful and I remembered her own mother had loved an altogether different beverage. *Way to go, Charlie.*

"I'm sorry about CHAPS," she said awkwardly. "That was an awful thing to have happen. It seemed like such a fun place." She hesitated. "They said on TV it was arson."

"So it seems."

"Do the police have any suspects yet?"

"None that I know of."

She nodded.

"What did you want to talk to me about?" I said encouragingly.

She took a sip of her tea before answering. "I just can't decide if I should tell anyone or not, Charlie. It's been a secret all these years, but if it would help to find the guilty person. . . ." She broke off, frowning. "I mean, I wouldn't want to besmirch Reina's reputation needlessly. I wouldn't want her secret to get out if it won't make a difference."

I took a chance. "Did the secret have anything to do with an adoption?" I figured if I'd guessed wrong, then I could cover up by saying I'd heard Reina was adopted.

Her breath left her in a sigh of relief. I hadn't guessed wrong. "You know about the adoption already? I thought I was the only one."

"I don't know the whole story," I said, fishing, and not yet willing to give anything away.

"I've known only since July," Becky said. "Reina and I ran into each other at a charity concert in San Francisco and we went out to dinner after, spur-of-the-moment thing. She seemed troubled and I asked what was wrong and she told me she'd been thinking a lot about her daughter."

She paused to remove the bottle from Thomas's mouth. He had dozed off. All babies look like cherubs when they sleep. Becky shook her head. "I was speechless. I'd never known that Reina had a daughter. But then she told me it was years ago and she'd given the child up for adoption the minute she was born."

"Did she tell you who the father was?"

Becky looked at me wonderingly. "You know, I never thought to ask. Isn't that odd? I was so shocked to think of Reina having a secret like that." She laughed. "I so worshiped Reina, I guess maybe I thought it was an immaculate conception."

I hesitated because I was about to give away information I'd been told by Bristow not to give away. But Becky already knew about the baby, so it couldn't possibly hurt, could it? I wasn't sure one way or the other, but I took a chance. "The person who told *me* about it said Reina had the baby almost twenty years ago."

Becky's eyes widened. "But that would be around graduation time."

"Shortly after, it would seem." I set my glass down and leaned forward. "Think back, Becky, it could be important. Do you remember anything happening with Reina in the months after you graduated?"

Her brow furrowed. "I didn't see her for a while after graduation. She went away somewhere to teach, some kind of teacher-exchange program. She was gone several months."

She paused and looked at me with light dawning in her dark eyes. "Oh," she said flatly.

I nodded. "She must have stayed away until she had the baby." I thought for a few minutes. "Do you remember anything while you were in school, anything at all that would indicate that Reina was having an affair with one of the students, one who graduated with you? One who was at the reunion."

"Oh, my," she groaned. "A whole tapestry is forming, isn't it? But what makes you think it was someone in our class?"

"The timing, mostly. And Reina's concern about the reunion. And her murder. And also, Dolores Valentino told one of my partners there was a rumor that Reina had an affair with one of the students during that last year you were all together."

Becky swallowed visibly, then brushed her hand over her face as though to wipe away cobwebs or stray hairs. "All the boys worshiped the ground Reina walked on. Well, the girls did, too. She was saving our lives and we knew it. I really hate to say this, but Forrest, well he's the one who comes to mind when I think of that time in connection with Reina. He was crazy about Savanna, but there was no doubt he had a crush on Reina. He'd get bashful when she so much as looked at him. He was always the first to help with anything she was doing—like when she locked her keys in her car and he found a coat hanger and opened the door for her. He was tall, so he'd reach things down off of high shelves for her and look at her adoringly when she thanked him."

She paused to think. "Perky adored her, too, in his own weird way. So did Mark Sandstrom. Mark got heavily into drugs in ninth grade. Started with marijuana, went into coke, then heroin, that's why he ended up at Dix's. Perky's folks were street people, didn't care if he went to school or not. Imagine that—brilliant as he was! Thad had some kind of illness—rheumatic fever? He missed a lot of school, couldn't catch up. Several kids came to Dix's for that reason."

She sighed, looking sad. "Mark wasn't at the reunion. I heard he died mixing drugs and liquor a few years back. He was a nice guy. Good family. Why do such things happen?"

"Did Thad have a crush on Reina?" I asked.

"Maybe not. One of the few. Not that I ever saw, that's for sure. He was like he told you—monkish and celibate. Kids used to tease him—say he was gay. He never got in fights about it, though. He was always kind of self-contained, sure of himself. He was a good student, certainly devoted to Reina's teaching, and respectful toward her."

"How about Jeffrey?"

She laughed shortly. "All I remember of Jeffrey was him pounding away on a punching bag in the gym, or on some unlucky kid in the ring. I think he wore boxing gloves all the time! I don't really connect him with Reina except for that dance he did at the reunion. It surprised me he could dance so well."

She went on to list a few other people, most of whom I barely remembered meeting. They hadn't made quite the impression on me that some of the others had.

"Tell me some more about Perky, Thad, and Forrest," I suggested.

She picked up her glass and drank some more tea. I did the same. The ice had melted, but it was still cool. It was very quiet in Becky's garden. I could hear the faint sound of someone's lawn mower some distance away, and occasionally a bird called out, but that was about it. Even though I'd been living in an apartment for only a few days, I was coming to a new appreciation of quiet. The Granada was upscale, but when walls were shared, there were bound to be some sounds that penetrated. One of my neighbors was fond of rap, another practiced karate in his bedroom.

"Perky got into some special art school. He used to draw all the time—caricatures mostly. In his own way, he was just as brilliant as Forrest. By the time we had our fifth reunion his cartoons were syndicated and he was weirder than ever."

She knotted her brow again. "Forrest went into his family's business—they sell furniture. He got married. He brought his wife to the tenth reunion. Nice woman. White. Looked something like Reina, now I think about it. Slender, long brown hair. She didn't have Reina's posture, though. I always admired Reina's posture."

I made a mental note to think about Forrest's wife looking like Reina. "And Thad?" I prompted.

She shifted in her wooden chair. "I don't think he ever married. But I never did hear for sure that he was gay. He was never obviously gay, you know, the way some guys are. I think he was just, what's the word—an ascetic? It may be he had gay leanings but just didn't give in to them. I'd heard he became a priest, but it turned out he was just a regular sort of minister. I believe his church is nondenominational."

She laughed. "I just remembered something. Reina got mad at him one day. I was in a room adjoining her office, and I heard them without seeing them—Thad and Reina—she was reaming him up one side and down the other, but I couldn't make out the words, just that she was really, really mad. Goodness knows what he'd done—as I told you before, I think, he was always righteous. Anyway, Reina was furious with him, which was totally out of character for her. I felt uncomfortable about eavesdropping, so I left the room. I guess Reina saw me. She shut up just as I left the room. I wondered for a long time what on earth Thad had done."

"When *was* this?" I asked.

She hesitated, then looked sick. Standing up, she hefted her sturdy little son to her shoulder and carried him into the house, presumably to put him down for a nap. When she returned, she walked over to a rose-bush at the side of the yard and pulled off a few dead heads and a couple of live ones, too, and crushed them in her hand.

I waited. After a couple more minutes, she came back, dropped the crushed flowers on the ground and sat down again. "I was blowing out eggs so Reina and I could decorate the shells for Easter," she said. "That would make it about three months before graduation."

She blinked. "Oh, dear God." She shook her head. "Look, that was twenty years ago. Reina could have been mad at him for any number of reasons."

She hesitated again, then said slowly, "Thad went away for a long time. He didn't even come to the previous reunions, this was the first one he attended." She brightened. "He was hardly acting at the reunion like someone who was carrying a torch, or a grudge or whatever."

"Where did he go after school?" I asked.

She thought about it. "Seattle."

I remembered then that Thad's face had struck a chord of memory in my brain when I first met him. Maybe I'd run into him in Washington.

"You surely don't think . . . ," Becky started, but didn't continue the thought.

"I'm not jumping to any conclusions," I said. "I'll think about everything you've told me and I'll pass it on to Detective Sergeant Bristow and let him work on the conclusions."

She didn't look reassured.

"Can you think of anything else that might be helpful?" I asked.

She pondered a while, then gave me the sweet smile I remembered from our last meeting. "I think I've emptied my whole brain, Charlie. There doesn't seem to be anything left in it."

"I'd like to ask you not to repeat anything we've talked about to anyone," I said.

"Hey, I wasn't even sure I wanted to tell you," she said. "I'm not a gossip, Charlie. I can be trusted."

"Good." I stood up. So did she. We shook hands. I could smell the aroma of the roses she'd crushed earlier. Some of it stayed on my hand and sweetened the air as I drove back to my new apartment. The bush she'd taken the heads from was a red rosebush, I remembered.

CHAPTER 18

Detective Sergeant Taylor Bristow showed up on my apartment doorstep at eight o'clock the following morning. I was barely awake. Now that I wasn't working at CHAPS until all hours, I went to bed earlier, but I'd had so much stuff muttering in my brain all night I had slept only fitfully.

Bristow cast an amused glance at my night-tangled hair and the long T-shirt I wore as a nightgown, but made no comment. I invited him in, put on a pot of coffee, and excused myself to get some sweats on and fight my daily battle through my hair with a wide-toothed rake.

We exchanged some small talk while I put out cereal and raisins and sliced up a couple of bananas. I didn't even ask Bristow if he'd had breakfast; he was always willing to accept food when it was put in front of him.

Once we were settled at the card table P.J. had donated, and I'd had a couple of good warming swallows of coffee, I raised my eyebrows at him. "When I asked Savanna to let you know I had something for you, I had no idea you'd arrive at the crack of dawn."

"I could have waited until later, but I thought you'd

want to see some evidence I picked up last night," he said. He tilted his head to one side. "And I was anxious to hear what you'd turned up," he added with his usual candor. "I didn't get home until two A.M. Didn't think you'd want me calling you then."

"You're still involved at Flood Creek?"

He shook his head. "Nope, got that straightened out finally. Guilty party got picked out in a lineup by several of the creek's residents."

He gave a tired smile. "Reason I was so late—I'm running a citizens' police academy course right now. Took three of the participants on a ride-along last night, showed them Bellamy Park's best in action. You should sign up for the next class, Charlie, seeing you have such an extreme interest in police business."

"I just might do that," I said airily, ignoring the pointedness of his comment.

He grinned at me. Taking a folded piece of paper from his polo shirt pocket, he handed it to me. It was a copy of an e-mail, addressed to ChapsDame@aol.com—the new address I'd switched to after having trouble with a remailer a while back.

I looked at the "from" line.

"Timothy Perkins," Bristow said around a mouthful of cereal.

Breakfast forgotten, I stared at him. "I don't—"

"One of the lab guys found it stashed in the mail program in Perkins's computer. In the send-later section. Only letter of interest in there."

I read the message:

Charlie, I'm writing what I plan to tell you
on our date. Maybe it isn't necessary, but
just in case. I'm not sure enough of the person
to accuse him, so I won't, but I think I know
who might have killed Reina—the same person who fathered her kid twenty years ago.
Reina told me the guy raped her.

I must have made some sound of shock. "Rape?" I
echoed.

"Affirmative," Bristow said. "Yet rape hasn't been
mentioned in this context. Not by anybody."

"Well, that makes it definite the killer was a man."

"One might think so. If Mr. Perkins was correct in
his assumptions. Seems he might have been, seeing he
was killed before he could tell you all this."

I gulped some coffee and read on:

Reina told me about it months ago. We met
in a bar and she had a little more to drink
than usual. She refused to tell me who the
guy was, but I think I've figured it out. Reina
gave the kid up for adoption and said she
never expected to see it and didn't want to
see it, not ever. I'd go to the police with this,
but if I'm right the killer would guess who
turned him in and maybe take revenge. The
police don't always act as fast as they should.

I glanced at Bristow and he made a sound of disgust.
"People always think they know how we should do our

jobs. We can't just pick someone up because someone else says they are guilty. And often the ones who make accusations are like Perkins, they hedge around who or what so we've nothing definite to go on."

I read the letter again, then put it aside and absent-mindedly fixed my cereal while I thought about Perkins's fear, which had turned out to be justified. I was feeling some of it myself, now that I was about to tell Bristow who I suspected.

While I ate, Bristow went into the bathroom and brought Benny out, stroking him gently as he watched me eat and waited for me to talk.

In the middle of thinking about Reina being raped and wondering what I'd do in such a situation if I turned out to be pregnant—an impossible question to answer—I remembered Becky saying Reina had been troubled and had said she was thinking about her daughter. "In July," Becky had said. Two months ago. A month before Reina was killed. Reina had told Savanna the flowers had started five months before. "Months ago," according to Perky's e-mail, Reina had told Perky about the rape and her subsequent pregnancy.

Several months back something had happened that had started in motion the events that had led to Reina's death.

I didn't realize I'd said that last aloud until Bristow made inquiring noises. I explained my train of thought. Which brought forth yet another conclusion.

"The photo," I exclaimed, setting down my spoon. "The photo Reina was clutching when she died. We took it for granted it was a picture of Reina, because it looked like a younger Reina. Remember Savanna said the hair was darker than it should have been? Could it have been a photo of the daughter?"

Bristow put Benny down on the floor and leaned back. I kept a watchful eye on the little rabbit as he hopped off to explore. He'd shown a tendency to try to burrow through the carpet since we'd moved in. Those cute little buckteeth were sharp enough to do serious damage. I didn't want to lose my deposit when I moved out.

"The age of the woman in the photo would be about right," Bristow said. "Twenty or so."

He squinted at me. "Okay, I'll grant you the smug look. But I have to tell you, Charlie, I've already got some publicity in the works, to see if we can bring the daughter in."

I might have known he'd already figured it out.

He mulled for a moment and I poured us both some more coffee. It was a Kona blend, my favorite, but it seemed tasteless to me right now.

"Darker hair," Bristow muttered. "Maybe I should have another talk with Forrest Kenyon."

Savanna was sure right about her darling husband. He seemed to have tunnel vision where this case was concerned. "The young woman in the photo didn't look black," I pointed out.

"Once the genes get mixed, a lot of different appearances can result," he said. "Look at Jacqueline. Her skin is much lighter than Savanna's."

About to stand up, he changed his mind. "What was it you wanted to tell me?" he asked.

"Did you get my message from Savanna?" I asked. "About Donald Ainslee, Reina's so-called boyfriend."

He nodded. "He called me yesterday. Just happened to catch me in the station filling out some reports. I asked him to come in and he did. Guy's got an alibi. He was in Alaska. I checked it out right away. Says Reina stopped seeing him a couple of months ago."

"She told him something had happened that upset her."

Bristow nodded. "Yeah," he said heavily. "There was certainly something going on that led to her death."

"Something to do with that baby that was born twenty years ago," I said.

"Seems like," he agreed.

"Did Ainslee tell you he knew nothing about the ring?"

"Affirmative." He looked at me in a grimly humorous way. "You have any idea what that ring has to do with anything?"

"Only the guess I made before. That she was pretending to be engaged. But there's no way of knowing if I was right."

I took in a breath and Bristow's eyebrows went up. His mental radar is sensitive. "I visited Becky Mackinay yesterday," I confessed.

To my relief, he smiled. "Anyone ever tell you you don't have enough to do?" he asked.

He had a point there. Since CHAPS burned, I'd been fairly idle. My mind shuddered away from that phrase—"since CHAPS burned." I'd been very successful so far at closing off the part of my mind that wanted to relive that fire. Sometime I was going to have to turn the memories loose and get it out of my system, but it was still too recent for me to bear to relive it.

"Becky's a nice woman," I said, as if that was the reason I'd gone to visit her.

"Sure, Charlie," he said, not buying it. Then he cocked his head to one side. "Did Ms. Mackinay tell you about Kenyon's late wife looking like Reina Diaz?"

I nodded reluctantly. "I suppose you think that's significant."

"Hard to tell," he answered. "I wondered at first, but it seems clear Mrs. Kenyon did die of natural causes."

I might have known he'd check.

I told him about Becky growing red roses, which seemed an unnecessary tidbit in the light of Perky's e-mail. I went on to tell him everything she'd had to say, including the stuff about Reina being angry with Thad.

"She couldn't make out what Reina was saying?"

"That's what she said. But you know the timing is such that . . . well, if Reina had that baby sometime after graduation, she might just have found out she was pregnant, which could have been why she was angry with Thad."

"That's a wild assumption on your part," Bristow said. "Thad O'Connor was her student. He might have turned in some unsatisfactory work. Who knows? There could be a hundred reasons for a teacher to take a student to task. Nothing in my investigation so far has pointed a finger at the pastor. I don't even see enough here for me to question him about that fight. He's been the most cooperative of all, so far."

"But you *do* see enough to question Forrest."

"Forrest sent her flowers, called her, had a crush on her in school."

"He says the story was exaggerated. He says he sent flowers four times, not every week, and likewise on the phone calls."

"He says."

"*And* that's all you found out at Tessler's."

"I'll be checking other florists. I've been otherwise engaged, but it's on my mind."

"Did you check phone records? Did he call her every week?"

"He could have called from a pay phone some of the time."

He was determined to convict Forrest if he possibly could, and nothing I was going to say right now was going to persuade him to look elsewhere. But I couldn't just give up, could I?

"You told me once that sometimes a law enforcement officer fixates on a certain individual, decides he's guilty and won't bother to look at anyone else. You were talking about your old partner, Detective Sergeant Reggie Timpkin, remember? You said he was obsessed."

He was silent for a while. "I'll admit I can't tolerate Forrest Kenyon," he said. "He irritates the hell out of me."

He looked at me, his expression softening. "I love Savanna, Charlie," he said.

"I know you do. Have you told her that lately?"

He sighed. "Maybe not in so many words. Things have been difficult."

"Telling someone you love them can make things a lot easier," I said. "I know actions are supposed to speak louder than words. But women want to hear the words. Specifically those three words. Not, 'I love you, sweetie,' or 'I love you, darlin',' you could say stuff like that to a friend. Not, 'I'm madly in love with you,' you can say that to anyone in a joking way. What women want are those three words, said with feeling: 'I love you.' They want to hear them often."

He gave me a weak smile. "Look who's the expert on love."

"Sometimes someone on the outside can see in more clearly than the people on the inside."

He stood up, came around the table, and kissed me on the forehead.

"Thad also has black hair," I offered.

"So he does," he said. "And so did Perkins. We'll see, Charlie. I'll try to keep an open mind." He looked down at his feet. "My man Ben seems to be fixated on my shoelaces," he said in a lighter voice. "You remove him for me, I'll be on my way."

I leaned down and scooped Benny up. "I still think you should take a closer look at Thad O'Connor," I said.

"We'll see," he repeated, then added, "thank you for the breakfast. I'll tell Savanna you took care of my inner man. And thanks for the helpful information."

Holding Benny, I opened my mouth, ready to argue some more, but just then my doorbell rang its dulcet chimes. I had a moment's regret for the *"Aroogah"* of the doorbell extension I'd had in my loft, but I pushed it out of my mind and opened the door to see a very large black man with a clipboard. "Plato?" he asked.

I nodded blankly, then realized this was Wednesday. "Stay and see my sofa and chair," I said to Bristow. "It's great stuff, you won't believe how soft it is. We can sit on it and talk some more."

He shook his head, then edged past the other man with a friendly nod. "Later," he said over his shoulder.

Benny and I sprawled on the new furniture and admired it for a while. It looked and felt great, though it made the rest of the apartment look emptier than before. It would be even more so when I returned P.J.'s futon.

Forrest was right, I was going to need at least a coffee table to put stuff on. And a lamp table for reading. Which would mean I'd need a lamp, too.

I couldn't get enthused about another shopping trip right now, all the same. I didn't feel like talking to Forrest and I wasn't feeling too positive about the value of talking to Bristow anymore. I wasn't sure what, if anything, I wanted to do about Thad O'Connor.

After putting Benny back in his cage, along with some veggie-flavored bunny bits, I wandered back into the kitchen and poured some more coffee.

Sitting down again on one of the card-table chairs, I pondered everything I knew about Thad. After a few minutes, I saw that there was one easy step I could take.

Picking up my cell phone, I put in a call to my ex-husband, Rob Whittaker. At first I thought it was a mistake to do it, he was so totally happy to hear from me. Usually any communication between us was initiated by him, and this was twice in living memory I'd called him. But he calmed down when he found out I was in search of information.

"Thad O'Connor?" he repeated. "Seems as if the name has some significance. Especially connected to a minister." He was silent for a while, then he said, "No, nothing's coming through the ether, Charlie."

"Could you ask around? See if you can turn anything up?"

One thing about Rob, he knew a lot of people. Like Zack, he tended to know more women than men, but he belonged to Kiwanis and Rotary and a couple of medical groups.

"I'll see what I can do," he promised, then asked if his son, Ryan, had been in touch with me, which he hadn't.

"Don't push him," I said, feeling guilty for saying it because it wasn't Ryan's welfare I was concerned about—it was mine. You wouldn't believe the mischief that sniveling kid had done to me when I was married to his father. "If he wants to call, he'll call. Let it be his idea."

Rob's voice was soft. "You're right, Charlie. He's a man now. I have to let him make his own decisions."

Sheesh. One thing I couldn't imagine was nineteen-year-old Ryan as a man.

"There you go," I said brightly, and Rob finally hung up.

* * *

It was the next day before he called back. "I asked a couple of my law enforcement friends about your guy," he said. "One of them remembered something and told me to talk to Sean Callahan."

"The fire chief!" I exclaimed.

"Yeah. You didn't like his wife."

"She's a snob and a racist and I thought you'd probably slept with her after you did her tummy-tuck."

He ignored the dig. "You remember Sean himself?"

"Yes, you operated on him." Sean had been badly burned in a warehouse fire that killed two other firefighters. Rob had put his face back together again. He'd done a fabulous job and Sean had been extremely grateful.

If Rob had stuck to firefighters and left good-looking female patients alone we might still be married.

"So what did he say?" I asked.

"Sean is a county fire marshall now," Rob said. "He remembers Thad O'Connor very well."

"They're friends?" I asked, noting the Irish surnames.

"Not at all."

He went on to tell me about a church north of Bellingham, Washington, that had burned to the ground a few years back. The insurance company had suspected that the minister of the church had set the fire, but couldn't prove anything.

"Thad O'Connor," I said.

"Himself," Rob agreed.

"I knew I'd seen him somewhere before," I said. "It must have been when I was living in Washington.

I must have seen a report on TV or a picture in the *Seattle Times*."

"No, Charlie, I don't think so. It was after you left."

"Well, then, maybe the story was featured here, with a picture. I just know I've seen him somewhere."

I was suddenly filled with a cold, cold anger. CHAPS. Thad must have set fire to CHAPS. It was far too much of a coincidence that he'd been connected to a previous fire for me to believe he'd had nothing to do with ours. And he must have set that fire, thinking he was killing me and possibly Zack. The only reason he could have had for that would have been that we were getting too close to finding out he had killed Reina and Perky.

"According to Sean," Rob went on, "it looked at first as if a spark from a gas lighter in the church kitchen—the kind you light a gas stove or a barbecue with—had caused the fire. But it wouldn't be difficult for someone to make it spark. Thad O'Connor hadn't taken anything out to save—important papers, credit cards, property titles, stuff like that. Happening to save such items is often a giveaway, Sean said. But in that particular case, all those papers were in the church office when it burned."

"Was he arrested?"

"Nope. Not enough evidence, Charlie. Investigators suspected he did it for the insurance money so he could build a new church. And that's exactly what he did do. Made the congregation very happy. None of them believed he burned the church down. He *told* them he didn't do it. He *cried*, they said. Within a year, he moved on down the coast. Said he'd had the call. And get this, Charlie, O'Connor became pastor of a Methodist church in Oregon, which also burned. Because of faulty wiring. Supposedly. God's will, according to O'Connor."

"*Sheesh!*"

"You think he burned your saloon down?"

"It's not a saloon, Rob, it's a nightclub."

"Whatever."

"I think it's very likely he set the fire at CHAPS. And that he was responsible for both . . . ," I hesitated. I'd meant to say "for both murders," but as far as I knew, Rob hadn't heard about Perky's death and I didn't really want to get into it, or to have him worrying about me some more. ". . . for both it and the teacher's murder," I finished smoothly. "Unfortunately, I haven't been able to convince the police to lean on him. I'll pass on this information, of course, but if Thad managed to weasel out of getting arrested twice before, he's liable to weasel out of this one, too."

"Where do you *find* these awful people?" Rob asked.

"Same way I found you, dear heart," I said, stung. "It's my karma."

"That wasn't very nice, Charlie," he said, sounding stung himself.

"You're right," I said, without taking it back. Adding fuel to the fire, I went on, "If you really want to know, Thad placed the winning bid in an auction with me as the prize."

Before he could comment, I thanked him very sweetly for getting the information for me and hung up. I felt rattled for a half hour. When you divorce a man he ought to have the good grace to stay out of your life.

Yes, I *know*—I was the one who called him.

CHAPTER 19

In the end, I called Zack and asked him to come over. It was no use talking about Thad to Savanna, she'd only go on about Forrest being innocent. And Angel was busy sorting through his worldly possessions, getting ready to move down to Salinas.

I set up some lunch on the card table, fully intending to keep Zack in the kitchen, but, of course, he first wandered along the little hall to the bathroom to visit with Benny, then poked his nose into the living room. "Very nice, darlin'," he said of my new sofa and chair.

"I bought them at Kenyon's store in Los Altos," I told him.

"Good goods," he said approvingly. "Does the couch turn into a bed?"

The man had an unerring instinct.

"Yes," I said, adding hastily, "do you want mustard for your sandwich?"

No answer. I heard a rustling sound and stepped over to look in the living room. Sure enough, Zack had pulled out the bed. Pressing on the mattress, he turned his head slightly and caught sight of me watching.

"Want to try it out, Charlie?"

My innards did their usual whomp!

Yes, I *know* it's immature, but that's what happens when I see him or he squints at me, or he makes suggestive statements. Apparently I have no control over my hormones. I'm trying to deal with it, okay?

"I'll be trying it out tonight," I said. I'd bought queen-size sheets for P.J.'s futon, they should work just fine for the sofa bed.

Taking off his cowboy hat and setting it on the futon, Zack sat on the side of the bed, pulled off his cowboy boots, and arranged himself flat on his back in the middle of the bed. "Very nice," he said again, clasping his hands behind his head. "What's that on the ceilin'? You got a leak up there?"

Fool that I am, I fell for a cheap trick like that, craning my neck and moving across the room in an attempt to see what he was seeing. I managed to catch myself before I got as far as the sofa bed, though. I looked down at my tormentor in exasperation, expecting to see the usual mischievous expression in his green eyes, but he looked unaccustomedly serious as his eyes met mine. And as usual, when our gazes met, a wave of heat arced between us.

"Charlie?" he said softly.

"Lunch is ready," I said, and beat a hasty retreat.

After we ate, I put the bed back up while Zack was in the bathroom, then got him established in the big chair with the ottoman when he showed up. He hadn't put his boots back on, I noticed. I entertained thoughts of having everyone take their shoes off before they entered the apartment. See what happens when you get *things*? You start worrying about keeping them clean, keeping them in good repair. We should all live in tents!

I sat on the futon, taking the high ground so to speak, so that if Zack moved, at least he wouldn't catch me stuck in the downy valley of that sofa. Such quasi-military strategies are necessary when dealing with our man in black.

I told him everything I'd learned about Thad O'Connor and that I was convinced he was our murderer and arsonist.

"You sure you're not sore because he turned you down for that date?" Zack teased.

I didn't bother to answer.

After a few minutes of thought, he decided he agreed with me. "So, do we talk to Taylor Bristow?" he asked.

"I'm not sure it will do any good," I said. "When I brought Thad up before, Bristow didn't show much interest. Besides which, Thad managed to escape the law the last two times, he might do it again."

"He might also be innocent," Zack pointed out. "Maybe the God's will he talked about was to punish him for some original sin."

Original sin was something Zack knew a lot about.

"If he *is* innocent, all the more reason not to go through Bristow," I said. "What we need to do is find enough proof to take to Bristow so he can't ignore our suspicions."

He nodded wisely, which probably meant he had no idea what to do next.

"We could invite the suspect over," he said at last.

"No way," I said. "We put ourselves and Benny in

danger last time we did that." This was a reference to
a previous murder case we'd become embroiled in when
we wanted to help a friend. I'd thought for several
minutes that Benny was dead. I didn't want to go
through that again.

"How about we go to Thad's church?" I suggested.
"Surely, he wouldn't get violent with us in his own
church? There must be people around. A secretary?
An assistant pastor? Somebody?"

There was a choir practice going on. Maybe twenty
people singing "On Christ The Solid Rock I Stand."

The choir had nice voices, but maybe not a lot of
training. One of the women was Asian. I thought it was
entirely possible she was Fred Nishida's wife, Sachiko.
She was petite and slender and very pretty. No wonder
Fred's face lit up when he spoke of her.

Pastor Thad was not in the room where the choir
was practicing. When all eyes turned to Zack, we with-
drew hastily and went in search of the office. Thad
wasn't there, either, but a woman who was frowning
into a computer monitor told us we'd find him in the
sanctuary, preparing his weekend sermon. He found
the atmosphere in there to be the most inspiring, she
said with an affectionate note in her voice.

Zack and I both paused as we entered the church.
Zack removed his cowboy hat. The far end of the sanctuary was a wall of windows, tapering upward to a
point. Not stained glass as you might expect, which
was good because the ranks of redwoods that showed
were more naturally beautiful than any stained-glass
designs.

The sun was shining at just the right angle to gild one edge of each tree and create dramatic shadows in the interior of the church. It was such a breathtaking sight that a couple of minutes passed before I realized Pastor Thad was sitting in what I guessed was the choir loft, head down, tapping away on a laptop.

He looked up as Zack and I moved forward past the polished oak pews. I might have imagined the darkening of his features in the shadows of the church. He smiled almost immediately, did some more tapping on the laptop, evidently to save his file, then powered down, closed the computer, and set it aside.

He was wearing jeans and a sweatshirt that said "Attitude is everything!" I owned a T-shirt with the same slogan, but mine didn't have an attribution to Norman Vincent Peale. I had an idea the emphasis might be placed differently.

"What a nice surprise!" Thad exclaimed, then added, as he shook hands with both of us, "Is this a social visit? Or are you two planning on getting married? We do a lovely wedding here."

I thought perhaps Zack turned pale, but again it might have been a trick of the light.

"We wanted to ask you a few questions," I said.

"You didn't get enough answers on the ferry trip?" A hard note had entered his voice, but his smile was still in place. It didn't quite make it to his eyes, though. They were flat, almost black, and very watchful.

I remembered reading a short story once in which a character was described as "a Sagittarian, eyes full of memories from the day he was born."

"When's your birthday?" I blurted out, feeling instantly stupid.

"July twenty-sixth," he said.

Leo. So much for astrology.

Zack was giving me a look. I didn't blame him.

"Maybe we should adjourn to my office," Thad said. "It would be a little more comfortable for you."

"Here is fine," Zack said, beating me by a split second. No way could we afford to take a chance on Thad bolting.

We sat on the bench in front of Thad's, turned around to face him. He leaned back, an inquiring look on his face, spreading his arms along the back of his bench, but he didn't look quite as much at ease as he wanted. His knuckles were white where they gripped the back of the bench.

I had no idea where to begin.

"I guess you know we're lookin' into Reina Diaz's death," Zack said. I doubted he had an idea where to begin, either, but he had a habit of just starting out without thinking about where he was going. In the past he'd used the same approach to women.

"I gathered that," Thad said. "Can't say I'm sure of your authority in the matter, however."

"We don't have any," I said. "Savanna asked us to help out." I paused hoping for inspiration. It came. "Savanna told me you know quite a bit about stalking."

He nodded. "I've counseled a few women during my ministry. Mostly the problem was a divorced or about-to-be-divorced husband. It's odd when you think of how many men are slow to make a commitment. Just as many seem unable to let go. Sometimes they get violent about it. *'If I can't have you nobody else can,'* that sort of moronic thinking. Sometimes, of course, stalkers are females. I've experienced minor stalking myself. Some impressionable women develop a crush on a minister. Lonely women, usually. It makes for a difficult situation."

He seemed inclined to stop there, and I had no idea what to say next, so I just waited and after a while he filled the vacuum. "I fail to see why everyone seems to think Reina might have been stalked," he said. "As I understand it, someone sent her flowers and called her. While it's true, stalking often begins with such friendly gestures, sometimes they *are* just friendly gestures. I've been known to send flowers to a woman myself. Though more usually on a birthday or some special occasion."

"Did you ever send flowers to Reina?" Zack asked.

Thad looked amused. "Are you casting me in the role of the stalker?" He shook his head. "Sorry, guys, you are on the wrong track there. I never did send flowers to Reina. I called her once or twice. Had lunch with her recently, as I believe I told Savanna."

He sighed, and moved a little on the bench. "I got the impression Reina might have been exaggerating a bit about the possibility of the stalker. But I was sympathetic, of course. And it's for sure stalking is a problem nowadays."

He went on from there to quote some of the statistics and anecdotes he'd told Savanna.

I tried to remember exactly what he'd told me when I questioned him on the ferry, but I couldn't remember.

Fine detective I was, maybe I should carry a tape recorder.

I did recall that he'd implied he was present in the main corral during the whole time frame that would cover Reina's murder. But if he had murdered Reina, how could he have been present in the main corral?

Someone, I didn't remember who, had said, "If the facts don't fit the theory, change the facts." Something like that. So—if Thad *wasn't* in the main corral, he wouldn't know what was going on there, right? Okay, so I'd told him myself about Francisca singing and the band taking a break, and he'd been present for the line dance, I'd admired his style.

Something flashed in the back of my mind, some quick vision of something previously forgotten, something moving.

What was it? I concentrated, aware that Zack had asked Thad another question, but not knowing what it was. Oh, yeah, he was talking about some *Prescott's Landing* plot that had dealt with stalking. The one he'd told Savanna, Angel, and me about, no doubt.

What had I been thinking at the moment that little flash of memory appeared? It was gone now. Perhaps it would come back if I just waited silently . . . .

There it was—the nude dancing instructors. Why on earth was I thinking about them?

I'd been thinking about Francisca singing her Tejano song.

"Do you ever see Francisca?" I asked Thad, interrupting Zack in full flow.

He shook his head. "I think she's a Catholic."

"I was thinking about that song she sang at CHAPS

the night of the reunion. Trying to remember what it was."

He looked thoughtful, then shook his head. "Sorry, the old memory must be failing. I remember it was familiar, but the exact title escapes me."

Was it really likely that a Tejano song would be familiar to him, I wondered. "I sort of vaguely remember it being an old Jackson Five song," I said. "I loved the Jackson Five when I was a kid."

Thad inclined his head. "You could be right." He smiled. "Sorry I'm not being much help. Is it important?"

"Not really," I said. Though of course it was. I was almost certain the Jackson Five had never sung Tejano.

Which meant Thad was *pretending* to have heard Francisca. While he was actually somewhere else.

"Did you know Reina had a daughter?" Zack asked, thus passing on information that had been given to us by Bristow and to me by Becky—both times in confidence. Evidently, Sheriff Lazarro hadn't ever learned that law enforcement people usually held back details about a crime so they could either surprise the bad guys with them, or rule out wrongful confessions.

Zack's question had surprised Thad all right, though he was sure trying to hide the fact. Standing up, he stepped gracefully into the aisle between the rows of benches and walked over to the *clerestory windows*, where he stood looking out at the trees for a couple of minutes.

His graceful movements had brought back another memory. Thad dancing at the reunion. Doing the electric slide as if he'd done it several times already . . .

Which he probably had! The two recent memories collided in my brain and made me gasp.

Thad O'Connor had been one of the dancing instructors who belonged to the Naturist Club. One of the nude dancing instructors!

No wonder I'd thought he looked only vaguely familiar. I hadn't exactly been concentrating on faces.

Talk about a double life.

No doubt about it. This man was not the man he pretended to be.

"What?" Zack whispered.

I shook my head. "Later," I whispered back.

When Thad turned around, he was in control, smiling. "Okay, Zack, you've managed to shock me. No, I didn't know Reina had a daughter."

"I've seen her photo," I said. "She looks just like Reina."

I don't know why I said that. It just came out. And it opened the door.

"The photo in Reina's hand," Thad said in a leaden voice. He came back to the bench he'd been sitting on and sat down again.

"Yes," I said.

I glanced at Zack. He wasn't keeping up. He was obviously unaware that Thad had just more or less confessed to killing Reina Diaz.

I looked at the pastor. He looked back with courteous inquiry.

"How did you know about the photo?" I asked.

He showed no discomfort, but the look in his eyes revealed that his brain was racing. "When I said the blessing over Reina," he said. "I saw the photo then."

"No," I said. "You saw a piece of paper. It was clutched in her hand. Only the medical examiner who did the autopsy was able to get it out of her hand. Even Detective Sergeant Bristow didn't know what was on the paper until after the autopsy."

"Someone must have told me about it then," he said. "Detective Sergeant North perhaps, or Sergeant Bristow." There was total confidence in his voice.

I wished I could check him for weapons. There was no way now to avoid a confrontation, and in my short career as an amateur sleuth I'd already learned that the most surprising people carried weapons.

Zack was leaning casually over the back of the bench we were sitting on, squinting at Thad in his wise Sheriff Lazarro manner. "We *know* you killed Reina," he said bluntly. He'd kept up after all.

The effect of his statement was amazing. Thad seemed almost to collapse in on himself, like a balloon that had suddenly lost all its air. Quite suddenly he looked worn and pale and much older than his thirty-eight years.

"We understand that you're under a lot of pressure," Zack said sternly. "You'll feel better if you get it all out."

Sometimes Zack amazes me. He comes out with something that ought to shut a guilty person up and instead of that, they start babbling their entire life story. Maybe it's the authoritative tone, or else he projects that Sheriff Lazarro image and they accept it as proof of defeat. They are in the hands of television series law and there's nothing they can do to escape.

CHAPTER 20

He cried first. Thad, I mean. Pitifully, productively. Real genuine tears.

We let him get it out of his system.

After a few minutes, I left Sheriff Lazarro in charge and went looking for a box of tissues, which I found inside a little kitchen in the building behind the church. I could hear the choir still singing right along. It sounded unreal to me, given what was going on in the sanctuary. I couldn't find tissues, but I found a box of paper napkins and decided they would do.

About to leave the room, I caught sight of a wall phone and decided it might be a good idea to call in the reserves.

Bristow wasn't at the station, the dispatcher said, but she could probably reach him, unless someone else would do. I debated asking for Liz North, but decided I didn't know her well enough to know how she'd respond.

"Get Sergeant Bristow as quickly as you can," I said. "Tell him Zack and Charlie need him at the Church of Enlightenment in San Francisco." I gave her the street address and suggested if she couldn't reach Bristow in a few minutes, she should send someone else. "We might have some kind of situation building here," I said, and hung up before she could ask me for more details. I didn't want to leave Zack on his own for too long.

Thad used up a lot of the napkins, ending up bleary-eyed and bloodshot, the way I do when I cry. But I wasn't empathizing one bit. I wanted to find something large and solid and hit him with it for killing Reina and Perky, and burning down his two previous churches, and spoiling the good life I'd just begun to achieve.

"It began in my sophomore year at Alger Dix," Thad said finally.

We waited. We'd both learned the virtue of silence in such situations. And what a tale Thad did unfold.

Halfway through his sophomore year, Reina had picked him out to have sexual relations with. He'd worshiped her, adored her, been so grateful to her. But he hadn't thought of her that way. He'd told her this and she'd laughed, and then she had taken advantage of him.

"It was rape," he said, his bleary eyes flashing to life for a moment. "What could I do? Who was going to believe me? Everyone else loved her the way I had until then."

Reina had told him if he didn't cooperate, she'd make sure he didn't graduate. If he didn't graduate, what kind of future was he going to have? "She was so cold," he said. "No one would have recognized her, the way she was when she was angry with me, she was so cold. It was never good. She just used me to satisfy herself."

Could a man *be* raped? I wondered. I mean, I could see how he could be molested. But if the woman was cold, would he have an erection even?

He wasn't looking at me, so he didn't see my expression. It had to have been one of disbelief. He wasn't looking at Zack, either. He was looking only into himself, either to concentrate on the made-up story he was telling, or back at the past that had actually happened.

Three months before Thad was to graduate, Reina had taken him into her office and told him she wanted him to stay in the San Francisco area. He'd thought once he was out of school his nightmare would be over, and here she was telling him it was going to go on and on. If he even thought of leaving, she threatened, she would tell people he'd raped her. They would believe her. Everybody always believed her.

He'd protested, but she'd kept on, getting more and more angry, telling him in no uncertain terms what she would do to ruin his prospects if he didn't stay with her. He *would* stay, she said. Everything would be fine then. Maybe she'd even arrange for him to marry her.

He was horrified, but she didn't stop describing the life they would lead together until one of the other students came out of the room next door.

Becky, I thought, but didn't say.

"As soon as the graduation ceremony was over," he said, "I took off, heading north. I crossed into Canada, stayed there for a while, working odd jobs, then I came back across the border to Bellingham, got a job and enrolled at Western Washington University. After I graduated, I worked for a minister of a large church. I studied theology, and finally had the call to enter the ministry myself, though not in such a hidebound religion as the man I'd worked for."

He'd invented his own, I guessed. I remembered my father once getting a package of materials advertising full-size baptismal fonts for sale. First he'd been outraged, then amused. If the restaurant failed, he might just start his own religion, he'd joked.

"I lived in fear that Reina would track me down," Thad went on. "But she didn't. I guess she hadn't really believed I would leave her and was too stunned to take action. She had such . . . power over me, it must have taken her by surprise when I disappeared so fast. I don't even know if she ever looked for me. Maybe she just found another victim. I never knew. I only knew I was free."

His head drooped. He was the image of the ill-treated victim, totally innocent of wrongdoing.

"So to celebrate your freedom, you burned down a couple of churches?" I asked.

I could almost see him debating whether to tell the truth about the fires or not. "Both of those churches were burned accidentally," he said firmly, lifting his head to show me innocent, though still bloodshot eyes.

"Not accordin' to the new evidence," Zack said.

Thad's innocent look gave way to wariness. "What new evidence?"

Zack looked mysterious.

Thad shook his head. "There was never any proof that those fires were anything but accidental."

Somehow I've always found it difficult to believe someone's innocence when they start saying, "There wasn't any proof." Tell me you didn't do it, I might start to believe. But saying there wasn't proof is not a convincing argument.

"I was never able to recover from what Reina did to me," he said. "While I was in Bellingham I fell in love with a wonderful woman and she loved me. But I couldn't make love to her. I was impotent. I've been impotent ever since."

The word made Zack wince.

Thad looked at me. "You remember, Charlie, I wouldn't accept a date with you because of the lifestyle I've had to adopt."

Monkish, celibate—yes, I remembered. "Where in all of that past history you just told us did you take up the nude dancing?" I asked.

He flushed. I was surprised he'd feel embarrassed. You wouldn't think a person who'd get embarrassed about nude dancing would do it in the first place. Maybe he was angry that I'd learned so much about him.

Zack was staring at him. Evidently, he hadn't recognized him before, either. I was willing to bet if the Viking woman had walked in he'd have remembered her.

"I had to put myself through college somehow," Thad said sullenly.

"Hey, I'm not knockin' it. It seems strange, though, that you've kept it up, seeing you became a minister and all."

"It's my way of letting off steam—relaxing. A hobby."

He'd never heard of golf? Fishing? Poker?

It didn't seem worthwhile pursuing, though it did make clear that this man had many facets to his character.

"What about that baby?" Zack asked. "If Reina forced you to make love to her, then it's obvious you fathered that baby. The timin' alone—we know how old Reina's daughter is. We know when you graduated. We know about the fight you had with Reina."

Thad was crumpling again. "The fight—the argument—was over her wanting me to stay after graduation. And saying she'd accuse me of rape."

"And you didn't know about the baby until you saw that photo?" I said with a falsely sympathetic note in my voice.

"That's right," he said.

"How did you know it was her daughter?" I asked. "When I saw the photo I thought it was a picture of Reina."

I could see he was searching his brain for answers again. And not coming up with any. Zack opened his mouth to say something and I frowned at him to stop him from speaking.

After a while, Thad sighed. "I ran into Perky—Timothy Perkins—in a computer store in San Francisco several months ago," he said without any expression in his voice. "We had lunch and he told me he saw Reina from time to time. I asked him not to tell her he'd seen me, she didn't know I was back in California and I didn't want her to know."

He paused, then shook his head a little. "Reina had told him that she'd been raped by one of his classmates just before we graduated. She'd had a baby girl, but gave it away. Perky asked me—with a very knowing look on his face—if I knew who the rapist might be."

"You told him?" Zack asked. "Is that why you killed him?"

I shook my head at him. Let's get this part finished, I sent subliminally through the space between us.

Luckily, Thad hadn't seemed to hear Zack's comment. He was back there with Perky, reliving that moment. "It was such a terrible shock," he muttered. "I knew at once that had to be my baby. And I hadn't even known Reina was pregnant. The fact that Reina was telling people these terrible lies didn't matter to me as much as her giving that baby away. As if she were nothing. That was the way she'd always treated me, as if I were nothing. But this was my baby, my daughter. Reina had ruined me for anyone else. I had no family. I was left on my own at an early age. On the streets, ill as often as not, until some social worker rescued me and sent me to Alger Dix. All those years I had *nobody*. And all of a sudden I had a daughter."

I speculated that a whole new scenario was about to show up here. "You went looking for your daughter," I suggested.

He didn't say yes right away. But he didn't say no, either.

Zack shot me a glance filled with admiration.

"I hired a private detective to find her," Thad said at last. "The PI tried a host of adoption agencies and finally was able to cozy up to a woman who told him, yes, they had handled the adoption, and yes, she would tell him the baby's name. Amelia. Amelia Renfrew. He subsequently found out that Amelia had signed on with an international reunion registry online, hoping to find her birth parents. She was in Canada, in a small town a hundred miles or so from Toronto."

His face lit up. "I flew out there to meet Amelia. She is charming. She looks almost exactly like Reina looked when she was younger, but there are traces of me in her, too. Her hair, her skin, the shape of her nose."

He laughed, an incongruous note given the circumstances. "She even has my *toes*. My big toes are longer than most people's, quite a bit longer than the other toes. I'd know her anywhere by her toes."

"Was Amelia happy to see you?" Zack asked.

Thad smiled. "She was thrilled. Very excited."

The smile faded and he sighed. "Right away she wanted to know who her mother was. She was going to get married, she said. She didn't want to have children without knowing something about her parents—their health histories and so on. When she saw I was reluctant to talk about her mother, she pleaded with me. How could I not tell her?"

"You told her Reina had raped you?" Zack asked, sounding horrified.

Thad shook his head wearily. "I meant how could I not tell her who her mother was. But before I could reveal her mother's name, I told her, I had to get her mother's permission. She agreed to that and we spent a wonderful couple of weeks getting to know one another. It was the happiest time of my life. I had a daughter. I met her fiancé and liked him. When she discovered I was a minister, she wanted me to marry them. She was planning on having babies."

There was great sadness in his voice now. And a ring of truth that hadn't been present earlier when he'd claimed Reina had raped him.

"What happened?" I asked gently.

"I decided it was time to forget old hurts. Twenty years had passed. For the sake of Amelia, I decided I would cast off the old bitterness and try to make friends again with Reina."

"You went to see her?" I asked.

He nodded. "Perky had told me she was still teaching at Alger Dix's. About a month before the reunion, I looked her up. I told her about finding Amelia. I told her about Amelia's fiancé and the planned wedding. I assured her that if she didn't want Amelia to know about her I wouldn't ever mention her name. I told her that for Amelia's sake I was willing to forgive and forget what she had done to me all those years ago."

The sadness was still in his voice and I thought I could sense what was coming. Zack looked at me and I shook my head at him. Silence was the best treatment here. Thad was most likely going to finish what he'd started.

Sure enough, after a couple of minutes of staring beyond us unseeingly, Thad continued.

Reina had refused to acknowledge that she'd had a child. Whoever this girl was she wanted nothing to do with her.

"She was adamant," Thad said. "I had no choice but to accept her decision and take it to Amelia. She was devastated. It broke my heart to see her cry. It seemed the couple who had adopted her had been very kind people, but elderly. They had both died within the last few years. They had told her she was their granddaughter and her mother had died giving birth to her. Just before she died, her so-called grandmother had confessed that Amelia was adopted. Amelia found the adoption papers after her death. They included the name and address of the adoption agency, but no parents' names. Amelia immediately started searching for us."

He paused again, this time for quite a while. I was afraid he was planning on stopping there and I had no idea what to do next. Bristow hadn't shown up. Should we try to make a citizen's arrest? Would Thad accept it more easily if Zack aka Sheriff Lazarro made the arrest? We couldn't just leave—there was no knowing what Thad might do.

"I decided to go to the reunion," he said, almost startling me. I'd been so sure he was through talking.

"I'd had Amelia send me her photo electronically. I printed it out and I asked Reina to meet me in the lobby at CHAPS and I gave it to her. I thought if she saw how much the girl looked like her, she'd change her mind and at least meet her, talk to her, answer her questions."

He swallowed audibly. "Reina agreed to meet with Amelia, but while I was thanking her, she said she would meet with her so she could tell her I'd raped her. I had no right to act like the girl's father, she said. Nobody could become a father through rape, it wasn't right. She had twisted the whole thing around and really seemed to believe I had raped her. I could see my whole new life getting ruined again, just when it had taken a turn for the better."

"So you killed her," Zack said flatly.

"I was so angry," Thad said. He hesitated, but he was on a roll now and I could see he didn't want to stop—confession was feeling good to him. Bristow had told me more than once that murderers are under great pressure to tell someone what they have done.

Sure enough, he continued. "Reina started to turn away from me and I grabbed her and pulled her through the first door I saw. I was shaking I was so angry, and I was shaking her. It all seemed to be happening in slow motion. I literally saw red, like a film in front of my eyes, as though my blood had gone to my eyes. She started kicking me and punching me and I was afraid someone would come in and see us fighting and then she started shouting and I just put my hands around her throat and squeezed."

He looked from me to Zack, with tears filling his dark eyes. "I didn't mean to hurt Reina. I wanted to make her be quiet and to slow her down so I could talk some sense into her. I guess I also wanted to scare her a bit so she'd take back her threat. But she just kept struggling and then she flung herself sideways and her knees sort of buckled and I heard her neck snap. I panicked."

"You were in the women's rest room?" Zack asked.

"I didn't really know where I was until then. When my head cleared, I pulled her into the end cubicle and ... propped her up and made her look as if she was using the toilet. I tried and tried to pry the photo out of her hand and succeeded only in tearing the edge of the paper. Finally, I gave up on it, locked the door and came out under it."

He shuddered. "I never meant to hurt her," he repeated.

He looked from me to Zack pleadingly, then straightened himself up in a sudden show of dignity. "I do admit that I have Reina's death on my hands and I'll never forgive myself for those few minutes of absolute insanity."

Ah, that's the way this was going to go, was it? The odd thing was that seeing how convincing he could be, I could also see that he might very well get away with pleading diminished responsibility if not outright insanity.

At the same moment I sensed a presence in the sanctuary. I glanced quickly at Thad, and saw he'd lowered his head again and was gazing glumly at the floor. Looking quickly to my right, I saw a shadow move behind the very last pew.

I could only hope.

"So how come you burned CHAPS out from under us?" I asked.

"I had nothing to do with that," he said, straightening up abruptly.

"Just like you had nothin' to do with the fires up north?" Zack asked.

"He's not going to admit to those," I said, trying a little sarcasm. "He wasn't man enough to own up at the time, he's surely not going to do it now."

Well, that was a mistake, I realized the minute it was out of my mouth and I saw anger take the place of sadness in his eyes. The pastor was more than a little sensitive about his manhood.

Up he jumped, so suddenly we were taken totally by surprise. As I started to rise, too—though I have no idea what I thought I was going to do—he knocked me to one side before I could establish my balance. As he swiveled to get out to the aisle, Zack reached for him and missed and he turned and delivered a punch to Zack's nose that made our man in black grunt like a wounded animal.

The blows didn't slow either Zack or me down, though. As Thad raced down the aisle, heading for the door, we both caught up with him and tackled him and landed in a tangle on top of him as he hit the floor.

"Call nine-one-one," Zack said, justifiably out of breath, as I was.

"No need," Bristow said, standing up at the back of the church, gun in hand. "The cavalry's already here."

CHAPTER 21

We were sitting around in Zack's enormous recreation room, in which just about everything reclines. Sofa, love seats, chairs. All of them done up in fine white leather. The carpeting is navy blue. All of the furniture is down-filled. Only one sofa doesn't recline—the longest one, I imagine because it can double as a love nest if the happy couple doesn't want to bother going to the bedroom.

There's an entertainment wall. Theater-size TV screen, stereo setup, a couple of VCRs. All very high-tech and handsomely surrounded by wood cabinetry and paneling. Amazing.

It was all very comfortable and soothing. Sybaritic is the word that comes to mind. But I missed our daily meetings at CHAPS almost as much as I missed the evenings of dancing and lessons.

We were all there—Savanna, Bristow, Zack, me, and Angel, who was planning on leaving for Salinas the next day.

"You could have let us know you were on the scene," Zack said to Bristow. "You'd have saved me a lot of grief." His voice was coming out plaintive nowadays, since his poor broken nose had been splinted.

I was lucky, all I had were bruises.

Bristow produced an apologetic smile. "Took me a while to get to the church. Gridlock en route. El Camino Real. Then when I finally arrived at the showdown at the O.K. Corral, I didn't want to interrupt while O'Connor was telling all."

"I knew you were there," I said. "I saw your shadow."

"Like the groundhog?" Bristow queried. "Does this mean it's going to rain?"

I restrained myself.

I guess I should bring you up to date. After Thad's arrest, I had told Bristow everything that had led me to decide Thad had murdered Reina and had received his usual lecture about taking the law into my own hands. "You were busy," I pointed out. "In any case, I wanted to be sure I was right before I bothered you."

"You could have been dead right," Bristow had said sternly. "We recovered a weapon from O'Connor's office at the church."

"He suggested we should go to the office when we arrived," I'd told him, feeling a chill climb my spine.

"I told him no," Zack had added—as if he could possibly have guessed there was a gun in there.

For this statement he had received an approving smile and had then been gently reprimanded for encouraging me to go to the church in the first place.

Maybe he was getting off light because of his injuries, I comforted myself.

That's about it. Except that Thad was of course

arrested and was being held without bail, pending his trial.

Back in Zack's recreation room, Savanna gave Zack the benefit of her sympathetic gaze. "You look like a wounded raccoon," she said.

He did, too. When the plastic surgeon had straightened up his nose, he'd also managed, at Zack's request, to make the jagged scar on his cheek less noticeable. "I can always paint it on if need be," Zack had said. "This way, I can cover it up easier for the camera."

The double procedure had blackened both of Zack's eyes. He kept his sunglasses on when he was out in public, but we weren't counted as public.

"I had to give up the job for now," he said mournfully. Actually, he might not have felt mournful, it was just that his voice came through that way.

"Job?" Angel queried.

"Francisca Gutierrez recommended me to her publisher as a cover model for her romance novels."

"Oh, yeah," Angel said.

I looked at him. "Dolores Valentino thought Francisca should have asked you."

He shuddered. "I don't mind having my picture taken cuddling up to a good-looking woman, but I don't want to owe any favors to Dolores."

"What about P.J.?" I asked. "You mind owing her favors?"

We all looked at him with interest, waiting for those telltale streaks of red to show up on his cheekbones, but they didn't. Instead, he gave me the wide white smile that showed up only briefly on special occasions. "P.J. and I are comfortable together," he said. Then turned solemn. "She showed up when I was in need of comfort."

If I could have climbed out of my reclining section of the sofa, I would have hugged him. He had indeed needed comfort after our last adventure, and I was glad P.J. was providing it. And getting some pleasure out of it, I was sure. I wondered if she'd be visiting Angel in Salinas, but managed not to ask. It's hell being nosy.

"You'll heal," I said to Zack. "I'm sure Francisca will wait for you."

"I should be okay by Christmas," he said, with a sidelong glance at me.

"Your probation is up then, is it?" Savanna asked.

Zack smiled for the first time since Thad had broken his nose, then winced with pain.

"Speaking of Thad," I said, turning to Bristow, who was reclining on my left, sipping on a beer.

"We found Reina's ring at his house," Bristow said. "Asked him about it. He's being very cooperative, hoping for a deal. Says she kept hitting him and he pulled it off her finger so she couldn't cut him with it. Kept it to give to Amelia, he said. He was going to hang on to it for a year or two, then tell her that her mother had died and had left it to him to be given to their daughter. He didn't know or care if the diamonds were real or not—he'd missed all the discussion—he just thought it would make Amelia feel better."

"I feel for that girl," Savanna said. "She just finds her mother and father, and one is murdered by the other. Tough to take."

"So, *are* the diamonds real?" I asked. Not that I cared, I just wanted to know.

"She didn't buy it off the TV shopping channel," Bristow said. "Yes, the diamonds are real."

"I love the shopping channel," Savanna said.

"You do indeed," Bristow said, but he was smiling fondly at her, I was delighted to see. Things seemed to be going better in the Bristow household.

"So who told the truth?" I demanded, anxious to cut through all the distractions, enjoyable as they were. "Reina said she was raped. Thad said *he* was. Who was right?"

"No way to tell so far," Bristow said. "No witnesses. Her word against his, which he is sticking to. We may never know who told the truth. Both of them had lied before. Thad about the previous fires." He paused. "I'm sure, however, that his lawyers will be bringing in psychiatrists and psychologists to prove it was all Reina's fault she got herself murdered."

"I can't reconcile the teacher I loved and admired with some monster who might have threatened and raped a sixteen-year-old boy," Savanna said.

"Most people have trouble believing when someone they loved and trusted is accused of improper behavior," Bristow said. "But people who molest children don't do it blatantly. They are secretive. They choose someone vulnerable. The individual's public image is often so positive the victim is afraid to speak out because he or she wouldn't be believed."

"Well, Miss Diaz wouldn't say someone had raped her if it wasn't true," Savanna said stubbornly.

Bristow gave her a sympathetic and very under-

standing smile. "I'll grant you the school principal said
Reina Diaz's record was spotless. He insists nobody
ever made any allegations or requested an investigation of the lady."

He paused again. "She lied about the ring being
relatively worthless, however. She lied about being
engaged. She lied about your boyfriend stalking her.
Obviously, she didn't always stick to the truth."

"She never said *Forrest* stalked her," Savanna said
hotly. "And he's not my boyfriend!"

"Admirer, then," Bristow said mildly. "And who can
be blamed for admiring you."

Awwwwww!

Savanna gave him a melting look and he acquired
a smug expression.

"You'll remember that according to Owen Jones,
Reina was very cold toward the baby," he went on.
"She called her 'it.' Doesn't sound too maternal."

"Well, if the baby was a product of rape...,"
Savanna murmured. Once you had Savanna's loyalty
you had it for life.

I decided to intervene before the argument esca-
lated again. "Okay," I said. "That's enough about Reina.
What about Perky? Thad did shoot him, didn't he?"

Bristow stretched his long legs out and smiled. "Not
yet proven, but most likely." He grinned at me. "Pastor
Thad is 'a gentleman, nurse, that loves to hear himself
talk.' "

The "nurse" gave me a clue. *"Romeo and Juliet?"*
I guessed.

"The same."

Thad had talked all right. He'd told that he'd followed Perky home from the Tiburon ferry, bothered because Perky had made a couple of comments to him that indicated he was highly suspicious of the pastor. Perky had guessed, it seemed, that Thad was the student who had supposedly raped Reina. Plus, the police had discovered clippings from the *San Francisco Chronicle* in Perky's house, clippings that told about the Washington church fires, and police suspicions of the pastor.

"You wouldn't believe the junk that guy had collected," Bristow said. "Perkins, not O'Connor. Piles of it all over. Closets full of it. Boxes in the attic. Theater programs, tickets to shows, magazines, newspapers."

"I'd understood he was recovering from his obsessive-compulsive complex," I said. "Becky Mackinay told me he was seeing someone and was cleaning house."

"Yeah, well, his psychiatrist told me the same story. But evidently, he hadn't finished the job. My guess is he'd squirreled those clippings away at the time because he knew the guy. Maybe he was thinking of doing a cartoon about him. Who knows? And then maybe he came across the clippings again while he was shoveling out, and showed them to O'Connor."

Thad's story was that Perky had insisted he hadn't told Charlie anything—and he, in turn, had convinced Perky that Reina had forced herself upon him when he was too young to know what to do about it. They had parted amicably, Thad had said. He certainly hadn't gone looking for him and then gunned him down.

"However," Bristow said, when I expressed disbelief, "we are confident we can pin Timothy Perkins's murder on the pastor. Liz North came up with a couple of neighbors who can place Thad's Mercedes in the area that morning. Tinted windows. A partial on the license plate. We're expecting a match on the murder weapon."

"A Mercedes yet," I muttered. "Whatever happened to his monkish life?"

"He *was* celibate," Bristow said. "According to his doctor, he was impotent and had been for many years."

"Which is possibly why he compensated by dancing in the nude," I said. "Bizarre, all of it." I'd already told everyone about Thad being one of the nude dancing instructors. Savanna wasn't sure she wanted to believe it.

"We have some great evidence to link O'Connor to Reina's murder," Bristow continued. He looked from me to Zack. "This is in strictest confidence, okay? I don't want you spilling this stuff on the television show."

"Television show?" I queried.

"You haven't told her?" Bristow asked Zack.

I discovered the way to get out of the clutches of this reclining sofa was to sit up and pull my feet sharply in. I sat bolt upright and narrowed my eyes at Bristow. "Told me what?"

"Seems your friend Perky talked to an old university friend of his in San Francisco the night before he died. Telephoned her right after the Tiburon trip. Said he thought you and Zack would make a great interview, the way you go looking for killers. The friend wasn't too enthused until she found out you were responsible for catching Perkins's killer."

"She?" I asked.

"The producer of 'Zappening,'" he said.

The Sunday evening live talk show that featured Alyssa Pearson, onetime news anchor, and a perpetually sunny brunette.

I groaned.

"October twelfth," Zack said. "Seven P.M. Don't wear white."

"You're willing to go on TV looking like that?" I asked.

"I'm not vain," he protested.

Ha! What he probably meant was that having the chance to be recognized as a hero outweighed his vanity. And of course, some smart director might just be watching and want to hire this hero for his next action movie. Even with a splint and raccoon eyes, Zack Hunter still looked better than most.

"You were going to tell us about your great evidence," I reminded Bristow. No way was I going to appear on TV to talk about catching killers, but I wasn't going to argue about it in front of the whole gang.

"Seems O'Connor spit on Reina during the process of strangling her," Bristow said.

"DNA?" Zack asked wisely.

"DNA," Bristow said. "We got a good match. The probability of such a match occurring randomly is approximately one in three million."

"You've definitely got him then," I said, feeling relieved. The thought of Thad on the loose was not one I wanted to entertain. I had a feeling he would not be a passive enemy. He'd already tried to broil me. Which he'd also finally admitted to, though strangely still denying the earlier church burnings. Maybe he wanted his former congregation to retain their good opinion of him.

He hadn't thought Zack was there, he'd insisted. He'd been hiding out in the cleaning crew's walk-in closet and had seen Zack leave the second time.

It's not a good feeling to know that someone would burn down a whole building just to make sure you couldn't talk. If I hadn't woken up . . . well, I wouldn't ever have woken up.

"All of this from something that happened twenty years ago," Savanna said.

"The past doesn't go away just because it's over," I said. "It's always there inside us, affecting what we do today."

"Yeah," Angel said and we exchanged an understanding smile. It wasn't too long ago that Angel had been forced to confront his past, so he knew the truth of what I was saying. I looked at Zack to see if he was agreeing also, but his attention was on Bristow.

Evidently, he'd asked a question about Bristow's HIV tests. I paid attention.

"Nothing has shown up yet," he said.

"I've joined a support group of people whose spouses are HIV positive," Savanna announced.

Evidently, this was news to Bristow. And he was not receiving it well. "I'm a police officer," he said flatly to his wife. "My private life should remain private. You had no business doing this without discussing it first. We don't even know that I'm infected."

"The way you've been acting, you might as well be infected," Savanna said tightly. "I thought I'd try to learn how to handle it without losing my mind the way you've apparently lost yours."

I imagined she'd announced this in front of all of us so he couldn't get too mad at her. He'd looked mad at first, but now he was mainly looking taken aback.

The two of them exchanged a long look, which excluded the rest of us. Apparently, they had forgotten we were there.

Angel was looking nervous. He feels very uncomfortable around confrontations. I didn't think he needed to worry too much. Already the vibrations between our two friends were settling down to a nice steady hum. I watched as Angel relaxed, too. Maybe their auras had taken on more acceptable hues.

"I almost forgot," Bristow said softly to his wife. "I brought you a present."

"I'll get it," Zack said, and went up the stairs. A couple of minutes later he reappeared, carrying a fair-size flat box that had been taped shut.

"What's the occasion?" I asked.

"My question exactly," Savanna said. "We already celebrated the anniversary of our first meeting."

"No occasion," Bristow said. "I was in the store, I saw this, it said it was for you."

Savanna opened it, with the help of her husband's Swiss Army knife, which he'd thoughtfully brought along. It was red, of course. Savanna dearly loved red. A suede jacket, with lots of long fringe.

She put it on, smiling at her husband, who was smiling at her in the same old loopy way.

Angel, Zack, and I all found it necessary to go up to the kitchen and get a fresh beer.

CHAPTER 22

Alyssa Pearson insisted I had to wear makeup. And I must admit I didn't look all that bad when the beautician got through with me. She'd even got my hair to look like hair instead of steel wool.

She used makeup on Zack's eyes. The swelling had gone down by now, and even though his nose was still splinted, he looked as macho and sexy as ever. Maybe even more macho. The wounded warrior.

Alyssa Pearson asked Zack the first question, in a very arch voice. "What's this I hear about you being married, you sly dog, you."

Turning to the audience, she added, "You heard it here first, folks, an exclusive from one of our frequent informers. Zack Hunter was married recently to a lucky gal named Buffy."

She looked back at Zack, showing surprise at the expression of shock on his face. "I guess you didn't want that fact revealed," she said cheerily. "But your fans want to know such things! So you just open up now, you hear, and tell us all about your lucky wife."

"But it's not true," Zack said faintly. "I've never

married. I don't have a wife. I don't even know anyone called Buffy."

He looked to me for help. "He's not married," I said, somehow managing to keep a straight face.

Some of you may remember that when I got tired of women calling for Zack when he loaned me his cell phone, I started telling them I was his wife, Buffy. Which I was never going to own up to. Evidently, one of my callers had reported it to Alyssa.

"He's not married," I repeated, when Alyssa showed disbelief. "Your informant was wrong."

Zack looked grateful.

Alyssa rearranged her lapel mike, and her face. She had very smooth hair. The kind that swings when you move your head. I'd give a lot for hair like that.

"Well, I'm sure we single gals are all delighted to hear that," she said with her trademark sunshiny smile, then segued into the proper topic of the day, addressing Zack again. "I understand you helped the police catch the man who allegedly murdered Reina Diaz, the acclaimed schoolteacher."

Zack bowed his head modestly.

"Thaddeus O'Connor, the well-known minister and lecturer, author of *Women Who Worry Too Much*," Alyssa told her audience, "we had him as a guest less than a year ago! Little did we know he'd be capable of murder!" She smiled at Zack. "And of punching Zack Hunter on his beautiful nose."

Zack bravely touched the proboscis in question and gave the camera the wry sexy smile that had brought him most of his fame and fortune.

"I understand it lost you your new opportunity as

a cover model!" Alyssa exclaimed. She had an exclama-
tory style. "I bet our listeners are disappointed about
that. We were about to see a big boost in romance
novel sales, folks," she added, beaming at the camera.

We hadn't stayed on topic very long, I noted.

"I didn't exactly lose the opportunity," Zack said.
"My agent called to say the publishing house will be
just as interested once I'm healed."

"Great, great news, Zack," Alyssa said.

Are you noticing something here?

Yes, you've got it. I'd become invisible again. Amazing how that happens when Zack's among those
present.

The two of them went on to discuss the capture of
Thaddeus O'Connor, while I wondered how idiotic my
smile must look now that it had congealed.

I have to admit Zack did not exaggerate his part
in the capture. Nor did he downplay mine. He just
failed to mention it. A moment of mental aberration,
no doubt.

But then Alyssa asked him if he thought Thad
O'Connor had raped Reina Diaz when he was a sophomore in high school, or if she had raped him. She was
quite breathless over the idea of a woman raping a
boy.

"Maybe Charlie should answer that one," Zack said,
and Alyssa gave a little tinkling laugh that indicated
to me she'd forgotten my existence.

"It's possible Thad raped Reina," I said. "He could
have kept her silent by threatening to tell everyone
she'd started molesting him when he was just sixteen,
just as he told us when we caught him out in a mistake

or two. That might have prevented her from reporting the rape."

"But it could have been the other way around?" Alyssa asked.

"I guess we might learn more in the trial," I said. "By all accounts Reina Diaz was an exemplary teacher, and according to the latest newspaper interviews with members of Thad's church, Thad was an exemplary pastor. I don't have any idea which of them told the truth."

"Reverend O'Connor's attorney says Thad's mental state is no different from that of a battered woman or an abused child who reacts violently after years of abuse."

I didn't know what to answer to that, so I adopted Zack's wise Sheriff Lazarro look and said nothing.

"Thank you, Charlie," Alyssa said, with an air of finality, then turned back to Zack and started complimenting him again on his handling of the situation, and his perspicacity in figuring out that Thad was the murderer.

Toward the end of the segment, Alyssa once again commented sympathetically about Zack's nose and what it had cost him.

"I lost out on a trip to Russia, as well," he informed her. This was news to me. "Seems *Prescott's Landin'* is enjoyin' unprecedented success in Russia these days. Number one show, I'm told. I was supposed to go to Moscow as part of the promotion for the show. Had to cancel out."

"What a shame," Alyssa sympathized. "You'd have made a wonderful ambassador."

Meanwhile, I, the ignored one, was trying to repress a shudder at the "Portrait of America," the Russian people would be getting from *Prescott's Landing*.

"All I can do now is help Charlie supervise the rebuilding of CHAPS," Zack concluded as a man at the back made frantic wrap-up gestures. "And wait for Christmas," he added.

Shocked, I looked around Alyssa at him.

Alyssa was looking at him, too, a bit uncertainly, for which she could hardly be blamed. "Christmas?" she queried.

"I'm expecting the best Christmas of my life this year," Zack said, raising his eyebrows at me and making my innards go whomp!

You begin to see why I always seem to forgive this man his transgressions?

Christmas. The end of Zack's probation. The end of suspense. The beginning of a new kind of relationship between Zack and me.

Maybe.

BOOK YOUR PLACE ON OUR WEBSITE AND MAKE THE READING CONNECTION!

We've created a customized website just for our very special readers, where you can get the inside scoop on everything that's going on with Zebra, Pinnacle and Kensington books.

When you come online, you'll have the exciting opportunity to:

- View covers of upcoming books
- Read sample chapters
- Learn about our future publishing schedule (listed by publication month *and author*)
- Find out when your favorite authors will be visiting a city near you
- Search for and order backlist books from our online catalog
- Check out author bios and background information
- Send e-mail to your favorite authors
- Meet the Kensington staff online
- Join us in weekly chats with authors, readers and other guests
- Get writing guidelines
- AND MUCH MORE!

**Visit our website at
http://www.kensingtonbooks.com**